BOXING CLEVER

BOXING CLEVER

Maureen Devlin

Boxing Clever

All Rights Reserved. Copyright © 2011 Maureen Devlin

No part of this book may be reproduced or transmitted in any form or by any means, graphic, electronic, or mechanical, including photocopying, recording, taping or by any information storage or retrieval system, without the permission in writing from the copyright holder.

The right of Maureen Devlin to be identified as the author of this work has been asserted in accordance with the Copyright, Designs and Patents Act 1988 sections 77 and 78.

Spiderwize
Office 404, 4th Floor
Albany House
324/326 Regent Street
London
W1B 3HH
UK

www.spiderwize.com

This is a work of fiction. Names, characters and incidents are products of the author's imagination. Any resemblance to persons living or dead is entirely coincidental.

The views expressed in this work are solely those of the author and do not necessarily reflect the views of the publisher, and the publisher hereby disclaims any responsibility for them.

ISBN: 978-1-908128-12-6

Many thanks to Dot, Gary, Mark, Phil, Terie
and to all those in the South Manchester Writers'
Workshop, for your good advice and
encouragement across the years.

CHAPTER 1

Tom Ashton grimaced as he descended the silver and black tunnel, wincing as he caught a glimpse of himself in a burnished steel mirror at the foot of the stairs. The pounding music from above made his misery complete. Bloody place. The interior designer had clearly run out of inspiration for the toilets, continuing the gothic theme but merely changing the black for purple. He just hoped Ellen wouldn't catch on that tonight was about work. That would just about be the last straw.

Preferring not to use the urinals, Tom chose a stall that was less dimly lit than the rest. He had just finished when he heard footsteps and a soft Irish brogue.

"It's good stuff, mate."

Well, well. Tom decided to stay put. Experience had taught him not to take any risks – he wasn't going to volunteer for a knife in the ribs and certainly not in a purple toilet. He craned his neck backwards, keeping the rest of his body as still as possible, to make sure he caught as much of the conversation as he could. The Irishman's companion was obviously slightly reticent, as after a responding growl, Tom heard the dealer press a little harder.

"Sure and y'know I wouldn't pass you any shite. Here, try this and I'll come and find yer tomorrow. I can get anythin' yer want, okay?"

"Gimme that," grunted the punter. "And I'll fuckin' pay for it – not being in debt to you, mate. And I'll find *you* if I like it."

2   *Boxing Clever*

Noiselessly, he twisted round and pressed an eye to the edge of the door. Peering hard into the designer dim of the urinal area, he could just make out the left arm of one of the two men. Which one? A dark jacket, smallish slim hand, nails surprisingly long. Aahh, that's more like it. Tom heard the twin rustle of paper, as drug and money exchanged hands. The arm in his view moved forwards, returning soon after with a crumpled note that the owner pushed into an unseen pocket.

By the time Tom had noisily zipped up, flushed the toilet and opened the door, he was alone. Washing his hands, he reflected on just how little both men had cared about the fact that someone might have witnessed the deal. He glared at himself in the mirror, his blue eyes almost black as they tried to pull in as much light as they could. He tried in vain to flatten his thick auburn hair with his damp hands and gave it up as a lost cause.

Finding an Irishman on the streets in Manchester wasn't going to be a breeze either – unless the bar staff had taken particular notice of the guy. Tom wasn't concerned; he wasn't nicknamed Duracell Man for nothing.

He rejoined Ellen at the table by the window that looked out onto the newly cobbled street by the canal. Her dark head was turned towards the scene outside.

"Another drink?"

"Is the Pope Catholic?" She turned to face him, her grey eyes brightening as she smiled in anticipation. Eight years younger, she seemed to be enjoying herself and he wanted to keep it that way. "Want me to come with you as protection?"

"That'll do, young lady," Tom feigned authority and moved away to the bar.

The Reyka was one of the older bars in the Gay Village, just a short walk from China Town and Manchester Piccadilly. It was as popular with the straight and curious as it was with the

Maureen Devlin   3

gay community, who were beginning to voice concerns in the press. While welcoming visitors, there was always the potential for misunderstandings.

Tom had been propositioned the first time he had been in here, but he was now on fairly good terms with the bar staff who delighted in winding him up ("oh, please – wear the uniform next time!"). There were clear rules in the Village. The police were tolerated as long as they didn't interfere.

She began chattering as soon as he sat back down. He hadn't told her he was working, just asked if she might like to meet for an early drink. He had only known her a few months and liked her company. The sex was a blessed relief too. His emotional armour plating, however, was still reassuringly intact. After Greg's death and the marital bruising he'd received from Greg's sister, intimacy could still only be skin deep. His mind drifted...

"Are you in there?" Ellen's voice cut into the void.

"Sorry." He played for time by taking a drink. "Tell me a bit more about this company you work for," he added, liking the way her face lit up at his interest.

He was only half-listening as Ellen began to explain.

The dead man had been dragged out of the water just like Greg. Broken and dripping. Who was he? And why did he end up pulverised and dumped in the greasy black waters of Salford Quays?

Tom barely registered that *Vanpharma* had offices around the world. It made medicines for all sorts of things but was increasingly specialising in diseases of the brain and nervous system, Ellen went on. But not for the sort of terminal brain damage inflicted on the man in the Quays.

"...and we have examples of successful advertising campaigns dotted about the building, even slogans printed onto the paper cups for water and coffee."

4 *Boxing Clever*

That brought him back to earth.

"Bloody hell! Talk about corporate brainwashing! More money than sense at your place."

Ellen started to protest that this was exactly the kind of thing that made people proud to work there – could he say the same?

"Don't even go there."

He kept his tone light but yes, actually, he did. He enjoyed the role of public servant, first in the army and now CID.

Ellen looked at him for a moment and then said quietly, "You don't give much away at all, do you? Always the policeman, asking the questions." She wriggled her slim body into a more upright position and carried on. "C'mon then. Why did you leave the army?"

He wasn't ready to tell her all of that. Norway. Not yet. He sidestepped the issue.

"Better prospects and prettier women."

Ellen hadn't accepted the brush off and kept at him until he had lost his temper. The row had bubbled all the way to her car and he only managed to salvage things when he caught her arm and gazed long and hard into her eyes.

"I'm sorry," he whispered. "Not ready, okay?"

There must have been a raw honesty in his face for she touched his cheek gently with her hand.

"You can drive," she said.

He was freezing cold. He could smell the vile stench of the bile that rose from deep in his stomach when he saw Greg, barely recognisable from the battering of the rotor blades that had caught him as the helicopter hit the water. Water gushed from the broken mass that had been his best friend, his best man...suddenly Greg's head turned as if to look at him and Tom's heart leapt with hope. But there was no face, nothing but blackness and horror.

Tom woke, sweating, heart racing. He looked around, disoriented by the images – where was he? Fear gripped him, waves of grief rising within him. Not again. He moved to swing his legs from the bed and his hand touched warm skin. Still shaking, he calmed his breathing and lay back down beside her. He knew why his memory was stirred but it didn't make it any easier.

He had been there when the ravaged corpse was pulled out of a side channel at Salford Quays, had seen the bloated body and mottled flesh. Biting damp had seared his skin and crept through the soles of his stylish but unsuitable shoes. He could recite the post-mortem report: 'Major soft tissue damage to trunk, arms and legs. Broken skull. Face disfigured; jaws, nose and teeth broken; eye sockets fractured.'

The guy had taken a real pounding. It was hard to know which of the blows had killed him, but the pathologist was sure he was dead before he was dumped in the water. He'd been in there for less than a week when he was found. That was nearly two months ago. All that Tom could say for certain about the anonymous victim was that it was male, white and with bleached cropped hair. Someone was responsible and he was going to find them. They never did decide who was to blame for Greg.

He left, unrefreshed and edgy, before Ellen woke. His working day did nothing to improve his mood and by late evening his neck was stiff with tension. Pulling at his shoulders in an effort to ease the growing pain behind his eyes, he grabbed his jacket and strode across the open plan office. A large white board on the wall next to the door showed the progress of each CID case. The moment it took to scan showed there was precious little he could add to it.

The door was suddenly wrenched open.

6   *Boxing Clever*

"Sir," Tom acknowledged. He had a lot of time for his boss; a decent man and a good detective. Behind his back DCI Frank Dawson was known as 'The Rodent' in salutation to his rather tight top lip that never quite made the connection south to cover his teeth.

"Tom," came the reply. "I've got a planning meeting with Region in the morning. What progress have we got?"

Tom leaned against a nearby desk in order to fully face his superior officer. He thought momentarily about bullshitting but could see from the shrewd gaze of the older man that he would regret it.

"Not much more I can tell you about the Quays case, sir. The guy's face was pulped before he went into the water. He doesn't fit any missing person descriptions and we are getting a complete blank from our contacts."

The Rodent obviously didn't like what he was hearing. He began to pace across the blue-grey carpet.

"I can't impress on you enough, Tom, that we need to have a clean patch here. The eyes of the world are going to be on this city in a few months and I want to be able to reassure region and, for that matter, the bloody Home Office, that we are on top of things." He began to smooth his thinning hair, a sure sign of anxiety. "What else could worry them?"

"We're trying to close down the shoplifting ring and get behind the increased activity on the drug scene but with the bloody canteen..."

Before Tom could finish he was interrupted by a raised hand.

"No buts. Get me good news." With a decisive nod, Frank Dawson pulled open the door and then was gone.

"Sod it," Tom announced to no one in particular. "I'm off."

"Where to? You've only been here five minutes."

Tom turned to glare at his friend and colleague, Dean Wilson, who raised his hands in mock alarm. "Too much bed and not enough sleep, Tom. That's your problem."

He battled to keep his eyes open for the last few miles of his journey out of Manchester. As he opened the front door and then shuffled towards the kitchen, the hard knot in his stomach reminded him that he hadn't eaten since noon that day and it was now nearing midnight. The sight of the congealed cat food in Jack's dish on the floor made his stomach churn. Bit of a difference from Ellen's spotless kitchen.

Jack, sitting in his favourite spot on the top of the washing machine, unravelled his sleek black body and stood, tail erect, to greet him with a silent mew. Tom scratched the cat's head in thanks for the moral support.

"Hey, boy – at least you're not giving me any grief. Best get us something to eat, eh?"

He opened a tin of tuna for the cat, and whilst waiting for the pasta to cook, Tom poured a large glass of red wine and reflected on his nightmare shift.

Two of the team were still off with food poisoning, courtesy of the staff canteen. His own workload, already heavy, was increasing by the day. It didn't help that a significant number of his colleagues were being re-assigned to provide security for the forthcoming G8 Economic Summit, and Frank was clearly beginning to show the signs of imminent mental and physical implosion.

He took another large slurp and then allowed his brain to rest as he concentrated on his preparations. The simple action of tossing the freshly drained pasta with home-made pesto and black pepper was like a meditation. He added more shaved parmesan. Fantastic.

8   *Boxing Clever*

Tom carried his meal and wine into the living room and flicked on the TV. He stared at the screen but his mind was elsewhere. His brain clicked through the case list: the shoplifting network, a car warehouse insurance scam, a vicious burglary and the murder. He always came back to the last case; the waterlogged body had turned up in Salford Quays at the end of January. Two of the water company workers dredging the area ready for the international visitors had made the gruesome discovery. Both were still having counselling. It had been a real battle to keep the lid on that bit of PR dynamite.

He took a large mouthful and chewed. Tom knew he had to get something soon, or he'd lose even more manpower. They'd met a deafening silence from the local community. No one matching the man's description had been reported missing, and dental and fingerprint records drew a blank. There was nothing in any of his pockets except sediment from the water. And the extent of the facial injuries meant they didn't even have a computer-generated picture that they could use. The initial press interest, using an artist's impression of what the guy's face might have looked like, had delivered a foray of dead ends. He needed a new lead. Like his engineer father, Tom believed that every problem had a solution. He also felt that every victim's family deserved to know 'why'.

CHAPTER 2

Thanking whichever god for a night of dreamless sleep, Tom grabbed a trolley and marched into the supermarket. Whizzing round the end of the pet food aisle, he had to execute a text-book emergency stop as an old lady suddenly appeared in his path.

"Whoa!" the sound was out before he realised he sounded like John Wayne. "Didn't catch you, did I?" She looked familiar, but he couldn't place her.

"Oh, no" she smiled at him, then peered down to review his selection. "Aah," she said, picking up and inspecting a pack of cod fillets before replacing them in his trolley. "Very good."

He was so surprised he almost said "Thank you." Not sure why he felt amused rather than irritated, he manoeuvred past her towards the checkout. Before leaving the store car park, he tried to contact Ellen, but could only get her confident voice on the answering machine. He left a message saying that Saturday was looking a definite possibility.

Back at headquarters after fitting in a much needed trim, Tom registered the level of manpower. No better.

In addition to the summary captured on the white board, each case had a dedicated buff-coloured file that held any paperwork pertinent to the investigation. Not only were all his case files sitting on his desk, but an additional two were waiting for him with a Post-it note on top stating baldly, "Had to go to

10   *Boxing Clever*

taskforce meeting re G8 – FD wants an update on these?" To add insult to injury, the coffee machine was on the blink. Tom stared out the window at the Manchester skyline and grimaced at his refection. Dean's sympathetic voice came from behind him.

"Still pissed off?"

"Let's just say that at times this sodding job is a cow's backside."

"It could be worse," Dean offered as they strolled back to the CID offices from the back-up coffee machine. "We could still be in the army."

Tom grunted in agreement. The decision to resign his commission was more to do with trying to save his marriage but he had never regretted his change of career. Dean survived less than three years as a PE teacher before he made the move.

Dean adjusted his jeans around his crotch with a satisfied grunt as he settled himself on to the corner of his desk, cradling a steaming brown plastic cup. The furniture groaned as it received his weight.

"Crap stuff, this," he remarked. "We were better off before the Super figured Investors in People meant buying desks and chairs that only come in noncey colours and midget size."

Tom grinned. He knew Dean was proud of his bulk and looked on his size as insurance in the job. Tom relied on red wine to keep his arteries clear, and his wits to protect his back.

"So, what's new? Let's pile it on."

"Seems that The Johnson has got a member of staff or guest with sticky fingers," Dean reported. The Johnson was a new four-star hotel next to the tired-looking building that housed the Granada TV Studios and close to one of the city's football grounds.

"Not our problem though, surely?"

Maureen Devlin   11

"Maybe, maybe not. Seems the latest victim is the agent of the London boxer hoping to fix a fight with Joe Murphy's latest find. The guy had quite a sum on him and he's well pissed off to say the least. Old man Murphy is going ballistic as well by all accounts – figures it makes him look like he's got no respect."

"Who's handling it?"

"Ryan and Elliott," Dean replied.

"Let's keep ourselves informed on this one, something smells interesting."

Dean nodded and almost in the same movement jumped away from his desk to avoid being on the receiving end of a major sneezing fit.

"Goddam, Rich!" he glared at their younger colleague. "Keep your snot to yourself."

Rich sniffed. "It's hayfever or allergy or something. Bloody eyes keep streaming too. A bit of sympathy," he pressed, "wouldn't go amiss."

"No chance, mate," Tom grinned. "First chance we get for some undercover work in a florist, it's yours."

"Must remember to warn Ellen about this stuff," Tom muttered later as he sat reading some activity reports. "Looks like we've got a spate coming up."

"What's that?" Dean looked up from his paperwork, obviously glad of the diversion.

"Another car's been broken into at the traffic lights on the Parkway near the brewery. Poor woman must have wondered what hit her. Same story - side window smashed and bag grabbed. Cards and cheque book probably sold on within the hour."

"How many is that now?"

12   *Boxing Clever*

"Four last week and this is the second so far this week." Tom flicked back to the previous page. "There was a gang pulling this sort of stunt about ten years ago according to the files. Obviously some bright spark figured memories are short and people don't think to lock stuff in their boot. And it could be rich pickings with all the people we're expecting for the Summit. It's no use relying on locking the doors – a quick elbow to some windows is all that's needed." He yawned and stretched luxuriously. "I'm getting a coffee. Want some?"

"Get me a Mars as well, will ya?"

Tom's exit was barred by the arrival of Frank Dawson.

"Right," the chief pronounced. "I'm getting earache because of national drug crime figures and I want you two to delve a bit more. We're a prime target with the student population and the clubs and as Region keep reminding me, Manchester must be a showcase for policing during the Summit. I want to make sure that we get to whatever's behind this ASAP." With that he hitched up his trousers, pointed to both of them and then jerked his thumb towards the door.

"No time like now, is there?"

Tom looked at his glass without enthusiasm. Mineral water had to be the least interesting drink, particularly when it was the fourth of your day. He'd toyed once with the idea of low alcohol lager but couldn't see the point. Like decaffeinated coffee.

Progress had been slow too. Not that his contacts were being unhelpful, just that in their view there were no new faces around. He decided to check out the student union bars (at a time when even the social secretary would be sober) and maybe finish with a visit to the new nightclub that was due to open shortly. Follow the crowds and the dealers, Irish or otherwise, wouldn't be far behind.

His mobile phone rang just as he was leaving the largest students' union, feeling like he'd just morphed into his father. Dean announced he was on his way to visit Joe Murphy's gym.

"I'll meet you there," said Tom. "Give me ten minutes."

Just after three pm, they strolled into Joe's Place, the only building in the locality other than the undertaker's that remained graffiti free. Tom delighted in the sullen silence that greeted their arrival.

Dean had tried using the gym the previous year. It was reasonably close to the HQ and didn't suffer from any of the trappings of new, and expensive 'health clubs'. He'd told Tom that apparently his attendance made some of the guys jumpy and Joe had had to point out that Dean was "bad for business and the psychology of his boys and would he mind terribly just fucking off?" Both policemen knew that not all of the gym owner's business was played out in the ring, and that Joe Murphy always had a good handle on what was happening on his patch.

"Mr Wilson," acknowledged the owner, moving across from his position near the practice ring to the door to greet them.

"Please, Joe, you can call me Dean. This is my colleague, Detective Inspector Tom Ashton." All ears were tuned their way.

"So, what can I do for you, Mr Wilson?" Joe Murphy asked, showing that he too was acutely aware of the audience and barely giving Tom a glance.

"Just passing through, you know. Heard that you had a new fighter that was beginning to attract some serious attention. Just curious, that's all."

The older man stared at them, one at a time, for just long enough to allow the tension to build. The unspoken message was clear – keep out of my business.

14   *Boxing Clever*

Tom lolled against the wall taking in all of the detail of the scene in front of him. For all except one man, any pretence of working out had stopped. The exception was thumping at the swinging punch bag with such force that Tom was amazed that the wiry old trainer straining to hold it hadn't already been launched skyward. He looked impressive. No wonder old man Murphy was a bit protective.

Tom noticed a guy nonchalantly holding a skipping rope near to the punch-bag. He looked like he was minding it for the big guy rather than intending to use it himself, but with a tighter grip than seemed necessary for the weight of the rope in his hands.

"That's right," Joe eventually spoke. "Franklin Raye," he added, unnecessarily nodding over to where the boxer had paused to talk to the trainer.

"You get many strangers in here to watch him?" asked Dean. "Anyone new hereabouts that I should know about?"

The older man pretended to consider the question and then asked his visitor. "What *exactly* do you want, Mr Wilson?"

"Heard an associate of yours had a spot of bother recently on trip up here from London. Lost some valuables – the trail seems to have gone a bit quiet."

Tom registered the flush of annoyance or maybe embarrassment on Joe Murphy's face.

"Everything here is just *fine*, Mr Wilson," he retorted with his aging chin thrust forwards.

"What's goin' on, Dad?" The three men turned to acknowledge the younger man who had appeared almost soundlessly at Dean's shoulder. "Any problem?"

Martin Murphy was tall, relatively slim and carried his clothes well. His air was one of self-assurance, his expression flat and uncompromising. Tom assessed him as the man who made things happen, seemingly content to do so in the shadow of his notorious father. Turning slightly to include the younger Murphy in his line of vision, Tom was about to ask about the rope-handler when Joe Murphy cut in quickly.

"Mr Wilson and his colleague are just about to leave, son. He was just doing some community policing and showing an interest in our boy, for which we are, as always, appreciative."

Taking the hint, Tom levered himself away from the wall. They left the building noting that the silence in the room was still broken only by the rhythmic punching of the rising star.

Ignoring the scrutiny of a young boy on a tattered skateboard, Tom crossed the broken tarmac outside the gym and two minutes later, as Dean pulled away, he sat in his car scribbling down the number plates of the four cars parked on the nearby scrub land. Instinct wasn't something you could quantify in your monthly report but Tom's antennae had definitely been tickled by the big man's side-kick.

CHAPTER 3

"What the fuck was that about?" Martin Murphy wasn't pleased.

"Nothin' to worry about – just sniffin' around."

"Well, just make sure there's no scent for them to follow. There's too much at stake."

"Don't you worry son. He's nearly ready."

Franklin Raye, giving a masterful performance of sporting focus, missed nothing. But because it suited him to do so, he played the game. He paused to allow the trainer to adjust his headguard and caught Joe looking over at him, satisfaction playing around his mouth.

He had been spotted by a cousin of Joe Murphy down in London and he was glad of the dedicated attention of the Irishman as well as the chance to get away. Franklin heard that Joe, brought up on bare-knuckle fighting, once said he'd give his mam away for the chance to face Franklin in the ring. Stupid old sod. Franklin was six-foot-two, black and proud, and nearly seventeen stone. And he was quick. Mean, too. His thoughts translated to his fists and he began to spar, relishing the power and speed of his arms.

"Break, break. BREAK, goddam it!" Sam Jones, head trainer, leapt into the ring and pulled Franklin away from the sparring partner who sank thankfully to his knees. "Don't go and kill the poor bastard – we're going to need him later."

Franklin continued pacing with enough latent energy to take out the rest of the gym, controlling the blood lust. He knew he would soon be ready. For all of it.

Fifteen minutes later, outside a relatively new café bar in Didsbury, Franklin Raye sat looking at his two best dealers, Otis King and Col Mawhinney. Visibly at ease in his surroundings, Otis King nursed a cappuccino and a cigarette. He could fit in wherever he was. A useful skill. Franklin also recognised in Otis a kindred spirit – his only desire was for money and what it could bring. Franklin was glad to have been given Otis as his 'loyal lieutenant'.

Col Mawhinney couldn't pass for anything but the Irishman he was. The two men suited him because they could access different groups of punters and open different channels of distribution. Franklin never divulged his source of supply. The less they knew the better.

Business was booming. Col was tapping into the pub scene in the city centre, focusing on the bigger places in the redeveloped Castlefield area. He could pass for gay, too, with his soft brogue and green eyes, so he was just beginning to work Canal Street, the main drag of the Gay Village. Otis, being a few years younger, was working the massive student market even if it had seemed at first that Col was better placed to work that patch.

"Keep it tight," was always Franklin's order. "Get demand up where we know it will keep on rollin'."

"So, guys," he murmured. "What've you got for me?"

As he spoke he glared sideways at the young couple moving to sit at an adjacent table. They wisely decided against it, noisily announcing that a "seat inside might be more cosy."

"End of term's coming up," reported Otis when the pair was well out of earshot. "July, August likely to be better this year -

18   *Boxing Clever*

am aiming to get more regulars who'll be staying in Manchester during the break. Then we'll get the returners to help with the new guys during Fresher's Week in September."

"How many punters we talking?" asked Franklin.

Otis shrugged. "Five ton a month I reckon."

"E's holding steady, K's on the way up, coke doing well and weed always needed," Col took over. "Hear there's a big conference or exhibition coming to the G-Mex next week so I'll make sure we've got some contacts with the organisers. That new club's opening on Saturday. Reckon we'll do loads there."

Franklin allowed himself a smile. "More coffee gentlemen?"

He watched as Col Mawhinney, in obvious good spirits, left the café.

"What's the word?" he demanded.

He was very pleased with how the Irishman was shaping up, very pleased indeed. Otis was going to face some stiff competition to stay as his main man and collect the bonuses that went with it.

"As we thought, doesn't touch the stuff, gets roaring drunk regularly, women all over him like a rash," Otis replied.

Franklin knew that Otis was a totally different animal. Lived with his mother and younger brother in a tatty little house with a bedroom full of designer clothes and jewellery. But he was a smart boy. He had found Col.

"Good. Now fuck off. I've got business." He waited until Otis was well away before making the call.

"Be at the Oldham drop. Nine o'clock sharp."

Franklin muttered his affirmative reply.

As instructed, Franklin Raye waited patiently in the lock-up, watching through an ex-army-issue monocular until he was satisfied that the van driver was well out of the way. He knew the man was cool.

Tonight he was resplendent in a long black leather coat, gloves and Sixties-style black leather cap; Manchester's answer to *Shaft*. He quickly opened the well-oiled inset wicket door and stepped outside into the shadows that covered the area to the rear of the neatly parked van. Franklin had chosen the place well. With economic movement, the fast hands opened the combination padlock, opened the van doors and transferred the two large Nike sports bags into the lock-up.

He emptied the contents of the bags into a large safe that had been bolted into the floor, replaced the bags in the van and secured the padlock against the closed doors. After placing an envelope, fat with cash, onto the driver's seat, he slid back into his store-room and began to sort out the little plastic pouches. Humming quietly a cajun rhythm he remembered from his grandmother's house, Franklin did not heed the rattle of small wheels across the uneven ground as the sound of the engine died away into the distance.

An hour or so after the meeting in Didsbury, Col Mawhinney was sitting in the same gloomy pub near the new Aquatic Centre where he had first got into conversation with Otis. The pub was beginning to fill up; Irish Theme Nite.

"A'right Col?" Bearded Pat, clutching his fiddle, was right in front of him.

"Right yer are," Col replied, then picked up his guitar and began to strum.

The Underground Club was hidden under the arches of the erstwhile industrial part of the city. London money, scenting a honey-pot, had moved north first into Sheffield and now Manchester with its multitude of grants available to attract new

20   *Boxing Clever*

businesses. The city was pulsing with a resurgence of vitality, with developments of new apartments springing up everywhere.

Tickets for the club's opening night had been delivered to a clearly defined local celebrity 'A' list who would be vital to the club's success. Some tickets would inevitably make their way elsewhere, but that was the way things happened in the club business. Besides, a ticket didn't always guarantee entry.

The place was cavernous, a maze of tunnels under the busy tram line that ran overhead. In the harsh electric light it was garish, with its purple, yellow and blue walls and silver fittings, almost like an old tart's stuck-in-the-Sixties make-up. But when the lights went down and the spotlights threw shadows across the club, it looked chic, expensive. The heating would be on low although the evening promised to be warm. Extra salted snacks would be placed on every surface to tempt the punters and increase their thirst.

"Oh, go on then," had been Ellen's jokey response when he'd called to confirm the plans for the weekend.

It was now almost ten o'clock and the club was still relatively quiet. Tom was enjoying the feeling of space as they leaned against one of the elbow-level tables and sipped at their complimentary glasses of champagne. He'd been gratified by the effusive welcome of the manager who had clearly made sure she knew which of her guests required a personal greeting.

"Remind me again why we're here with the saddos?" He nodded over to the bar where a few naive clubbers, who had got there even earlier than they had, were standing in a pathetic cluster at the main bar with the four barmen behind it trying to look busy.

"So we can see who comes, who with and what they're wearing!" Ellen exclaimed. "I thought you were supposed to be a detective?"

"Now that you mention it," he said, suddenly recognizing one of the barmen. "Back in a minute." Leaving Ellen people watching, he walked across to talk to him.

"Good evening, sir!" Tom was almost blinded by the intensity of the barman's grin. "What can I get for you?"

"Nothing at the moment, thanks." Tom raised his half-full glass. "Just wanted to introduce myself. DI Tom Ashton, Manchester CID."

The barman's grin became a wry smile. "Thought I recognised you from the Village. Not expecting any trouble tonight, I hope?"

"I would hope not. My being here is part duty, part pleasure. Just keeping an eye out as I'm sure your boss would expect."

The barman continued to look at him.

"Could I take your name? So we're even?"

"Rob," the man replied. "Hope you have a good evening." With that, he nodded in Tom's direction and moved to the other end of the bar to issue some order or other to one of his staff.

"What were you talking to him about?" Ellen asked him as he came back to her side, one hand appreciatively stroking the right cheek of her red silk-clad bottom.

"Just checking in." Tom replied as he looked around. "This place is a bit bloody slow, I must say - shall we have a look further in?"

Two hours later the place was heaving. Much to Ellen's delight, there was a substantial sprinkling of TV personalities.

She suddenly grabbed his arm. "Look, that's Mike Robson from the local radio station talking to the manager. Let's hear what they're saying."

Tom eyed her vibrant face with some amusement.

22   *Boxing Clever*

"I feel like a pillock," he tried to yell discreetly into her ear as they elbowed their way towards the radio man who had now attracted a small listening crowd. "We look like groupies."

"I thought you had no qualms about how you get information?" Ellen retorted. "Besides which, you can stand close behind me and get both hands on my bum."

Tom laughed. He tried desperately to tune into the conversation in front of him.

"You've certainly drawn a crowd, Jan," Mike Robson yelled in her direction above the pumping music. "Any problems?"

The manager shook her head and motioned towards the door. "The local gym owner, Joe Murphy, has provided some intelligent door staff that just send out the right message. One or two punters have been turned away because they looked like they haven't tried hard enough with their appearance. We want to make this *the* place to be seen in Manchester."

Tom could see her interviewer nodding appreciatively and thought that she had answered his query very cleverly. And no doubt a good radio report and write-up on its website from tonight would guarantee the radio station a regular supply of entrance tickets.

It was way past midnight when Ellen came back from the toilets and reported that she was very impressed with the decoration and how the light was good enough to redo your make-up but still managed to be flattering. Having no idea what she was talking about, Tom merely responded with a vague, "Oh, right."

Undeterred, she carried on. "I thought you said this opening bash was for celebrities and the Manchester's who's who?"

"That's what I'd heard. Why?" He couldn't help the yawn that choked his question. He was knackered.

Ellen, somewhat miffed, described the two girls giggling in the ladies' who were obviously students and even more star struck than she was.

"Apparently they managed to get tickets through a 'friend'. I wouldn't have thought they could afford to buy one drink in here, never mind stay all night."

"Were they taking anything?" The club was bound to attract drug dealers but he knew they would be hard to pick out in a crowd like this. He turned to face her head on. "Any mention of trying to get any drugs?"

Ellen sighed.

"Might have known you'd kick into work mode when I'm giving you some gossip. At least you've woken up a bit." She paused. "No they didn't. Not that I heard anyway."

"Can you see them?" His senses quickened, keen to see if there was any sniff of dealing activity going on.

"Bloody hell, Tom. You don't ask much."

Ellen moved his head around so that he could take in the heaving mass of people now gathered in the stylish gloom.

After a couple of hours of dancing, drinking and observing, Tom admitted defeat. It was impossible to move freely and when they found a couple of seats near a small bar in one of the side areas away from the main section, Ellen laid claim and refused to budge until her feet stopped throbbing.

Col watched as the two girls edged towards the main bar. One, slim and taller, pulled at her ear against the onslaught of the sound. The two girls pointed at a long-legged and long-haired young man who was gyrating at the edge of the dance floor and began to laugh.

He watched as the smaller girl tried to say something into her friend's ear. The friend laughed and hoisted the tiny scarf

24   *Boxing Clever*

top up over her breasts and grabbed the other girl's arm. They moved alongside the man and began to dance.

Col moved in. Wordlessly, he moved the friends apart, dancing with such nonchalance that the girls began to mirror his indifference. The tall girl flicked her long auburn hair and grinned suddenly at him moving in front of her, his arms raised to shoulder level and fingers splayed. Col Mawhinney smiled. No problem. Eye contact at this stage of the evening meant he was definitely on form. In fact, Col was feeling pretty good. His entry to the club was his first reward for sales from Franklin who had been given two tickets from the local newspaper's sports editor, and it was a chance to check the information that Col's contact would be providing.

The girl, Lisa, had been easy right from the start. Mind you, he'd had to pay over the odds for two vodka mixes, but she was pretty and, well, sort of *enthusiastic*. Not much conversation, naturally, clubs weren't designed for that sort of thing. Still, she'd stuck with him for the rest of the night and had been really easy to persuade.

"How about one of these, lovely Lisa?" he had yelled in her ear, swigging carelessly from his bottle as he did so. "Wanna feel good?" he rolled his eyes and laughed while pretending to throw a white tablet from his hand to his tongue in a practised movement. A few minutes later he began to push his feet into the floor, rhythmically stomping and writhing with such energy that the girl was transfixed.

"Hey!" she pulled at his sleeve. "Where'd you go? What've you had? Hey!"

Just as she was about to move away he pulled her to him, his arm around her waist, his eyes half-open.

"Come and play where I am?" he murmured. He saw her look around quickly, her face feverish with excitement and reckoned she was thinking – hell, why not? She put her hand out.

"How much for one?"

Col smiled. "Buy me a drink," he said as he passed her the E and watched as her innocent, bright face swallowed the kick.

In the early hours of the morning, Tom, who discovered he was relatively sober in the cool air, struggled to support Ellen to the taxi rank.

"I'm not drunk," she kept insisting. "It's just that my feet hurt."

As the pronouncement was given with her eyes closed and a vice-like grip on his arm, he wasn't convinced. Balancing Ellen as they staggered along the uneven pavement, they were overtaken by a group of friends, who'd obviously also had a good time. One, a tall girl, shouted as she hopped on and off the kerb.

"Hey guys," she whooped, skipping alongside them. "What d'ya say we have a moving-in-together house party?"

CHAPTER 4

Jack eased his way through the cat flap into the small yard at the back of Tom's house. With senses on full alert, he padded past the dustbin and paused before leaping on to the top of the brick wall that formed the boundary of Tom's property and the alleyway that separated it from the next terrace. He took his time surveying his territory from the vantage point on the wall.

Satisfied, he strolled as carelessly as an acrobat along to Mrs Roberts at No. 87. She expected him about this time, for a chat about the day and maybe to give him a bit of chicken or fish. He reached her back yard and jumped nimbly onto the lean-to roof and in through the open window in the kitchen. Right on time, as always.

Alice Roberts was seventy-six years old. Sitting in her cluttered but tidy back room she smiled as she heard the familiar tapping of her kitchen blind as the cat hit it on his way in. She sipped at her tea and waited for his company.

The next morning was grey and drizzly, although the weather forecast promised that the day would brighten. Alice carefully placed her freshly washed cup, saucer and plate away in the cupboard that had never quite sat true against the wall of her kitchen. It was twenty years since Jimmy had died and she still hadn't quite got used to seeing so few items on the draining board next to her sink. A heavy sadness clung about her and she hung her head gently, respectfully and with a barely audible sigh.

She missed her Jimmy, and still ached at her inability to bear their children. He was kind and gentle, especially each time she had miscarried but her 'dabbling', as he called it, made him closed and anxious. "I'm a witch," she used to say, just to get a rise out of him. It always worked though, a flick of the newspaper and a careful sideways glance that indicated his discomfort. She had known nothing else, as a child she had learned to welcome her strangeness rather than to fear it.

She knew the day that Jimmy died that he wouldn't come home to her from work. She wished she could have been with him at the end, but she'd seen the accident only minutes before it happened and she was truly glad not to witness it for real. Alice shook herself and briskly put on her raincoat and gloves, reached for her bag and went out, checking the door out of habit rather than concern. There was no mischief around her that day. It was Thursday. One of her bingo days.

As she made her way along the road from the house that had been her home for fifty years, she heard the joyous sound of youthful laughter coming from the alleyway that was alongside her back yard. The old houses were becoming more and more popular; the same houses that Tom's grandmother might have lived in with hopelessness and an outside lavatory, were now in one of the right parts of Manchester. One of the nearby streets favoured by young professionals even had its own website now.

On a whim, Alice decided to follow the sound even though the diversion would bring her out on the main road a little further away from her bus stop. She smiled as she saw two pretty girls teasing a tall young man who was clearly protesting in vain.

28   *Boxing Clever*

"Honestly, Pete!" The smaller of the girls said. "The place is minging – we're going to have to give it a good spring clean before we move in."

"What's wrong with it?" came the plaintive reply, which set the two girls laughing helplessly again.

"Look, we'll be round tomorrow to make a start," the girl said.

"Oh, not me," said the taller girl who had lovely auburn hair. "I'm going home for the weekend, remember? I'll be back on Sunday so let's do it on Monday, Mel? Not fair for you to tackle this on your own."

Alice learned, as she affected a slow walk that befitted a lady of her advanced years, that the tall girl was called Lisa and that Mel would more than happily wait for her friend's return.

Two days later, Alice watched from her small back bedroom window at the activity in the house across the alleyway. The balmy early summer air was perfect for sound to travel.

"Shall we get started then?" Lisa called from the back door where she was looking at the overflowing rubbish bin. Mel came to the door to join her friend.

"We'll have to give this place a clean *before* we think of putting our stuff in, don't you think?" After a few minutes' discussion, Alice watched as the two girls set about cleaning the house. She enjoyed observing their vitality and hearing their cries of "Yuk!" and "That boy is gross!" She almost wished she was fifty years younger.

She pottered around her home with the noise and music from the other house providing a welcome background. It was nearly seven o'clock in the evening when she realised that all was quiet. She was back in an unwelcome, heavy, elderly silence. She began to feel increasingly unsettled, a feeling that did not lessen at Jack's arrival. The cat must have sensed her

Maureen Devlin 29

mood for, instead of using his languid gaze and throaty purr to evoke some calm, he paced restlessly with her around her generously furnished living room.

"I'm all out-a-sorts, Jack," she muttered while slowly shaking her newly washed and set grey head. "I can't seem to settle...it's as if I've got so much energy I don't know what to do with myself, but it's not a good feeling. It's a bad feeling, Jack."

Alice turned in her slippers towards the chair, then grasped her head, moaning. She could feel the pulse rushing in her ears, her stomach was churning...the room was swaying...lights dim with the sound of talking and laughter all around her. She could smell an unfamiliar sweet, but not unpleasant scent. There was smoke. She was dimly aware of her breathing coming in short gasps, sweat forming on her brow and her back. Her jaw locked. Voices came and went. They sounded anxious, fearful – a girl's voice, pretty faces just out of clear focus. Calmly, she accepted that she was going to die – she was sinking into a fat, glorious, forgiving blackness....

"Aaagh!" Alice put her hand to her cheek where the cat had scratched her, and opened her eyes. Her heart thudded. Where had she been? Something dreadful was going to happen but she didn't know where. What was she going to do?

Alice got shakily to her feet to get to the window for some fresh air, breathing deeply as she did so. Hearing the cat yowling in the kitchen to be let out of the back door, she followed him, intending to put the kettle on for a cup of tea. She opened the door and as she idly followed the cat's leap onto the yard wall, she noticed a girl at the window of the house across the alleyway and to the right. The girl was laughing and clearly talking to an unseen friend.

Oh my dear, thought Alice. What am I going to do?

30   *Boxing Clever*

She was still agonising over her breakfast tea the next morning. Hardly aware of Jack's reappearance, she found herself idly stroking his soft, black head muttering over and over, "I have to do something, before it's too late."

Resting her head backwards on the old Dralon chair, she closed her eyes and cursed her frail indecision. Seconds later, her eyes snapped open in reaction to the heavy tread of Jack's paws on her chest and the thrust of his head under her chin. She gazed at him, their eyes locked for an indefinable moment. The next second, the cat had gone, out of the open kitchen window. "Back home, I suppose," Alice mused. "That nice young man must wonder where his cat disappears to. Oh! You stupid woman," she shouted at herself. "He's a policeman, he'll know what to do."

Filled now with purpose, Alice hurried from her house in her slippers (not the done thing, but just this once) and was soon knocking on the green door of the house where Jack lived. She was still holding the knocker when the door was opened by the handsome young freckled man dressed only in trousers, with wet hair and a slightly irritated expression.

"Oh," she stammered, flustered. "You see, well the thing is, I live round the corner and Jack comes to visit and something dreadful is going to happen and I really don't know what to do?!"

Tom looked at the worried old face and the angry scratch on one cheek. What on earth was she talking about? For a moment he couldn't place her, then remembered the near collision in the supermarket.

"Please, calm down," he began, not wanting to appear rude.

"I'm Alice Roberts. I'll come in." The woman had obviously regained her composure and pushed past his naked chest into the hallway. "We must work out a plan of action. I think someone is going to be very ill, even die, in that student house at the back. I've seen it."

Tom could feel his eyebrows dance towards his hairline and he worked very, very hard to mask his disbelief.

"Er..." He was stumped.

"Don't you understand, young man?" she demanded. "There's no time to lose." She began to wring her hands. "Let me explain."

So, over the next few minutes she told him of her experience, describing a girl's face and the dread in her heart that was growing heavier by the minute. And all the while, Jack sat at her side, his unblinking gaze never leaving Tom's face.

"Did he do that to your face?"

"He brought me back," she replied simply. A minute passed.

"Tell me again, slowly, how you felt while you were having this... experience, Mrs Roberts," Tom asked, interested in spite of himself. As he listened to the old lady's graphic description he realised that she was giving a text-book account of a drug-taker's nightmare. He almost shrugged as he thought, well, yes, students, parties, drugs – it's how it is. But with the words of his boss ringing in his ears and the weight of the woman's intelligent gaze, so sure of impending tragedy and his ability to prevent it, that instead he took her hand.

"It's like this. Apart from the fact that I'm off duty now, I have precious few powers to go across and even *talk* to the students let alone look round for any drugs–"

Her eyes flashed with what he read to be the intent to go herself. She pulled her hand away, folded her arms across her chest and glared at him.

"Mrs Roberts, please don't think I don't take your concerns seriously but there is really nothing I can do."

"Hrumph."

32   *Boxing Clever*

His visitor made no move to leave and he was beginning to think he'd be stuck all day with her unless he did something.

"Look, "he said. "I know the last thing you would want is to be seen to be interfering–"

"For goodness sake! This is not about me, it's about that young girl over there. I have to say I'm very disappointed in you, Tom. I rather expected you to be more helpful."

Why she made him feel ashamed was beyond him, but he was more puzzled by how she knew his name. He hadn't told her. He began to ask her when she cut him off.

"Well?"

Tom sighed.

"I can't promise anything but if you're really concerned.... It'll have to wait until the night of the party and when it is in full swing. I'm sure it'll be fine."

The woman considered him for awhile, and then nodded her assent.

Tom gave her his card and explained what she had to do.

The phone began to ring just as she was leaving. He smiled at her encouragingly, gesturing for her to see her own way out and picked up the receiver.

"Tom Ashton–" barely had the words hit the telegraphic wire than a sobbing gasp came back into his ear.

"Tom – it's me, the bastards, oh..." He stiffened in alarm, his visitor forgotten.

"Ellen? What's happened? Are you all right?" The breathing in his ear was still coming in short gasps. "Tell me what happened! It's okay, it'll be okay."

"My car," came a sniff. "Some thug caved in my car window when I was at the traffic lights at Moss Side – they've got my bag – I was so frightened–"

Maureen Devlin   33

"Are you hurt?" Tom was mentally thumping himself for not warning her weeks ago when the threat first appeared.

"No, no – no cuts or anything," her voice was calmer now. "There was glass everywhere. I just didn't believe what was going on, it was so quick. They knew they were going to frighten me..." Her voice began to catch again.

"Where are you?"

"I'm at the police station!" Ellen's voice lifted at the irony of the statement. "Will you come for me? I need to get the car fixed and locks changed on the house and cancel cards and everything. Bloody hell!" She was getting angry now. "It's all so sodding inconvenient."

When he arrived at the station, it was to find Ellen looking glum.

"Thanks for coming," she raised a half smile. "I've just realised how I stupidly carry around nearly my whole life in my handbag. I'm totally lost without it." She sighed. "It had taken me until now to get used to the electronic organiser my parents gave me last Christmas and *everything* was in it. Phone numbers, diary stuff, notes. My mobile phone has gone too."

"Does your neighbour still have a set of house keys?"

A nod.

"Right – you call her now and I'll follow you to the garage and then take you home. We should be able to get the locks done in a hour or so – have you spoken to your office?" With that, he helped guide her to her feet and out towards the car park.

The flat black and silver case was cool to the touch. Diary, notes, addresses, telephone numbers. With nothing better to do, the boy began to surf through Ellen's life.

CHAPTER 5

"Hello? Is that Col?"

He paused. Not familiar, but female for sure.

"You are?"

"Lisa. We met a couple of weeks back? At the opening of the Underground Club? There's a party coming up and I wondered..." The girl's voice tailed off.

"Well, hi, Lisa! Didn't recognise you." Col's brain connected the names and voice to the face. "Glad to hear the plan – when and where?" He noted down the address and hung up after assuring her that he would be there. Time, he thought, for a bit of parallel trade.

It promised to be a glorious evening. Manchester had surpassed itself with unbroken sunshine and an unexpected 81 degrees Fahrenheit. Leaning by the slightly open window in her small back bedroom, Alice watched the comings and goings in the student house. Absent-mindedly she stroked Jack's head. The cat was rarely with her during the day and she was glad of him. Her hand continued its rhythmic motion as she watched the busy preparations, the odd burst of laughter bouncing along the nearby walls to suddenly fill her little room. Not long now.

As time went on, she had to admit to being more than a little puzzled. Was she mistaken? She saw the dark-haired girl close the windows and door at the back of the house and suddenly all was quiet. What if her vision wasn't clear and she had just assumed it would happen in *that* house because she recognised the girl? No, no. She had to be right – she'd seen them, heard them preparing. All she could do now was wait. The evening wore on and Alice maintained her vigil, rewarded eventually by the building noise from across the alley.

Soon, over twenty people were crammed into the small walled space at the back of the house. Alice saw Jack jump up onto the alley wall and pass unnoticed. Talking, music and laughter combined to fill the local area with the unmistakable sound of youth. Still more people appeared via the alleyway and pushed in towards the tiny kitchen and back room, no doubt drinking and beginning the delicate negotiations that would determine the sleeping arrangements for the night. Alice was older but by no means ignorant in the ways of the young.

Col had taken considerable care in choosing which clothes to wear. Not too flashy, but it was obvious he was no student. Light, black linen trousers, white designer t-shirt and black trainers. Anyone there able to recognise the brand of watch on his slender wrist would assume it was fake. It wasn't.

The auburn hair was easy to spot, even in the gloom. He scanned the group, exploring the potential. He eased his way towards her and waited until she turned and saw him. She smiled.

Without a word, he steered her away from the kitchen towards the quieter front room.

"Lisa," he said, looking at the young woman with blatant admiration. "You look gorgeous – anyone special here for you tonight?"

The girl blushed. He knew that he'd been noticed by the other girls nearby and was enjoying the glances coming his way. She laughed.

36   *Boxing Clever*

"Tell you later! Look–" Her voice lowered. "Have you brought the stuff?"

Col feigned hurt.

"Now, do I look like the kind of man who'd let you down?" Then, catching her in an embrace, he danced her into the back room toward the open window.

"Who's the first customer then?" he whispered into her ear. "Do I have to work this thing or am I expected?"

He allowed her to manoeuvre him around the room in time with the music, so that a small group came into his line of sight.

"The girl with the short hair, pink top, is Mel. She wants some and so does Pete. The guy next to her with the long hair."

"Are they cool?"

"Yep. Can I have one too?"

He smiled at her.

"First on my list, sweetheart," he said.

Alice watched and waited. Not yet. Time ticked by in synch with her elderly heart. Soon.

One-thirty am and the party was in full swing, noise reverberating around the Victorian walls. Hearing the flick of the blind in the kitchen, Alice reached for the phone.

"Which emergency service do you require? Police, Fire or Ambulance?"

Alice was firm in her reply. "Police please. I'm an old woman on my own and they've been making a racket for hours now – thump, thump. It's the middle of the night and I need my sleep."

There was a pause, no doubt as the officer began to log the call, and Alice was sure she heard the sound of a drink being taken.

"Are you still there?" she said stridently.

"Of course, madam," came the reply. "Could you give me your details and the address of the house making all the noise?"

"You will send someone round right away, won't you? It's very important."

The two young officers knocked at the front door of the house.

"They're never going to hear us," said the first officer to his female colleague. "Reckon we should try around the back." He turned to Alice who was hovering nearby.

"You don't need to be here, Mrs..."

"Roberts," she cut in. "And I think I do."

The WPC tried again. "Really, Mrs Roberts. We'll sort it out, you go back home now."

Glaring her indignation, Alice jerked her head and said, "The back is that way."

The two police officers followed her direction, and made their way to the rear of the house. Alice stayed close behind.

A voice was shouting for "Help – someone do something!"

"Pete!" came a cry. "Pete!" The girl's second call coincided with a brief respite between one ghastly piece of music and another. Hearing the scream, the two officers ran towards the sound and began banging at the gate.

The commotion in the house was centred on a small figure curled up on the floor in the back room. As the police pushed their way through the dazed and ignorant party goers, Alice felt sick as she stared at the horrible state of collapse. It was the small dark haired girl. Mel.

"What's she had?" The police woman shouted into the room. "Come on, someone, quickly!"

Alerted by Alice, Tom arrived at the busy Accident and Emergency department of the Royal Infirmary just as the steel trolley was rushed in. At least his elderly conspirator hadn't

38   *Boxing Clever*

said "I told you so" but she had insisted he let her know what happened.

A couple stumbled behind the trolley, unsure of what to do. Tom saw the girl wince involuntarily as her senses adjusted to the light and the young man seemed to be early stages of sobering up. He was shaking his head repeatedly, muttering "What the fuck...? Shit...."

Tom could feel the anxiety in the air. Cream walls and bold prints couldn't ease the worry of efficiency and trauma that typified this part of a hospital. All elements of humanity seemed to be represented here, a snapshot of the city's cosmopolitan population. Young and old, male and female; black, white and brown faces; arms held protectively, eyes closed in pain, the occasional shout of abuse.

The young officer who had brought the girl's friends to the hospital spoke briefly to the receptionist, pointing over to where they stood. He then returned to the two young people and motioned them over towards Tom who was standing near the large front doors.

"I'm DI Tom Ashton." he said. "You are?"

"I'm Lisa Waters, he's Pete Garvey."

"First, we need the name and address of her parents. Second, whatever you know about what happened."

"Her name is Mel Chadwick," the boy replied, his senses clearly sharpened significantly on exposure to the frenzied efficiency of the A & E. "Her folks live in Sussex somewhere, can't tell you where, though."

The young officer looked at Lisa. "Can you add anything, miss? We don't need to impress on you how urgent this is."

The girl's eyes were full and liquid. She bit her bottom lip and shook her head.

Maureen Devlin   39

"Call in and see what there is at the house, Wilkins," ordered Tom, then "Where's he going?" as Pete began to lope away from them.

"I don't think he's feeling too well," Lisa said, apologetically.

Tom sighed inwardly. Bloody students, no common sense. He agreed with his father. Bring back National Service.

"Right. We're going to have to get a full statement from you both later, but what can you tell me now?"

"Do you think she'll be all right?" She looked round, wildly. "I mean, no one is telling us anything."

"They're used to people like your friend in here," Tom replied, though not unkindly. "They'll talk to us when they need to. Now," he paused as Wilkins rejoined them. "Tell me what you can remember. We know she took a tablet that you think was E, and had been drinking. Who did she buy it from?"

The girl looked terrified.

"It'll not help your friend if you keep quiet," Tom warned, but recognising her distress and his own thirst, he added, "Look, right now I suggest we go through to the canteen, get some tea, and you can start by telling me about the guy who gave or sold this stuff to Mel. All right?"

"What about Pete?" she asked looking over to where her friend had slumped in a chair, his head in his hands.

"Doesn't look like he's going to run off anywhere." Glancing at the young man, Tom figured that his comment was a glaring understatement - he looked near to collapse. Leaving Wilkins to babysit, Tom guided Lisa along the green and grey corridor to the public canteen.

"Actually, this tea's not bad," he said watching Lisa as she stared sightlessly into her cup. It was obviously a big shock for

40   *Boxing Clever*

her. A brutal introduction to the real world. A good time to get some answers.

"Right," he changed his tone, harder and no nonsense. Her head snapped up, eyes widened in alarm. "I'm listening."

She swallowed and, sitting up straight in her chair, began to speak.

"I met him at the Underground Club a couple of weeks ago."

"Did he give you a name? And what date was this?"

"Col. And I think it was a Friday, I can't remember." Lisa shook her head as if to try and clear the fog away. "Oh!" she exclaimed. "Of course. It was the opening night, a sort of launch party. Pete had got some free tickets."

"Did he now?" Tom made a mental note, remembering Ellen's observation. "Carry on."

"Mel, Pete and I went," she recounted. "It was packed, and there were quite a few famous people there. Mel and I were dancing and Col just started dancing with us, well, with me."

"Did he sell you anything? Did *he* take anything?" he pressed.

She flushed. Taking a deep breath, she replied "Yes, I'm sure he did. A white tablet; he gave me one to try." Her tone was a little defiant now and her chin lifted. "I enjoyed it. I..." she hesitated "...I didn't know..." Her voice tailed off.

"What was it, Lisa? E? Can you describe the effects?"

Tom was struck suddenly by the incongruity of the situation they were in. Sitting in a bright hospital canteen, drinking orange tea and discussing the voluntary ingestion of poison whilst all around them many poor souls were reliant on other drugs just to stay alive.

"I think it was E," she replied. "I've never taken anything before. We talked about it the next day and then when we decided to have a party. We wanted Col to come with some stuff for everyone."

"So then, what can you tell me about this Col?"

Lisa described the man she knew, her lip trembling. Tom figured she had been a bit keen on the guy who had helped put her friend in a coma. She painted a picture of a dark-haired and good-looking individual, very self-confident.

"He had an accent. Gentle. Scottish I think. Or maybe Irish. I'm not very good at telling the difference."

"We'll need you to look at some photos at the station."

Lisa nodded in assent.

"How did you contact him or did he find you?"

"He gave me a slip of paper – with a mobile phone number on. It's in my purse at home."

"Right, that'll do for now. Are you happy for my colleague to look for it now?"

Lisa nodded and after having given details of where to find the purse in her bedroom, she rose stiffly from her chair and walked back to reception. Tom instructed Wilkins to radio through to the officer still at the house.

"Get them to ring the number through to CID will you? I'm going to speak to one of the doctors, see how she's doing."

Apparently she was proving difficult. As he stood by the door waiting to attract someone's attention, the tired-looking young doctor called for a SATS check. Tom knew this helped to describe the status of the patient.

By the frown on his face, the figures provided did nothing to reassure the doctor that she was improving. A nurse suddenly noticed Tom's presence in the doorway. As her mouth pursed ready to ask who the hell he was, he pulled out his ID card and quickly introduced himself.

42   *Boxing Clever*

"We have gotten hold of the parents' number and the local police will be informing them as we speak. How's she doing?" He looked down at the tiny figure, dwarfed by the paraphernalia of intensive care.

"If she can hold her own for a few hours until the alcohol is out of her system, her body might have a chance. We really need to know what she's had although we think it's probably E. Have you any more on that?"

Tom shook his head. "Her friend seems to think that's what it was. We're trying to find the dealer." Not being able to add anything more, he backed away, feeling useless.

CHAPTER 6

T he briefing room was crowded and getting hotter and more pungent, a combination of coffee and a rising undertone of hot bodies.

Tom eyed his colleagues as they shuffled into chairs and onto desks, chatting easily with their neighbours; tension levels low. Dean, as ever, feigned indifference and gave all his attention to cleaning the fingernails of his left hand with a crippled paperclip. Rich, near the door and in the grip of a bout of hayfever, had the appearance of a heavy drinker who'd just had some very bad news.

Copies of the incident report had been circulated within CID before the meeting.

"Right," he said, calling the meeting to a start. "First, let's look at what we've got on the drug case. Student party, just about everyone who was there and can remember their own name either bought or was offered drugs. One girl, Melanie Chadwick, nineteen years old, is now lying in a coma in the MRI and not looking good. We know from her friend, Lisa Waters, who lived in the house with Mel and a guy called Pete–"

"Lucky bloke," somebody quipped.

"–Lisa Waters," Tom continued, ignoring the comment, "had arranged for a guy called Col to be at the party with the express view to supply. Now, you've seen the report. She met this guy at the opening night of the Underground Club. He turned up at the party alone, at about midnight. Lisa is coming

43

44   *Boxing Clever*

down later to look at some mug shots but we've got a mobile number for this Col – what's the progress on that? Rich, was that yours?"

Rich was momentarily halted in his reply as Ryan made her usual late entry, bringing a haze of cigarette smoke in with her. He coughed.

"Not great," he reported, looking glum. "From what the phone company tells me, the mobile was registered to a guy called Davies who'd apparently had it stolen some weeks ago and–"

"Hang on," interrupted Dean. "How come this Davies guy didn't get the account stopped and the SIM made obsolete? Why was this dealer still able to use it?"

"I had a chat with Mr Davies this morning," Rich replied. "It turns out that although the mobile was registered in his name, it was funded by his company and he had just been told he was being made redundant. A bit aggrieved to say the least. His view was that they could sort it out if they were bothered, or stand the cost. We spoke to the company – least of all their worries."

"You did ring the mobile, didn't you?" queried Tom to be met with a withering glance.

"Of course. Dead or dumped."

"Great – so all we've got is that the guy's name is Col and that he has a Scottish or Irish accent. Dean – when is the friend coming in to look over the rogues gallery?"

"About eleven."

"Okay – let's meet again if and when she finds our man. In the meantime, crawl over the incident report again with the descriptions the students gave us on the night – see if any bells are rung."

"Half of them were seeing triple never mind double when they were asked," muttered a voice. "Doubt they could recognise their own mother; fat chance of anything useful on a dealer."

"It's all we've got right now," Tom snapped. "This may not be the only comatose teenager we get this year and, as our leader keeps reminding me, we need negative press like a hole in the head. Right, let's move on. Elliott?" He perched himself on the corner of a nearby desk. "Where are we with the shoplifters?"

"About the girl," said Dean later as they left the room. "What else could we look at?"

"This Lisa said she had first come into contact with matey-boy at the Underground. We need to see what they've got. Talk to the doormen, look at any CCTV tapes, try and get a visual if we can." He paused. "You get over there and see what you can come up with. I'll catch up with you later. There's someone I need to talk to first."

Dean gave him a quizzical look. "Who is?"

"Just an anxious neighbour who called 999 on the night because of the noise." He was damn sure that he wasn't going to admit to using the paranormal as a tool of preventative policing.

"Very community-spirited of you, I must say," Dean observed. "Trying for more promotion?"

She was waiting for his arrival. The front door of the neatly kept terraced house opened just as he raised his arm to knock.

"Is she all right?" Alice asked anxiously as he walked into the sun-kissed front room. "It was as I said, wasn't it?"

"She's in a bad way," he replied. "They think they know what she took, but with the heat and alcohol...they're giving her the most up-to-date treatment. She's still in a coma, though–" he softened his voice "–they're not sure she's going to make it."

"The poor girl," Alice muttered. "Such a ghastly experience. I wish I could have done more." Wearily, and showing some signs of her years, she sank into one of the two brown floral armchairs, livened by pieces of crisp, white linen on the arms

46   *Boxing Clever*

and backs. Tom, not waiting for an invitation, sat in the other, his frame blocking some of the bright late morning light.

"Is there anything else you can remember? From the other night or the other day?"

Alice pondered. "I'm afraid there were just too many new faces and noises for me to pick out anything in particular." She studied her hands. "The only thing that was relatively clear was the face of the other pretty girl who lives there. With the reddish hair. Lisa. I saw them the other week as they were moving in. I hadn't seen any danger then..."

Tom nodded agreement. "She's had a big shock. It was her idea to get the guy selling the drugs along to the party."

They both sat quietly for a moment, the stillness broken suddenly by a sharp sound in the kitchen. Tom looked quickly at Alice and made to get up when he saw a small smile playing on her lips.

"He's a regular little visitor, your Jack," she said. As the small black figure leapt onto the side of her chair she added, "He was round here most of the evening of the party, keeping me company. He popped out once and I could see him on the back wall of that house – almost as if he was looking..." she tailed off, stroking Jack's appreciatively curved back.

Tom promised to let her know how Mel was doing and then left, patting his errant friend on the head as he passed by to the door. It was only as he stepped out onto the pavement that the thought struck him. He hadn't told her Jack's name either.

An hour later, Tom was in the station's main interview room. Lisa, looking pale and younger than her nineteen years was flanked by her equally wan parents. The father was tight-lipped, while his wife alternated her gaze between her clenched hands and her daughter who was sitting next to her father. Ryan stood by the door.

Maureen Devlin   47

"Lisa, Mr and Mrs Waters," Tom began. "Thank you for coming in today – we appreciate it. We need all the information we can get to track down the man who has put Mel in hospital." He spoke kindly, and his tone was enough to bring about a relaxing of Lisa's shoulders and a direct gaze from both parents.

"Now, you know what we need you to do Lisa?" he asked.

She nodded. "You want me to look at photos to see if I can pick out Col." Her voice was flat but strong. "Can we get started? The sooner you get him, the better."

"Thanks Ryan," Tom said on receiving the call. "Keep them there for a minute, will you?" And when the phone was switched off, muttered, "Sod," under his breath.

"Nothing?" asked Rich, standing near the water cooler in the corner of the CID office.

"Nope," affirmed Tom. He paused. "This might be a bit of a long shot...is John Andrews still in?" John Andrews, police artist, was borrowed occasionally from a neighbouring force despite the advance of other technologies. "A quick sketch could be useful and while we've got the girl and her family here...." Tom tailed off as his colleague tapped a number on a nearby desk phone and asked the desk clerk if John was around.

"You're in luck," Rich reported. "He'll be there in a few minutes."

John Andrews wriggled his large bulk onto a chair next to Lisa and carefully arranged his A3 white pad in front of him at an angle that she could see comfortably. He began to draw an initial pencil outline.

"Face, thin or rounded?" the artist enquired, all the while making light charcoal strokes on the pristine white sheet. Tom looked on, admiring the skill.

48   *Boxing Clever*

"Sort of round, but not fat. And he had a sort of a neat nose? But not girly?" she tried to explain.

"Eyes?" came the next question. "Deep set, hooded, round...?" John prompted and drew as Lisa in turn agreed and challenged the shapes appearing on the page.

Time passed, lines added and removed, shadows and definition applied. Then, at last, a face was looking out from the artist's pad.

"Yes!" Lisa said. "That's him."

Tom moved quickly to take hold of the pad and concentrate on the face captured in front of him. Bugger. He didn't recognise it. Judging by the sag of Ryan's shoulders, neither did she.

Dean called in as he was leaving the Underground Club.

"Nothing at all?" Tom queried.

"Zilch." Dean's tone was dull with frustration. "I did catch sight of the three friends going in and coming out of the club but they didn't have anyone else in tow. The film from inside the club only clocks the entrance – guess it's too dark inside. Saw you and Ellen. Anything from the mug shots?"

"No, but we got John Andrews to do a sketch. Not ringing any bells, though. When are you coming back in?"

"Day after tomorrow. I'm shadowing Martin James over in Leeds tomorrow, remember?" Working alongside other, more senior officers from different police forces was part of the Commissioner's strategy for performance improvement. "I've put it off twice already."

"No problem. But I'll fax a copy of the sketch over there so you can check it out." Tom rang off, already turning his mind to the pile of other case files on his desk.

CHAPTER 7

Tom was rather enjoying *The Archers*. The drama of an affair between the vicar and the village GP kept him quite entertained. He wasn't a follower of the country soap; it was unusual for him to be listening to the radio at seven o'clock at night and even more unusual for him to be sitting in his car outside the large modern offices of Vanpharma.

He'd promised to pick Ellen up from work. Her car was still being repaired and although she had the use of a 'pool' car, she had accepted his offer as it would be the only time they would see each other this week. It wasn't just Tom's work getting in the way this time, Ellen was working increasingly crazy hours. Something to do with a new drug the company was about to launch.

He watched as smart be-suited men and women left the main entrance in front of him. Not a bad place to work, he mused, taking in the landscaped grounds, the glass and chrome facia of the buildings and the modern sculpture near the gates. Clearly well-paid as well, judging by the generous smattering of BMWs and Mercedes still in the car park. Hard to believe that a few years ago this place was a rubbish tip.

Time wore on and his stomach began to growl. By eight o'clock, Tom's curiosity about the place had completely worn off and he was getting narked. He'd booked a table at a new restaurant in town he was keen to try. No doubt Ellen would want to get changed before they went and they were running

50   *Boxing Clever*

out of time. He flicked open his mobile and rang her extension number.

"Hi, it's me," he said immediately the phone was picked up.

"I'm sorry, who are you?" came back an unfamiliar voice.

"Tom Ashton – I was wanting to speak with Ellen?"

"Oh right!" Recognition. "She's just left."

Tom raised his eyes towards the door as he thanked the man and saw Ellen hurrying towards him.

"Sorry, sorry," she gasped at him as she plonked herself on the passenger seat, struggling to arrange her briefcase and handbag in the well at her feet.

Tom leaned across to kiss her flushed cheek.

"Forgiven. I'm starving – I've booked a table at Umba's. Eight-thirty. We'd better get moving if you want to go home first?"

Ellen considered.

"Nah. I'm in need of a drink and I guess you've done enough waiting around. I'm going to have to come in early again tomorrow so I can't really do a late night. Let's go straight there."

Tom, hearing the subtext that he would be sleeping on his own tonight, wished he wasn't driving. He could have done with at least enjoying a few drinks.

The restaurant was tucked away down a side street near the imposing white columned buildings of the financial district. The walls were cleverly decorated with what looked like balls of cotton wool stuck onto a red-and-gold-painted surface and the mood was relaxed. The place was comfortably full and the service was just right. Tom was looking forward to seeing whether the chef deserved his reputation and he could see that Ellen was impressed.

Maureen Devlin 51

"So," he said as they waited for the dessert menu to arrive. He didn't really need one, the roasted brie and garlic followed by seared tuna and black olive mash was sitting quite contentedly in his stomach. "How come you're so busy?"

He listened as Ellen outlined the complexity of launching a new medicine. She was responsible for pulling together meetings for doctors so that they could hear all about it and she also was involved with getting the sales teams up to speed with the marketing and clinical information.

"That's why I'm going to be away so much over the next few weeks," she announced. "We are launching to the sales force first. In Barcelona. Then I'll be going to medical launch meetings in Leeds, Belfast, London, Cardiff and Glasgow."

Tom was surprised to feel that the news bothered him. He tried to do a quick analysis as they waited for the chocolate bread and butter pudding to arrive. Hhmm. Worrying.

"Well, all right for some. All that excitement, away from the daily grind." His tone wasn't quite light enough.

Ellen gazed at him, the candlelight reflected in her eyes.

"Believe you me, Tom. It's no picnic. Anyway, you'd hate it. No nasty stuff to get your teeth into." She sipped her wine. "Oh, yes, that reminds me..."

She was interrupted as the two bowls arrived. Amid a satisfying munch of the fluffy concoction, with vanilla custard, Tom asked, "What were you going to say?"

"Oh, it's nothing really. Just that I've been getting a few nuisance calls."

She described how she had got home from work one evening the previous week to see her machine flashing, letting her know that she had eight new messages.

"One," she smiled at him, "was you, but the rest? Silence. I did 1471. Nothing."

52   *Boxing Clever*

Tom actually laughed out loud when Ellen then told him how she had dealt with the calls. Her chance had come at the start of Friday evening's edition of Coronation Street. On registering the silence coming loudly through the earpiece, Ellen had formed a ring with the thumb and middle finger of her right hand and blew, hard. With considerable satisfaction she reported how she had heard the caller's phone slam down.

"Ha!" she crowed. "Weirdo. Probably trawling through the phone book and seeing who he can worry. That'll have cleared his earwax."

On Saturday, though, Ellen clearly wasn't quite so self-assured. She called him at work, which was a rare occurrence, and asked if he could meet her for coffee.

"Now?" he had asked. "What's up? Can't it wait until tonight?" Both divorced, Tom and Dean occasionally made up a four with Ellen and her friend Fiona. Nothing too heavy, but no complaints from any of them so far and they were meeting up later.

"Suppose," she didn't sound too happy about it. "Maybe you could come on your way home? I want to show you something."

The note, which had been lying on her doormat when she got back from the gym that morning, was certainly something. A nasty little note. Tom looked at it again. It was handwritten on cheap, lined notepaper.

"We know what you do and where you go. Your friends are scum. You kill animals. You'll pay."

The note had been pushed through Ellen's door with no envelope, no stamp. By hand. Tom could see that Ellen was shaken.

"Doesn't the company have a procedure for this sort of stuff? Have you reported it to them?"

Ellen explained. Vanpharma, like every other pharmaceutical company, had a sophisticated policy for managing pressure groups such as the animal rights lobby that were often behind this type of activity. Before Tom's arrival, she had called the emergency number provided by company security.

"They asked me to fax a copy through so they could see if there was anything to tie it in to any groups they know about. I've to take the original in on Monday before I go to Barcelona."

"Have you any idea how these guys could have got your personal information?" he asked without thinking.

"Well," Ellen spoke slowly and between clenched teeth. "I did have my car broken into while I was driving into Manchester a few weeks ago. My Psion was stolen, and my mobile. I did let the office know at the time. Oh, and you were involved too!" Her voice became a shout.

"Sorry, sorry." Idiot. "Surely you don't think it could be those thugs behind this? They tend to sell on stuff they steal."

"How the hell do I know? Fat lot of use you are."

For once, unsure of a clever answer, Tom pulled Ellen to him and held her, stroking her hair. As he felt her relax into him he whispered that it would probably best if she stayed with him for the rest of the weekend. She gave a small sniff and then pulled away and looked up at him. Her lips moved in a wobbly smile and she coughed as if to regain her composure.

"Thanks. Yes, I will. Look, I know you've got stuff to do so I'll share a taxi in tonight with Fiona. Can you take a few things in a bag back to yours for me now?"

He tried a sheepish grin as he slid into the booth next to Ellen who was looking stunning in a blue and black gypsy-style ruffled

54   *Boxing Clever*

blouse topping a pair of white jeans. She barely acknowledged his arrival. Dean raised his eyebrow in sympathy.

"So much for eight o'clock," Ellen snapped waspishly, unable to let the lengthening silence remain unfilled. "We've all got bloody hypoglycaemia."

"Sorry," said Tom, hands raised in abject apology. "Had an unexpected visitor and I just couldn't get away. She..." he tailed off as Ellen's laser glare beamed full onto his face.

"Spare us the gripping tale until we've eaten, Tom. Please?" He'd forgotten how Ellen suffered a severe loss of humour when she was hungry.

An hour or so later, wined, dined and relaxed, he felt brave enough to venture an arm around Ellen's waist. He squeezed. Leaning back against him Ellen sighed with pleasure.

"Oh, I see the fifteen rounds are officially off then?" Dean quipped. "Was rather looking forward to a bit of post-prandial sport."

Replying with a most un-ladylike poke of the tongue in his direction, Ellen rose and sashayed across the restaurant and up the open stairs to the ladies, Fiona in tow.

"Why do they always go to the bog in pairs?" Dean asked. "I've never understood that one."

"Going for a pee is a side line," Tom replied, philosophically. "Did Ellen tell you about the threatening letter she got?"

"Yeah. And the nuisance calls. She tried to give the impression she wasn't bothered but I think it had got to her. Reckon there's much behind it?"

"Bit early to tell but it's pretty nasty when someone's targeted you directly. She's staying with me for now and then we'll see what the guys at her place come up with."

The two men sat in easy silence, nursing a pint each as the noises of general conviviality washed around them.

"How was the job shadow then? Worth the trip?" Tom asked.

Dean grunted. "Guess. Picked up some ideas and they've got a new Chief Inspector who sounds like she's going to shake things up a bit." He paused to take a good two inches from his glass. "Just remembered, I didn't get that fax from you. What happened with that?"

"Shit! I got caught by The Rodent and it slipped my mind. Sod, Tom," he berated himself.

"Well, I'm sure it'll keep till Monday," Dean puffed his chest appreciatively as the girls approached the table. "Day off tomorrow and I intend to spend the entire time in bed with this delightful fox." Fiona caught the end of his remark and looked delighted rather than offended.

"Okay, guys," Ellen stayed on her feet. "Where next? I fancy a bit of a bop."

"Doesn't that new club have live bands on a Saturday as well as a disco?" asked Fiona. "I'm sure I read something about it. What do you reckon?"

"Well, let's get another drink in a pub first," ventured Tom. "A pint in that new place is going to cost a week's salary and I'm going to need to be pissed to pay for it."

Pushing through the growing crowd, he made his way to the bar while Dean placated the two women who were both keen to move on to the club.

"One, two – one, two," intoned a thick northern voice over the pub's PA system. Tom glanced idly across to the small raised stage dwarfed by two vast black speakers where four men in jeans and t-shirts were preparing for a gig. God, this bar was slow. Having had his raised hand ignored for the second time, he gazed back at the band and watched them shuffle around checking their gear without any great desire to hear their output.

Aah. At last.

56 *Boxing Clever*

"Two pints of bitter and two G&Ts," he yelled. Waving across to his friend for assistance, he paid for the drinks, passed the spirits to Dean and then muscled through the crowd behind him with the two beers.

There was a niggle in his mind. Something had just connected but he was damned if he could pin it down. Tom craned his neck to look backwards in order to survey the heaving mass of people. Was it a face he'd caught in his peripheral vision? Mmm, nothing obvious. Looked again. Frowning slightly, he anchored himself against the ochre plastered wall next to Ellen and ran a final visual check over the pub. Nope.

After the shaky start, it was a great night. Ellen purred on his shoulder as they shared a taxi back to his house and his eyes drifted to a lazy close. Click, click – his brain ticked over the images in his head...that was it! Tom's eyes snapped open as he realised what had caught his attention at the bar in the pub. Nails. The guy tuning up his guitar had noticeably long nails on one hand. Like our man in the Reyka. So, maybe our dealer was a guitarist as well, eh? Bit of a long shot, but maybe he did a few gigs himself. Worth following up. Satisfied that he had scratched the itch in his consciousness, Tom gratefully closed his eyes again and rested his cheek on Ellen's fragrant head for the rest of the journey home.

CHAPTER 8

He didn't see too much of Sunday morning. Not that he was complaining. Bed was a very satisfactory place to be; Ellen was snuffling into his left shoulder and his nostrils welcomed the scent of her perfume that was suffused with undertones of sex. Moving slightly so as not to disturb her, he traced the arc of her shoulder, then down to her waist with his right hand, fingers splayed to maximise the contact with her skin. She murmured and rolled over to face him, eyes barely open. He kissed her and once again, lost himself in her.

He dozed. Waking properly, Tom peered at the clock in disbelief. Midday had long passed and it was nearly one o'clock. He hadn't done that for years! Chewing the coating in his mouth, he grunted and moved to the edge of the bed, swinging his legs towards the floor. Bugger. Definite toxicity rating in the head, stomach and liver and a pressing desire for the toilet. As he pushed back the duvet, he gave Ellen's deliciously exposed bottom a playful slap.

"Sod," came the muffled response. "You'd better be getting up to get me some tea." She repositioned the duvet. "And I'm afraid I need a glass of water, and some paracetamol." Pause. "And if you've not got anything scrummy for breakfast, you're in big trouble."

Smiling, he made his way downstairs after relieving his ballooning bladder and grabbing a towel to wrap around his waist. Jack was waiting for him at the bottom of the stairs, an

58   *Boxing Clever*

expression of extreme annoyance on his face. He yowled to further remind Tom that his bowl was empty and had been for some time. The cat managed somehow to walk across Tom's foot with outstretched claws on the way to the kitchen.

"Okay cat, I know you're miffed. Bit of a late night and I've been preoccupied this morning." Reaching for the kettle, his leg was tickled by the flick of Jack's impatient tail.

"Tinned stuff this morning I'm afraid." Tom instantly regretted bending down to plop the rectangle of meat and jelly in Jack's dish as the odour of the 'mouth-watering meaty chunks' hit his nostrils. His head swam.

He rested his gaze at the small window as he waited for the swinging feeling to pass and the water to boil, mugs at the ready. The small yard outside his kitchen was filled with sunshine and his attempts at urban gardening were beginning to show; herbs green and vibrant in the window box. Sunday afternoon stretched before him and the day was warm.

He delivered the tea, water and painkillers to a pale but grateful Ellen. It was remarkable to see the transformation in her eyes as the chemicals hit her system.

"Feeling better?"

"Getting there. What'll we do today? I've got to get packed later but we've got hours before then."

Tom thought. It was quite a novelty this. Most Sundays, if he wasn't working, would be spent either playing around in the kitchen or reading. War books mainly. When he was married he had had a few flying lessons with a small outfit over towards Liverpool, but money had become a bit tighter after the divorce and he had lost his confidence. He kept promising himself that he would pick it up again, like all the other hobbies he'd tried and given up. But not today.

"Plan A," he issued decisively. "Freshly squeezed orange juice, Italian coffee and croissants for breakfast. Then we catch the bus into town and visit the new art gallery that's opened. Followed by a stroll down to one wine bar or other for a glass of chilled whatever and then back here for one of my special stir-fries and a DVD."

Ellen furrowed her brow as if considering the idea. "Plan B?"

"I watch the sport all afternoon and you can do my ironing in the back room."

"Oooh, a tough one!" she laughed, pulling back the duvet and leaping out of bed. "Get that coffee on and I'll be down in a minute."

"What's the matter with this cat of yours? He's not normally so friendly," Ellen observed later, wiping croissant crumbs from her cheek. Jack was behaving rather oddly. He had howled as she had sat at the old pine table and had tried on a number of occasions to get up onto her lap. By the time they were ready to leave the house she had nicknamed him 'Velcro cat'.

"It's as if he doesn't want to let me out of his sight," she commented.

"Maybe he thinks you'll look after him better than me. His mealtimes might be more regular if you're around."

Some days you could forget how shitty the world could be and how people could damage one another. Some days, there was just something in the air that encouraged smiles and palpable well-being. Maybe it's just me, he mused as he walked along a sunny and buzzing city street, hand-in-hand with Ellen. Maybe it's just a reaction to good sex that makes the world look a better place. He cast a side-long glance at the woman beside him. She was smiling too. Clearly his technique was responsible there.

They didn't spend too much time talking about the note. Ellen was putting her faith and trust in the company and Tom

60   *Boxing Clever*

was glad that she would be away from home for much of the following few weeks. He reckoned whoever was behind it would soon get tired of any lack of response and move on to something or someone else. He didn't tell her too much about his workload either, thanking God that the nightmares had become less frequent. His ex-wife blamed his job for many of their problems and hated him bringing his work home, even if he really needed to let off some steam. He and Ellen were keeping things light and it was good but he was beginning to feel that he wanted to open up to her. To tell her about the botched investigation into the accident, the crucifying grief and eventual resentment of his ex-wife that Greg was dead and he, Tom, was still alive. To be able to enjoy his life without guilt.

Monday morning dawned bright and clear. Tom was in a buoyant mood as he drove, or rather crawled, along the city ring road but for once he didn't mind the delay. The extra time was not wasted as he indulged himself in the memory of Ellen. Earlier, she had silently followed him into the shower, her lathered hands waking a hunger in him that surprised them both. They had had a glorious hour without saying a word, even if the necessary second shower had nearly made them both late. He had said goodbye to her as the taxi arrived to take her to work, reassured that she seemed in a calm and confident frame of mind. She had promised to call him as soon as she had been to see Vanpharma's head of security.

He noticed that the railings and lampposts of the central reservation were hung with flowers. Brought in for the Commonwealth Games in 2002, the displays were always good but clearly the Council wanted to make an extra effort for the delegates arriving for the Summit. Most of them would come along this road from the airport and the bold, bright colours lifted the whole area with a rainbow welcome. As he pulled into the car park and killed the engine, he realised he was whistling.

He made a quick detour on his way to Frank Dawson's office. The Rodent was insisting on daily bulletins of progress and Tom wanted to pick up his notes from Saturday. At least today he had some good news.

"Yes." The response to his knock was not delivered as a question but as a command to enter.

Frank continued to look at the pages spread over his desk, leaving Tom wanting to pull faces at the bowed, balding head. He couldn't resist it, crossing his eyes and baring his teeth like a teenager in a photo booth for a few glorious seconds. Satisfied, he corrected his vision and stared over his boss' dome at the unimaginative faux Constable print on the wall behind the desk as the minutes past. His cheery mood began to evaporate.

"I've got about ten minutes only this morning," Frank announced as he collected files together and at long last, met Tom's eyes. "I'm having a refresher media training session this morning." He could barely hide his enjoyment at the prospect of the public eye. Tom hadn't had him down as someone to be seduced by the media, but there was increasing evidence of new ties. It would be the hair next.

"No problem, sir. I'll give you the good news first in case we run out of time. Dean and Rich came up trumps with the stakeout at the car warehouse. You remember we thought it was the Theake brothers who were behind it?" Frank nodded. "Turns out they were the link but were being shafted too. They decided to take the situation into their own hands. Thanks to the nod from one of Dean's people, we were there when it all got lively. The real guy behind the scam was a Mark Livesey who had set up this pseudo business providing insurance for used cars. Had done something similar in Southampton apparently."

"Good. What else?"

62   *Boxing Clever*

"Burglary on Beech Road. Looked opportunistic but was down to a group of teenage girls who decided to pinch some stuff from one of their parents' houses. Unimaginatively stashed the stuff at one of their grandmother's until they could get rid of it – the woman is almost stone deaf but not stupid and she called us."

Tom paused to check his notes.

"Still working on the shoplifting network. Hours of CCTV tapes to work through and those behind it are cute. No faces, nothing to use in the press. We're talking again with the shops that have store detectives and making other enquiries."

"And the Quays case? Drug girl?" Frank had linked his hands on the desk and was leaning forwards as if to fend off the lack of news.

Tom drew a breath ready to answer when a sharp rap sounded on the door behind him.

"Yes?!" The question was shouted at the interruption.

Dean's head appeared round the door. "Sorry to interrupt sir, but thought you both should know. Call from the MRI. Mel Chadwick has just died."

"This is all we need." Frank was smoothing his hair. "We don't want the press to be all over this. We'll need to get a briefing organised for tonight's news – what can I say?"

"We've a name and description of the dealer. None of us here recognise the guy. I'm going to..." Tom was thinking quickly. "The friend met this guy at the opening of that new club. No sighting of him on the tapes but we'll review the invitation list and start talking to those there. You could appeal to them directly. We'll need a photo of the girl to jog memories. I'll interview the friend again."

Frank was standing, signalling that the meeting needed to be over.

Maureen Devlin   63

"Before I go, sir – the Quays case? We're also going to go back to those we talked to when the body was found. Time has passed. It might be that loyalties have changed. All we need is one tight lip to be loosened." His hand found the doorknob behind him, feeling like he was in a TV police drama. What else could he say then except "I'll keep you informed"?

The news of the death had obviously been circulated through the team. Someone had written 'Died' alongside Mel's case notes on the white board. What a stupid waste of all those years of parental nurturing and new-found independence.

He was by no means a puritan or killjoy, and thankfully not yet embracing real middle-age but at times Tom despaired at the stupidity of human beings, and particularly the young. Programmed to self-destruct. He'd never been keen to talk about having a family with his ex-wife which she had naturally taken as a major personal rejection. He had thought his feelings were so strongly opposed to the idea because their relationship was lacking but now he wasn't so sure. Maybe he just wasn't the paternal type – or too afraid to take the risk as well as the joy. Jack was responsibility enough. Thank the lord for his relationship with Ellen. Uncomplicated.

With her in his mind, he walked across to his desk to check his messages. Sure enough, she had called earlier. He dialled her number.

"Hello, Ellen Warner speaking," her tone was business-like and brisk.

"Hi, it's me."

"Oh! Hi – glad you called now. I'm going to have to leave for the airport in about an hour and I wanted to speak to you before I left." Still business-like, but no longer brisk. Warm, as if she was smiling.

"How did you get on this morning? What was their verdict?"

64   *Boxing Clever*

Tom sat back in his chair, bending the backrest to within an inch of its specification. He'd tipped himself over on one quiet afternoon, a feat that had sent Dean into such a fit of glee that he could reduce himself to giggles at the simple memory of it. Now Tom made sure he positioned the chair in a way that the backrest would come into contact with the wall behind him, not the floor. He listened as Ellen took him through her morning.

As usual when she was in the office, Ellen had dumped her laptop and briefcase on her desk and gone in pursuit of fresh coffee and two slices of toast (with Marmite) from the restaurant situated on the level below. Fifteen minutes or so later she had run down the spiral stairs from the restaurant to the lower ground floor that housed the maintenance and security services for the site. Tom smiled at her need to give him the unnecessary detail.

Ellen reported that the head of security said it was rare for this particular Vanpharma premises to be a target for protesters as the facility that housed the rats and mice for drug testing were located some two hundred miles south in Cambridgeshire. Nonetheless, any threat, however small, was treated very seriously indeed. Some scientists working on novel drug delivery systems for a small affiliated biotechnology company had been targeted in recent years, one attack leaving the victim unable to walk or recognise her husband.

"I spoke with a guy called George Barnett. He's an ex-policeman from the London Met and he was very interested to hear that you were in the force. Reckon he misses it."

"What kind of stuff did he ask?" Tom probed, conscious of time.

"Where I'd had the note stored, and how many others had handled it. He knew about me losing my laptop and organiser. He is going to send the note to his contact in the Serious and

Organised Crime Command at the Met for fingerprint matching."

Tom's respect for the guy grew as Ellen listed the questions he'd asked her, and the strategy he had suggested for dealing with the situation. The company would be checking with their sources which activist groups could be responsible. George Barnett thought it could even be the work of a rogue player who had come by her personal information after the robbery, however unlikely. Apparently it was good timing that Ellen was leaving the country for most of the week and that she would be away intermittently for the following two.

"Would you be able to do me a favour?" she asked, after some twenty minutes.

"If I can," he was cagey, anticipating a request for a lift to the airport.

"Well, thanks." Her tone was instantly chillier. Ploughing on, she said, "I would appreciate it," pause, "if you could find the time to pop into my house maybe once or twice this week to check if any more notes have been delivered. That's all."

"Sure. Sorry. Just meant today was a bit tight. What about keys?"

"You'll have to come over to the office. I haven't time now to get to you. I'll leave the keys and alarm code at reception in an envelope for you."

"No problem. Do you want me to check your messages as well?"

"No, I can do that remotely. I'm back on Sunday. I'll give you a call then or you can try me, if you like." She still sounded rattled.

He spent the next few minutes trying to make amends in a tone quiet enough to be inaudible from his colleagues and he wasn't sure either was entirely successful. He wished her good

66   *Boxing Clever*

luck and safe trip, intending to send a text message that she would pick up when she arrived in Spain.

"Okay, guys," he announced to the room. "Dean?" The big man lifted his head in anticipation. "You take Rich and go and talk to Mel's house mates and anyone else from the party. See if we can fill in any more details of our dealer. Ryan – get in touch with the manager of the Underground Club and get a list of all those on the invitation list for the launch party. Trawl through, see if anything rings a bell." Heads nodded at the prospect of getting out of the office.

"What about you?" Dean was typically blunt.

"I'm going over to the Quays office again. Talk to the security firms there and see if anyone has suddenly remembered something about the night our guy went for a final swim. Elliot, I need you to look at the tapes again." The request was met with a groan.

"I've been looking at bloody tapes for the last week. How come I get stuck in here again?"

"Because you've got sharp eyes. And besides," Tom paused to show just how thoughtful he was being. "You've got a change of programme. No more shops, instead–"

"Yeah, right," Elliot interrupted. "Now I get sodding building sites." Still chuntering, he got up to leave. "I need coffee and chocolate for today's performance. And you lot put your phones through to voicemail. I'm not going to answer those as well."

CHAPTER 9

Ellen's company wasn't exactly on the way from HQ to Salford Quays but the sunny day was too much of a temptation. Tom decided to chance the likelihood of ice-cream stains on his polo shirt and bought a massive chocolate and nut concoction on a stick and a bottle of mineral water from a garage. Chomping vigorously, and with necessary speed, he manoeuvred his aging BMW towards the business park, the hourly radio news bulletin washing around his ears.

The man at reception was courteous and efficient, asking to see some identification from Tom before he passed over the A5 brown envelope containing Ellen's keys. Knowing that the head of security at Salford Quays finished his day at five-thirty, Tom decided to talk to him first and then stay around to talk to the night watchmen, hoping it would be at least the same contracted firm, if not the same blokes. He would drop by Ellen's house on his way home.

A programme on Radio 4 provided some useful education on the eradication of potato blight and the art of re-potting ancient orchids as he made his way back across the city. He'd been introduced to the joys of national conversational radio during the hours he had sat with his weakening father. It was great for bizarre tit-bits of information, which he liked to use when forced into conversation with humourless individuals who then never quite knew how to read him. One of life's pleasures, being able to bore dull people rigid.

68   *Boxing Clever*

The road towards the Salford Quays site office swept him past the magnificence of Old Trafford. Tom had been through the turnstiles many times with his father, a lifelong supporter of the club. He never had the heart to tell his parent that he actually preferred cricket to football. Perfectly maintained, the club ground overlooked one of Greater Manchester's most deprived areas, tensely alongside designer offices and prestigious homes for young professionals. No wonder property crime was rife here. Wealth was right in the face of the disadvantaged.

Leaving the football stand winking in his rear-view mirror, he turned left off the main road, the elderly chassis juddering across the tram lines that criss-crossed the tarmac. The sun twinkled on the surface of the canals, water blessed blue thanks to the virtually cloudless sky.

Brilliant day to be out and about, he mused, and a lifetime and universe away from that grey morning when the body had been pulled out of the black and icy water.

Since that morning, the Imperial War Museum had re-emerged from behind its scaffolding and netting. The ultra-modern building was positioned eyeball to eyeball with The Lowry Art and Entertainment Centre, a stretch of canal between them. He had been to a concert or two there and had enjoyed the energetic and airy feel of the place though God knows why they'd decided on orange and purple décor.

He made his way to the Quays Heritage Centre and cut through the narrow service road to the site office. Leaving his linen jacket in the car, he trod the familiar path towards the security guard's cabin. Tom knocked as he turned the steel handle of the door, ready for the blast of hot air that would probably hit him. It did.

"How the hell do you stand this?" he demanded of the resident, as he stood sweating gently in the barely circulating air.

Maureen Devlin   69

"And good afternoon to you too, Mr Ashton," replied the man. "You get used to it. Store up the heat in your bones ready for the winter. Tea?" he pointed towards the kettle, perched on a filing cabinet.

"No thanks, Dave. Just wanted to have another chat with your people about the week our man was found. Maybe we missed something last time."

"You must be desperate," Dave observed. "You've talked to them at least three times already. What about the guys from the water company?"

"We're in touch with them through mediators. They are both still getting counselling and they'll let us know if anything comes out during sessions." Unable to cope with the temperature, Tom opened the door and wedged it ajar with his foot, glorying in the breeze that caressed his sticky shoulders. "Take me through the systems that were in place that week. Is there anything we could have missed? Could there be anything else from the museum site?"

Although the body had been found close to one of the solid stone walls near The Lowry, there was no guarantee that it had been dropped in there. Tom knew that the water level in the nearby basin was generally stable, affected only by rainfall or if the Ship Canal Company needed to divert supply from one area to another through a series of locks. The Manchester Ship Canal also ran alongside. They had checked the weather over the week prior to the discovery and the heavy rain and high winds may have affected the position of the corpse. There was also a possibly that it could have been moved around due to the activity of the dredger, waltzing it through the silt and slurry.

Dave described again, patiently, the surveillance equipment on the site. As more and more acreage was developed, individual companies took over the major responsibility for protecting their premises.

70   *Boxing Clever*

The Lowry, the nearby shopping complex and the Imperial War Museum had installed additional lighting and cameras to reassure their visitors but with the result that most of the lenses were pointing away from the water and towards the pavements and car parks. When these facilities closed and the staff had left, well after midnight, the total site was patrolled by security guards in locked vans. They would generally make one full circuit per hour through the night.

Even though the body must have been brought there in some form of transport, there had been plenty of time and dark places to provide cover. The CCTV footage of the access roads from the nearby housing estates had shown nothing of interest and all the cars recorded had been passing through, nothing more. Tom couldn't believe that anyone could be that lucky or that clever. The murderer must have had some help.

Thanking Dave for his time, and yet another reminder to get in touch if anything came to mind, he went alone to stand at the edge of the water where the body had been located. Visitors were milling about on both sides of the canal, strolling in the sun and marvelling (or tutting) at the changing architectural landscape. The investment here was part of an overall drive to see Greater Manchester recognised as a truly international commercial and tourist destination.

Tom sat for awhile on one of the cast iron benches welded in place at regular intervals along the bank. The calm afternoon warmth was like a massage and he let his mind wander over the facts of the case. Try and order the info.

Alone and in the clear light of day he knew this case was becoming a personal quest, atoning for Greg – or was it in order to lay his own painful memories to rest? To move on? Slightly uncomfortable, but acknowledging the thought, he dragged his mind back to the facts.

A young man, savagely beaten, no identity, ends up in a man-made waterway. Nobody has seen anything, no one has reported him missing. Tempting though the thought was, there was absolutely nothing to tie this guy in with any of the local thugs. For all he knew, the body could have been brought here from anywhere.

He rang the office.

"Elliot," the reply was brusque.

"I'm at the Quays. Anything from the tapes?"

The sigh reverberated through the ether. "Naff all. I've seen water by moonlight, water in rain. A couple who obviously get off on doing it in uncomfortable places and a couple of nocturnal joggers. I'm still working through the stuff from the week before we reckon the body was dumped. I decided to start that way round instead of working back from when the body was found this time."

"Good idea. Anyone else back yet?"

"Ryan has just got back from seeing the manager of the Underground Club. She's working over the invitation list now. Want to have a word?"

Tom did.

"Nice to see you made it to the big time, sir," Ryan was obviously impressed by the names in front of her. "Just about anyone who is anyone is on this."

"Don't suppose by any stroke of luck and divine intervention there is a Col someone on it?" Tom rose from the bench and leaned against an ornate lamppost, his face appreciating the sun's rays.

"Not that I can see so far." The sound of rustling paper accompanied the reply. "She told me that they had sent out over six hundred invitations – some just for PR knowing not everyone would come."

72   *Boxing Clever*

"Let's go through this tomorrow. We'll need to talk to as many as possible, but make a start on noting who might be the most useful to get to first."

Tom flicked his phone closed and returned to his seat on the bench, staring at the water. He reflected that he had more leads for the drug dealer than he did for the poor guy in the morgue. Both crimes tragic and probably just as pointless. He called The Rodent.

"Mr Dawson's office." Margery was getting very protective of her boss now that the media were beginning to contact him on a regular basis.

"Margery, it's Tom," he said. "Can I have a word with him?"

"Not here at the minute, Tom," came the reply. "He has got his mobile with him though, if it's urgent."

During the next few minutes, Tom began to feel warmer and warmer, not entirely due to the sun on his back. Despite his best efforts, he was getting nowhere in his request for additional help to redo the door-to-door checks around the Quays.

"Can we at least get the local boys to ask around when they're out and about?"

He listened as his boss reminded him (again) that the city centre needed as much of a street presence as possible in the coming weeks and he would have to do what he could in the meantime.

"Use your initiative, Tom." With that, the phone disconnected.

Taking that as a carte blanche to shatter the departmental budget on allowable expenses, Tom rang Dean to instruct him to fish for information, by any means, from his friends in the physical fitness circles. Thinking of keeping fit and healthy living, he decided to go and visit the local health centre while he was in the neighbourhood. Sometimes people who were afraid would use the medical profession as a confessional.

Maureen Devlin 73

Particularly if the fear was longstanding. Locum doctors on call may have seen something. He was clutching at confidentiality straws and he knew it.

The surgery was situated behind a high concrete wall, imprisoning the staff who worked within it. He had read that the place was run by a nurse under a scheme introduced by the government, with GPs employed as needed. Apparently the first thing the male nurse had done was to contact the local gangs for protection. Wise man. And certainly not stupid.

"I understand what you're asking, Inspector," he said. "But I can't help you. Many of those who live around here have anxiety and depression. If any of this is because they have been a witness to murder, they are unlikely to say. All we can do is our best for them. Please rest assured that if anyone asks us to act as intermediary to you with information, we will do so."

Resigned, Tom left the building, absorbing the wary curiosity of the jaded clients in the waiting room. He had much to be thankful for.

The smug voices of middle-England radio annoyed him as he started up the car. Pressing the off button, he drove in relative silence to find the security patrol, believing that they held the key to a vital, if seemingly irrelevant, piece of information. He had talked to the men a number of times in the days immediately after the body was found. Even accepting that there was bound to be an element of protectionism because all guards doze off at some point during a shift, or take a quick trip to a takeaway, they still had given up nothing. He refused to let it go. Someone was holding out on him.

The security van was parked alongside the museum. Tom could see that it was empty and he looked around the vicinity, knowing full well that the occupants wouldn't have walked far. Sure enough, the two men, in grey and black uniforms, were

74   *Boxing Clever*

leaning on the rails facing the swooping steel edifice of The Lowry.

"Evening, gents." He enjoyed the little inadvertent hop given by the larger of the men.

"Not you again," the other man said as he turned to face their intruder, managing to blow cigarette smoke into Tom's face at the same time. "Don't you ever give up?"

"Stan and Eric, isn't it?" Tom said. "Impressive building, eh?" He nodded at the museum. "Must get round to a visit."

The men looked at him, not rude in their silence, but not exactly thrilled to see him either. They waited.

"We're still working on the murder case as I'm sure you'll appreciate. Wonder if there is anything you've remembered since we spoke to you last? Anything that now strikes you as odd?"

The men looked at each other and then Eric, the larger of the two, turned his head to stare at the canal, as if for inspiration.

Tom recalled Elliott's observations from the tape. "Did you ever see anyone jogging round here during those weeks?"

"Always someone running around this area," Stan replied. "Am sure I told one of your people that at the time."

Indeed you did. It was in the notes.

"Would you be able to recognise any of them? Anything distinctive about them?"

"Hardly," the response was more of a guffaw. "One track suit looks like another, and they all had hoods up or hats on. It was the middle of bloody winter, don't forget."

How could he? He'd had to throw his shoes away after the freezing water had knackered the uppers. He'd not dried them out properly and they'd grown mould.

There are times when you knew you were doing the equivalent of pushing custard uphill and this was one of them, so he decided to call it a day. Wishing them a quiet shift, Tom strolled back towards his car and a visit to Ellen's.

Her house was small and modern but boasting semi-detached status. The grey wheelie-bin looked out of scale as it nuzzled to the left of the garage door. A blue glazed pot housing a dark pink feathery plant stood sentinel by her doorstep. Neat. The road was relatively busy as his arrival had coincided with the mass of young professionals returning home from the office or gym, but he was able to park on the small drive as Ellen had stored her car in the garage. She was one of the few people he knew that used their garage for a car.

He opened the front door and tapped in the alarm code on the panel to his left. He felt a little uneasy as he entered the bright, airy hallway. His unaccompanied presence there was almost too intimate, as if he was invading her private space. There was a faint fragrance of perfume and even without knowing who lived here, the atmosphere was feminine and inviting. Hell, he was getting quite poetic.

He bent to examine the small pile of white and brown envelopes near his feet. Taking a slim, chrome pencil from his jacket pocket, he crouched near the letters, flicking first one, then another across the cream carpet. All, thankfully, were easily identified. One from the bank, a charity circular and a postcard from someone called Ali who was having a fabulous time (writ large) in Corfu. Nothing else. No scrappy note. No unwelcome handwritten missive pushed through the brass low-level letter box.

He picked the envelopes up and placed them on the window ledge by the telephone. The answering machine light was flashing but he knew she would be accessing any messages herself from Barcelona. Suddenly unable to resist it, he began to nose around the house.

He poked his head into the immaculate kitchen. Then into the living/dining room and the bathroom with the usual bewildering array of bottles and jars. He lingered slightly longer at the doorway of her lilac and ivory bedroom where he

76   *Boxing Clever*

had spent a number of very pleasant nights. The second bedroom had been arranged as an office and even here, Ellen's organised nature was evident. Nothing amiss.

He closed all the interior doors before pressing in the code to reset the alarm, glad to have made the visit. He would send Ellen a text to let her know all was well.

"Oh, shit!" A glance down verified that the squishy sensation under his foot was just that. "Just great." He disliked dogs at the best of times.

The smelly pile had been left on the path just in front of the step and out of his line of sight as he came out of the house. He wiped his shoe on the small patch of grass and tried to scrape the remnants from the sole on the little stone edging of the drive. He was so engrossed in his task that he was unaware of the woman standing beside him until her shadow cut across the ground in front of him.

"Can I help you?" Her voice wasn't exactly friendly.

He looked up to see a short, dark-haired and rotund figure, sharp eyes peering at him from behind surprisingly flattering square glasses. Her arms were folded in the archetypal stance of defence.

"I'm...er...a friend of Ellen's. Tom." He explained. "I've just been in to check the house. Are you a neighbour?"

"I'm Anne, I live next door." She motioned to the other side of Ellen's garage, not at the adjoining house. "I could have checked the house. She's asked me to water her pots while she's away." She was clearly still a little wary and, by her tone, a bit suspicious.

Tom shrugged as if he wasn't privy to the workings of a woman's mind and smiled ruefully.

"Don't suppose you know which mutt left this little gift?" He pointed at the squashed turd near the door. "I managed to step right in it coming out of the house."

Maureen Devlin 77

"We haven't got many dogs round here, too many single people, I guess. Must have been a stray. I'll get some hot water to throw on it otherwise it will stick there. Will you be checking the house again?"

Tom nodded and moved towards his car.

"Probably Thursday or Friday. She's back on Sunday so that should do. Cheers."

With that he opened the car door and slipped into the driver's seat. He didn't want to get onto further conversation about why he was there. He gave the neighbour a cursory but friendly wave as he reversed out of the short drive and onto the road.

It took less than a mile for him to realise that he hadn't been quite thorough enough in his shoe cleaning. He pulled into a garage and rinsed off his shoes with the water provided for windscreen washers. He grappled with a pair of disposable plastic gloves and some paper towels in order to wipe down the pedals and mat, giving himself backache into the process. Without getting any petrol, he bought an extra-strength car freshener that he attached to the rear-view mirror. After opening all the windows, Tom headed for home.

Alice arrived within five minutes of him shutting his front door. Her nostrils wrinkled a little as he invited her inside so he hurriedly grabbed his shoes from the mat near the door and threw them outside.

"She's gone, hasn't she?" The grey eyes were misty and sad.

Tom wasn't surprised at her knowledge. He nodded and moved towards the kitchen to make tea. "This morning," he added. "From what I understand, she didn't regain consciousness."

"How very sad." Alice was clearly moved. "Such a shame when it is a young life. I wish..."

"There are plenty more tragedies that go unnoticed. And you did all you could."

78 *Boxing Clever*

"All I did in the end was watch," she said, in defeat. "I've had these visions all my life and what use are they? Or me come to that?" Her kind face crumpled and he was terrified that she might begin to cry.

"You cared enough to come and tell me about it. Others would have tried to ignore it. Now, would you like some tea?" In truth, he was looking forward to opening another bottle of the surprisingly good Merlot that had come through the wine club but didn't think she would appreciate it.

"No, thank you. I haven't slept well lately and I feel maybe an early night is called for. Before I go – do you know who sold her the drugs?"

"Not yet but we've got a few lines of enquiry going on." In an effort to raise the old lady's spirits he added somewhat jovially, "anything you see that could shed some light would be gratefully received."

"It doesn't work quite like that," she sighed. "But of course, if there is anything I can do."

"Actually, there is something," he thought out loud. "If you get a minute... maybe you could have a word with the friend? Lisa? I'm sure she'd be glad of the chance to talk it through and she should still be here tomorrow. She may just have some detail in her head that hasn't come through to me yet."

"Of course. I'll go round in the morning." Her expression lifted. "Thank you."

Alone again he turned his attention to the lamb cutlets he was going to marinade in a bitter plum sauce. Reaching for a couple of sweet potatoes, he began to peel, his mind emptying as the orange flesh emerged.

CHAPTER 10

"How come there was nothing about the girl's death on the news last night?" Tom quizzed Frank Dawson as they each pointedly stared at the patch of wall above the urinals. "I thought we'd agreed the coverage would help?"

"As I keep reminding you, there are other things going on round here." The Rodent took great care in washing and drying his hands. "I gave all the information out at the briefing but we're not really going to be able to compete with the Summit for airtime. Not exactly the news they want to be giving out a couple of weeks before we're overrun with visitors. The *Evening News* did a piece."

"I saw. About one column inch and the thinnest description. Could apply to half of the male population of the North West."

"What we need is positive results to get into the news." His boss was terse. "Not trying to use it to ask for help. The public need to have confidence in us."

Tom, never good at brown-nosing, could hear the voice of the regional commander in the other man's words and for a fleeting moment felt a stab of pity for him. The Rodent's neck would be on the block if there were any high-profile cock-ups this summer.

"Message understood, sir," he offered, with an admirable lack of cynicism.

80 *Boxing Clever*

Less than a mile away, Franklin could barely hide his fury at the fact that either one of his guys was connected to that girl lying in a mortuary or someone was muscling in on his patch. He didn't care about the stupid female, he just wanted no trouble, nothing to link back to him, nothing that could lead elsewhere. The death was not exactly headline news but he didn't like it all the same.

"Tell me again what you know." His neck was thrust forwards towards his two companions in ill-disguised aggression. "The description of the guy they're looking for could be either one of you two and I don't want any interest coming my way."

Otis shrugged. "I've not been working that area – the word is that it was a rogue trader at a house party. Maybe another student. A one-off."

He wasn't going to let them get away with it that easily. He balled his fist and placed it carefully on the table in full view. He said nothing and waited for more.

Otis, wriggling around in his seat began to speak again, but with less confidence. "I'm going down to the student bars later. See if I can find out who's getting in our space. If this girl keeling over hasn't given them enough of a fright I'll make sure they know they're not welcome."

Col, inwardly relieved by this report but suffering increasing bowel cramps, considered his Guinness. He decided to be bullish and met Franklin's fierce gaze.

"Not picking up anything useful yet. Students not really my thing, but I'll ask around."

Franklin was only slightly mollified. He appreciated a bit of fighting talk and he had no doubts they were loyal. And they had better be. He wasn't fooled by their apparent calm. He knew he terrified them both. Good.

Relaxing back in his chair, he caught sight of a young boy reflected in a large mirror directly opposite the window that exposed the street. Skateboard clutched under his arm, he was staring at Franklin with an expression of open curiosity. Franklin smiled. He'd seen the youngster hanging around outside the gym, wanting to catch a glimpse of his hero? Yeah, he'd give him a few quid next time he saw him, brighten up his day. Maybe he'd get the lad to keep his eyes on these two goons from time to time. The more eyes and ears he had to protect his patch the better. Now, back to business.

"Tell me what we need," he commanded. "I've got a warm-up fight coming up and I don't want to have to be thinking about what you two are doing while I'm otherwise engaged. You with me?"

Col and Otis began to reel off their requirements. Franklin's eyes didn't leave their faces as they spoke, nor did he write anything down. This was one branch of mathematics that he figured he could compute very ably indeed. He knew the boss had been stung once before and it was never going to be his fault if it happened to him again.

He was taking the run-up to his first major fight seriously. Negotiations were proceeding well; the London promoter was due to visit the gym later that day. Why Martin Murphy had chosen an opponent in Scotland for the warm-up fight Franklin wasn't sure, but he trusted him to be doing what was best. Franklin had never been further north than where he was now. His time for seeing the world was dawning and soon he'd really be travelling in style.

He realised that Col had finished speaking. Both men were looking at him with slight trepidation but no longer alarmed.

"Good," he said. "Don't call me. Understood?"

Indeed they did and as he rose to his feet to go back to his training, he took a moment or two to tower over them from his

82   *Boxing Clever*

full height. No extra words were required. He strode away from them towards his black Mercedes, looking forward to the next few hours at the gym.

Training was his drug. He loved the fact that his body obeyed his instructions, that his muscles were hard and bulging. He particularly relished the adulation on the faces of the other men in the gym, and the envy that was not very far beneath. He basked in the glow of his manager and trainer, but nothing – nothing – matched the glory of crunching bone and bruising flesh.

He could do it, here, right now in front of them all.

He'd been working out for almost an hour before he had gone into the ring to spar against the only guy who could cope with him for the required ten minutes.

The promoter knew his stuff.

"Christ! I wouldn't want to face that big bugger. We'll get a good crowd for this one. He's the first serious contender we've had against Tyler." The mood in the gym was buoyant, alive with the anticipation of success.

"He was fucking impressed," Joe Murphy could barely contain his glee. "We're going to get a bloody good purse out of this one and I reckon Franklin can do it." He looked to his son for endorsement as Franklin held out his hands for his gloves to be removed.

"Well, certainly not like him to be so positive," admitted Martin in a considered tone. "It's not in his interests to put on a meet if the pair won't give a good fight."

"Jesus, son! Don't fall over yourself with excitement will ya?" Joe was clearly rattled.

"Just making sure we don't get carried away with appearances, Dad. I want everything to go absolutely according to plan." Martin's jaw was set and his eyes hard as he looked at their protégé. Franklin reckoned that the Murphys needed this fight even more than he did. That they needed their boy to win, big time. Well, they'd better be fuckin' grateful when he did.

The typed pages read like a northern Who's Who. Ryan had sorted out some photocopies so that the rest of the team was able to scan the list when time allowed. It was certainly an exercise in detection.

"Who the hell is Graham Noyce?" Dean sounded peeved. Not all of the names had an explanation listed next to them as to why they had been invited to the launch of the Underground Club.

"He's the new editor of *Living City*," replied Ryan. "I checked that one yesterday."

"Have you come across anyone that might fit the description of our man?" asked Tom. "Apart from the obvious." About half of the names clearly belonged to females.

"To be honest, the only ones I can be sure of are you and that guy from the radio station that you mentioned. Just because these people are listed doesn't mean they actually went. I'll have to give them each a ring."

"I'll give Sam Halpern a bell," Dean chipped in. "I've met him a few times and want to tap him for some tickets for the weightlifting." Sam Halpern, as the list said, was the sports editor for the *Evening News*.

"There's something else we need to look into." Tom rocked his chair back and forth. "The guy I overheard in the Reyka had an Irish accent and I reckon could be this Col. He had longish nails. Could be a guitar player. The long nails were on his left hand. Ask around."

Dean nodded in assent, then asked, "Why can't we just get a uniform to keep an eye out?"

84   *Boxing Clever*

"Don't go there. The Rodent goes pale every time I bring it up so I'm doing as he suggested. We'll find another way to get the information."

Tom spent the rest of the day discussing the findings from the CCTV tapes with Elliott. He scanned the figures that appeared again and again in the vain hope that one of the joggers would suddenly whip down their hood and become visible. He began to feel quite depressed, inhabiting this world of grey and black shadows.

He almost felt sorry for Elliott. No wonder his waste bin was full of chocolate wrappers and discarded coffee cups. The tapes from the cameras covering the city centre, soon to be covered by the new state-of-the-art surveillance system, had more activity but just as little hard data.

"Stop killing yourself on these." Tom sat back, his spine protesting. "Go and talk to the store detectives again. I'm going to have one more look at the Quays footage." He paused. "After I get myself some lunch."

He stood for a few minutes hoping that the time delay would somehow magically increase the selection of pre-packed sandwiches in the vending machine. A choice of pale egg mayonnaise on white bread or spicy sausage (orange) on brown. His guts growled at the thought of either combination so in the end he settled for two packets of crisps, an apple and a can of Diet Coke.

If he could stand the ribbing (and get a small fridge installed) he'd bring in his own. He'd tried it once with a mackerel salad that he'd left in his desk drawer by mistake. Then he'd gone away for the weekend.

Crunching on the apple, all noise and no flavour, he sent a text to Ellen, letting her know all was well with the house.

Crisps long forgotten and on his third cup of coffee, Tom's eyes began to ache with the need to absorb some colour. The dark and light contrasts of the films were giving up no secrets; maybe they had none to give. Tom had been nicknamed Duracell Man when he first came to CID as he kept going long after others had called it a day. Sometimes it bore fruit, more often than not his tenacity just resulted in him getting a headache. Like now.

He stood for a moment to stretch his back and turned to let his gaze fall to the horizon through the large window that had been behind him. His eyeballs relaxed with pleasure on the bliss of long vision, red and chrome buildings and a blue and white sky massaging his optic nerves. He decided to review the case file again and then look at the tapes one more time before he finally admitted defeat.

"Tom?" the question cut across his thoughts.

"Uh?"

"You don't remember seeing the new boxer at the club that night, do you?" Dean's hand was still on the telephone handset; clearly he had just discovered the possibility.

"No. I'm sure I would have seen him even though the place was heaving. The guy's hardly wallpaper. I didn't see him on the invite list though."

"I've just spoken with Sam at the *Evening News*. Turns out he couldn't go so he passed the two tickets he had onto Franklin. Rates him pretty highly. Apparently Franklin was discovered by a cousin of Joe Murphy in London. I thought he was a local boy."

"Worth talking to the big man again then. Anything else?"

Ryan, who had been listening to the exchange, added, "The only thing I've got is that the manager remembered the group of students as they weren't strictly what she was after. As far as

86   *Boxing Clever*

who they mixed with, she couldn't help. Apparently she'd been too busy making sure her key guests were happy."

"You able to make another visit to the gym then?" Tom looked at Dean.

"Yep. Possibly later but more likely tomorrow. Want to make a few other visits today. Have got the feelers out about our man in the water."

Tom had a sudden thought. "Before you go, mate, have a look at these tapes from the Quays. There are a few joggers out. Tell me what you think."

Dean willingly hoisted himself out of his chair, moving swiftly for such a big man. "Are we still on for a drink later?" he asked as he stood by the grey AV console.

"Too right." The tape machine whirred as the spool reversed to the section where the first couple of joggers were seen. "This one's from the week before the body would have been put in the water," Tom added, tapping the remote control to 'Play'.

An hour or so later, Dean had slumped into one of the older chairs in the office. It creaked and groaned as he rocked away from the screen to rest his eyes and then back towards the monitor to get a closer look at the grainy figures when they appeared. Finally he spoke.

"I reckon the second couple of guys we saw are more experienced in keeping fit. Something about how they pace their run, the relaxation in the shoulders. Other than that, I can't see bugger all that would help. Couldn't see anyone pause to size up the canal as a dumping ground, that's for sure."

"Could the more experienced types scan their surroundings without breaking stride? One of them turned to jog backwards at one point." Tom had been puzzled by that when he'd first noticed it. Hard enough going forwards, in his opinion.

"Yeah, I guess so - but they do that in order to stretch different muscle sets," Dean advised as he rose from the confines of the chair. "Let's be honest, it's hardly suspicious behaviour."

Tom sat nursing a pint of Guinness as he waited for Dean to join him. He always did when he was hungry, a view that had grown out of his mother's belief that stout was bordering on the medicinal. A tiny beeping came from inside his jacket that he'd carelessly thrown on the chair beside him. A text message. From Ellen.

"Thnx 4 msg & 4 going to house. V busy here! Call sn. E xx" He smiled. Modern communications were quite remarkable; a little note sent and received over thousands of miles in no time at all. Pity others weren't so timely. It was way past seven o'clock and Tom was beginning to feel the effects of thick beer and a lack of food. This pub wasn't his favourite haunt by any means and he wasn't inclined to get a third pint. He pulled up Dean's number on his mobile and, against the competing cacophony of the TV and piped music, listened for his friend to pick up the call.

"Tom!" Dean's voice was distant. "Listen, I can't talk now, mate. Count me out. I'll call you later." And with that, he was gone.

Faced with an unexpectedly free evening, Tom realised that he had begun to rely quite heavily on his relationship with Ellen for his social life. For a sickening moment, he couldn't think of what to do with his time.

Before they had met, he had been quite dedicated to developing a different life after his marriage. He'd begun cooking again and had even started an evening class in Russian, purely because he thought it was the hardest thing he could try and he also knew it would astonish his soon-to-be ex-wife. It had been a real revelation when he had finally understood the alphabet and been able to string a sentence together. He had

88   *Boxing Clever*

found the regularity of the classes hard to manage though, and had finally admitted defeat just before he met Ellen. Maybe he would pick it up again, plan a trip to the place to give himself a target to aim at.

He carried on his personal review all the way to the small bistro near his home, through the delicious olive bread, wild mushroom risotto and bottle of Chilean cabernet sauvignon. During coffee, black and sharp, the questions mounted. Where was he going to be in a few years time? Who would he be if his job was taken away from him? Would he ever let anyone get close to him again? He eyed his empty glass, uncertain of the role of the wine as counsellor or critic but recognising that he was sinking into a plummy well of self-pity.

He paid his bill and strode out into the warm, light night. He breathed deeply, inhaling the peculiar urban scent that comes from a multitude of homes, restaurants, cars and buses. Most of the houses had a smattering of pots or hanging baskets and a vague floral whiff came to him every so often as he walked along the tidy streets to his home. As he turned into his own road, a little black shadow shimmied along the pavement towards him. Jack. Much the same as when he had first appeared soon after Tom had moved in. He had followed Tom into the house one day and decided he would stay.

"Hello, boy," he scrunched the top of the cat's head in greeting. Jack leaned against Tom's leg as he opened the front door and then somehow managed to be in front of him, pointedly showing the direction of the kitchen. "I'll feed you in a minute, just let me get in."

He closed the door behind him and saw that there was a small white envelope mixed in with the free newspaper sticking through into the hallway. Tugging them out of the letterbox, he separated out the envelope and read the enclosed note as he walked through the house.

CHAPTER 11

E ven without taking in a word of the handwritten text, Tom knew who it was from. The tidy, slightly flowery script, carefully written in blue ink, was characteristic of an older hand. He walked through to the kitchen carrying the two sheets of white paper and switched on the main light to read them properly.

Alice wrote that she had seen Lisa and her parents that morning. Apparently they had been more than happy to talk to her, and grateful that she had called the police on the night of the party even though it had not, in the end, prevented the tragedy. The parents were clearly devastated that their daughter had got involved in such a situation. They had offered tea, which Alice had accepted.

He turned the page and read on, absent-mindedly stroking Jack's head, vaguely registering that he was allowing the cat onto the work surface next to him. He should really nudge him off.

It seemed that Alice had kept the conversation with the family going by describing how she had enjoyed watching the young people prepare for the party. Alice reported that Lisa had been talkative, more as a way of reaching some sort of understanding within herself, rather than to explain to them. That the boy selling the drugs had been charming and attractive, and had had a sneezing fit at some point out in the back yard and Lisa had joked that he must have been allergic to a good time. At this point in the story, the girl had begun to cry and

90   *Boxing Clever*

exclaiming that she was stupid and had been trying to impress this boy and it was all her fault. Alice had taken this breakdown as a good time to leave.

Tom was impressed. That she had managed to take all this in whilst playing the concerned old lady was something.

He had reached the final paragraph of the note. "Maybe this bad lad gets hayfever or similar? I'm sorry there was no more."

Jack was impatiently nudging his hand as he closed the note thoughtfully.

The office was deserted when he arrived the following morning. A white board had recently been installed showing people's movements and he could see that Dean had gone back to talk to Franklin at the gym, Elliott was getting some retail therapy and Ryan was on leave. Rich was nowhere to be seen. Tom spent the morning pulling together the monthly report for the team, ready to be included in the routine crime figures. He also managed to read through the mass of paper in his in-tray and scan the e-mails that had arrived over the past couple of days. His own brand of paperwork feng-shui left his waste bin satisfactorily full.

He finished his rare burst of administrative fervour just as Dean sauntered back into the room, glistening with perspiration.

"Shit, it's hot out there," he announced, yanking a tiny cone of waxed paper from the tube besides the water cooler and filling it with liquid. As he drained it and bent to refill it, Tom asked him what he had found out from the rising star of the boxing world.

"He wasn't there. Seems he's gone up to Scotland to prepare for a warm-up fight on Sunday. Joe has gone with him but I did manage a word with Martin. He's a surly bugger, that one." He paused and drank again. A few moments passed.

"Well? In your own time." Tom twiddled his pen between his fingers.

Dean considered. "Nothing I can put my finger on, but he was seriously pissed off that I had gone to try and talk with their boy. Said that there was no way he was going to allow Franklin to go clubbing when he was in preparation for the most important fight of his life. Not this warm-up, but the one planned for October. That Franklin had obviously passed his tickets on somewhere and that was the end of it. He got even more sour with me when a journo from *The News* turned up and saw me there."

"Do we know who Franklin hangs around with? There was one guy when we went last time who looked really edgy."

"Like I said the other day – the guy was discovered by a relative of Joe Murphy. Franklin's only been in Manchester since last November."

"See if you can find anything more out about him. Ask around about who he's seen with. See if you can get an idea about the guy who was holding the rope for him last time. I've got the numbers of the cars that were parked there. Try the Met, as well, and your journalist friend."

"Bit obsessive, isn't it? There's nothing to tie him in to this."

"Any better ideas? I've got a meeting with The Rodent tomorrow to go through these figures," Tom stabbed the paper in front of him, "and I could do with some Teflon coating."

"Sorry, mate," Dean looked rueful. "That's why I had to blow you out last night, was out and about, passing the word again. The place is a bloody clam; I got nothing except an empty wallet. Little sympathy for the girl. It's like, well, what do you expect? As for our stiff, nobody seems to be missing a mate or if they are, they like it that way. I'll keep diggin'."

The whirring beep of the phone cut across the exchange.

92   *Boxing Clever*

"CID, Tom Ashton." He heard a sharp intake of breath and almost a giggle in response. No voice and then the line went dead. Thinking no more of it, he replaced the receiver and stood in order to stretch his back.

"Did we get any other leads from the list?" he asked as he walked across to Ryan's vacant desk.

"Don't know. Didn't get chance to talk with her before she went off."

Tom retrieved the relevant folder from Ryan's desk and began to thumb through it, leaning against the wall and pressing his shoulder blades back to help his muscles. A red scrawl decorated the list with useful notes such as 'didn't go'; 'said couldn't remember too much, i.e. pissed'; 'passed ticket onto sister, gone on holiday'. He saw next to a P. Garvey, 'friend of barman, three tickets', and the explanation that these were the friends, Mel, Lisa and Pete. Scratch one. Next to his own name was a scribble to say, 'lucky bastard'.

Each of the obviously female names had been crossed through but as he scanned down the pages, Tom realised that some of these names had the number two next to them. If they had been issued two tickets, it was pretty likely they would take a male friend along with them. Even though this Col guy had appeared to have been operating as a singleton when he approached Lisa, that didn't necessarily mean he had gone on his own. Jotting a note to this effect on a Post-it pad, he stuck it on the front cover of the file for Ryan to find the following day.

The rest of the week passed fairly uneventfully. Enquiries were proceeding and Frank looked like he was keeping a lid on his blood pressure. Tom was looking forward to seeing Ellen on Sunday, even if only for a short while before she headed off again. He sent her a text to say he would check the house on Friday evening and got a message back to say she would try and call him on Saturday afternoon. Giving in to the fact that he had become a sad bastard, he spent his Thursday evening working late on more paperwork before mingling with other beleaguered souls at the all night supermarket. He was going to try his hand at paella at the weekend.

He had arranged to meet an old friend for a drink on Friday night in Chester, so he called round to Ellen's house on the way home from work. It was all as he'd left it, and clearly the neighbour had been doing her duty as the potted plants looked happy and full.

Realising that it was getting to be a habit, he was again tuning in to *The Archers* as he reversed away from Ellen's garage. *Bang!* Tom jammed his feet on the clutch and brakes. He jerked up his head to see a figure just to the side of the back of his car, a slim mixed race boy who must have been crossing the drive on the pavement. Tom opened the window to check that the boy was okay but all he got was a departing back. One hand was raised in a two-fingered salute as the teenager strutted off, no doubt alarmed but too cool to make a scene.

The motorway was heavy with Friday night traffic as he made his way west. The car seemed to appreciate the change of tarmac under its wheels; the engine purring throatily. He turned off the radio and opened the window, letting the sound of speed fill the interior.

He was always struck by the uneven landscape here. To his left was a gentle green hill that angled itself towards the motorway, dotted with houses and a tiny church, whilst on his right stood the massive petrochemical works at Port Sunlight glistening in the evening sun, looking for all the world like a movie set for a sci-fi adventure. Slender steel towers and a mess of pipes were speckled with black snakes of ladders as if there was no earth supporting the complex, just pipes upon pipes.

94   *Boxing Clever*

He was meeting one half of a couple that he and his ex-wife used to see quite regularly. Paul and Sue had been diplomatic since the split, dividing their allegiances. The two men did not see each other often, but it was always an enjoyable event when they did.

Sitting in a Belgian beer bar near the Old Cross where the Town Crier still entertained visitors, the two men glossed over old times and friends. During a rather disappointing sausage casserole served with leek mash, Tom answered his friend's query about how work was going.

"Just beginning to feel like we're on top. The chief is determined to keep bad news out of the public eye so that Manchester looks good for the next few weeks. At least this week we've sorted a few biggish cases and found quite a few leads on a drug dealer who sold to a now-deceased student. My main headache is a murder that happened well over two months ago and not a sniff." Paul listened attentively as he made his way through a large piece of steak, offering no opinions but acting like a mirror reflecting Tom's emerging thoughts. Refusing another beer and opting for a coffee, he moved the conversation on to Paul and Sue's first child, expected towards the end of the summer.

Asking after Sue's health and knowing that she would be reporting back to the former Mrs Ashton, Tom happily informed his friend that yes, he was seeing someone and yes, she seemed pretty keen on him and no, it wasn't serious.

Driving back to Manchester awhile later, Port Sunlight looked almost beautiful as the tiny lights all around the site made the pipes look as though they had been bejewelled in his absence. The motorway was blessedly clear and he was home in less than an hour. Shrugging off his jacket, he pressed the Play button on his answering machine, alerted to new messages by the winking red light.

"Hi you," Ellen's voice rang across the hallway. "I know I said I'd try and call tomorrow but I just wanted to try and catch you while I had a minute. Look, I'm not going to have time to see you on Sunday after all. I'm going to have to get home and re-packed and set off to Birmingham almost at once for the Monday meeting. I don't want to trouble you for a lift from the airport," well, that's a bit harsh, "so I'll share a cab with Matt." Who the hell is Matt? "I'll try and reach you tomorrow. If you want to try me, the number here is–" He found a pen and paper in time to scribble down the elongated number and two-forty-three, which was her room. He tried it immediately. No reply.

The receptionist cut across the ringing tone, "Would you like to leave a message, sir?"

"Would you please let Miss Warner know that Tom called? That's all, thank you."

He replaced the receiver and pulled at his lip. Well that's it then. Ellen had said she was going to be all over the place for the next week or so doing these road shows. Looked like he wasn't going to have sex for the foreseeable. Just great.

It was a perfect day for washing the net curtains. Alice sat with a cup of tea after the exertions of bringing through the small aluminium ladder, taking down the nets and setting them in a basin of water to soak for an hour or so. She had added a full sachet of the special whitening powder.

She was tired today. Her sleep had been disturbed over the past few nights and it was catching up with her. Sometimes this happened when her dreams became prophetic but she hadn't woken this week with any notable images playing in her head. Maybe she was just getting old. She sat in her favourite chair, her china cup and saucer (plus one ginger crisp biscuit) carefully placed on the linen square protecting the little table by

96   *Boxing Clever*

her side. She didn't approve of mugs; in her view they made the tea taste funny. Cheap.

Jack was already sitting in the front room when she came through from the kitchen. He looked up and chirruped in her direction before making himself comfortable in a new position in a patch of sunlight on the carpet. Round and round he went, shuffling his back end until he decided on the right spot and then sank, liquid-like, into apparent sleep. Alice smiled as she watching the little feet ease forwards and claw at the carpet in a blissful sun-kissed stretch. Just for half an hour, she thought as she leaned back in her chair closing her eyes, I'll do the same.

It was dark where she was. No lights or any noise. She knew somehow that she was in a small place and she was hot and uncomfortable. Her head began to hurt and her brain felt fuzzy as if the nerves no longer connected properly. Her senses began to scream that there was danger; her wrists didn't feel right. Petrol. She could smell petrol. Was it fire that was warming her back, her head? The temperature was rising...

Alice's head jerked as her eyes opened, her mouth gasping for the air. The chair was bathed in sunlight, a shaft of heat cutting across her chest. But that wasn't it. That wasn't why she had felt hot, couldn't explain the smell that still resided in her nostrils. Who was it? Where were they? Alice rubbed her forehead and tried to remember all of the detail. Was this happening to someone she knew?

Over the years, she had seen premonitions of events that sometime later would appear in the newspaper or on the TV. That she had seen the girl so soon after her last vision was unusual and it had only been with her Jimmy that she had known absolutely who was involved straight away. She did a quick mental check and was reassured to feel quite calm. The danger was probably not close or immediate. She would wait. If it was important, it would come again.

As she rose, she realised that Jack must have gone out of the open kitchen window whilst she was asleep. Picking up her cup and saucer, she went back into the kitchen and carefully washed and rinsed her refreshed curtains. There were fewer more pleasing sights than fresh, clean white fabric billowing in gentle daylight and she stood for a moment in her back yard just to enjoy it.

Her days were always full even though she had no one other than herself to look after. It was not in her mother's nature to be idle, and this maxim had burned in Alice's brain ever since she could remember. She lived by the same rhythm as countless other women of her generation. Monday was washing day, Tuesday was ironing; Wednesday meant bathroom and kitchen cleaning, on Thursdays she dusted and polished her collection of porcelain figurines, and on Friday she did her main supermarket shop for the week. On Saturdays she pottered, sometimes catching the bus into Manchester to look at the shops and enjoy the atmosphere and company of busy people. Sunday she kept as a quiet day.

She liked to join the congregation in the local parish church for evensong on occasion; she enjoyed the colour and sounds of the service. It also helped to salve her conscience when she joined her neighbour at the bingo session for pensioners that the church ran on Tuesday afternoons. The orange tea they served there was a downside but she had won twenty pounds the last time she had played which had covered the cost of replacing her old wooden clothes dryer.

"Are you ready, yet?"

The distant voice came across the top of her yard wall. She recognised the sound of Lisa's father. They must be taking her home today. Poor girl. What a horrible thing to happen so early into her life and what a journey she would have to forgive

98   *Boxing Clever*

herself and limit the guilt of her own survival linked to the loss of a friend. Alice didn't think she'd see her again.

Turning the corner towards the bus stop awhile later, she cannoned into someone reading a newspaper. Her alarm and initial annoyance disappeared when she saw it was Tom. He'd clearly been oblivious to the rest of the world.

"Alice!" He greeted her with genuine pleasure. "Where are you off to? Shopping?"

"Not really," she admitted. "I just like to wander around looking in the shop windows and watching people."

"Can I give you a lift into town?"

"No thanks, I hate to waste my bus pass. Are you busy today?"

He grimaced. "Friend is dragging me off to the gym." He lowered his voice as a young girl passed alongside. "Everything all right with you?"

She nodded. "All quiet."

Well, it was almost the truth.

CHAPTER 12

The phone was ringing as he came in, and Tom dropped everything to grab the receiver. It was Ellen. It was good to hear her voice and he felt a sudden rush of affection for her.

"How's the conference?"

"Usual boozy night in the bar last night, but my talk went well."

She sounded guarded. Was someone there with her?

"Something bothering you?"

"No – well, I'm not sure. Just someone being a bit weird."

Tom waited for more.

"Look, it's not easy to talk right now? I'll fill you in when I get back."

"What kind of weird?" There was a pause as Ellen told an unseen colleague that she'd join them in a few minutes.

"Honestly, don't worry Tom. It's something and nothing. I'm going to have to go - the final dinner tonight. Black tie. Apparently the rumour is that they've booked Lenny Henry to do the cabaret."

"Don't change the subject. Who's being weird? Is it this Matt guy?" He tried to check his jealous tone.

"Matt?!" Her laugh sounded genuine. "Now *you're* getting paranoid. But...well, thanks."

"So, will I see you tomorrow after all then? Pick you up at the airport?"

100   *Boxing Clever*

"No, best not. But are you free on Thursday night? I'm up and down the country till then, and my next meeting isn't until the weekend."

"Call me as soon as you can in any case," he insisted, sensing that she was still troubled. He was rewarded by noises of kisses. He wished her a safe trip home.

Thursday it would be then. Not too long. Checking his watch, he reckoned there was time for a pot of strong coffee before he had to meet Dean. Who needed exercise when caffeine got your pulse rate sky high?

"For fuck's sake!"

Tom could just about breathe enough to spit out the curse. His arms wobbled as he struggled to keep the weighted bar above his exposed throat and not on it. Dean tutted as he effortlessly retrieved the bar and placed it back on the rests.

"You really are out of shape, mate." Dean sounded truly disappointed in him. "You'll be fifty before you know it and facing your first heart attack. What have you been doing?"

"Well, thanks for the death sentence." Tom heaved himself to a sitting position on the blue padded bench. "I'm not that bad – have just got out of the habit of doing stuff since the divorce." He used to pound the streets for hours on most nights towards the end of his marriage as a way of getting out of the house.

"This," he tapped his flattish but no longer taut stomach. "This is a sign of my new found contentment."

"You won't be content when you can't see your feet."

"You can't see yours! Your bloody neck's got so much muscle it can't even bend properly."

Tom was petulant. And, an hour or so later, very, very sorry that he'd opened his big mouth. Dean knew every other guy in the gym and made sure that he announced that "this is my mate,

Tom... in training for the next Great North Run" to each one of them. Saving face had never been so painful.

"Okay, okay. You win. I'm a lazy, unfit git." Tom would have sung an aria from Puccini if that was what it would take for Dean to say they had finished for the day. "It's a good job I'm not seeing Ellen tomorrow – I'm going to be good for nothing."

"Won't be tomorrow that you'll feel the worst. Just wait until Monday."

At least Dean's approach to keeping fit didn't rule out alcohol after a work out. They both had drunk plenty of water in the gym and an electrolyte drink before they retired to the upstairs bar. There was a glass viewing area there and as they enjoyed a cool beer, Tom watched in fascination as two guys got redder and redder in pursuit of the tiny squash ball.

"Quite fancy getting back into that," he observed, liking the satisfactory sound as the ball was thwacked around the court.

"Not yet, buddy. You've got to get fit to play that game. You'd be knackered."

"I can do knackered." Tom now had the self-satisfied glow of someone who had *been to the gym*. "Do you play? Or know how I can get started?" Enthusiasm. Yep, that was what was stirring. He liked the atmosphere here although it wasn't the most convenient place for him to come. He'd take a look at the new place nearer home. Could be a way of meeting new people as well as doing him good.

Dean eyed him suspiciously. "What's going on in that head of yours? I've never been able to drag you within spitting distance of this place before today and now you're wanting to play squash."

Tom explained briefly that he thought his life was too much work and Ellen and nothing else. He didn't admit to the pang of

102   *Boxing Clever*

jealousy he'd felt earlier, just that he didn't want to get too involved, needed to try different things. The confidence was offered and accepted without fuss and would not be mentioned again.

Inspired by the vision of his new self, Tom drove straight to the new sports centre about two miles from his home. He liked it and decided to apply for membership on the spot, taking note of the number to call if, as a member, he was interested in joining the squash ladder. Now all he needed was the kit.

With the redemption of the newly fit, he prepared himself a large stir-fry with king prawns, chicken and vegetables tossed in a special Thai sauce. Surprisingly, there was no sign of Jack, who normally appeared within seconds of the sound of a packet of meat being opened. He had just finished a massive bowlful and was sitting nursing a second large glass of fragrant white wine, video control in his hand, when the nudging beep of his mobile phone came from the kitchen. It was Frank.

"Tom," he cut straight to the quick. "I need you in here right now. All hell's breaking loose. And try and find Dean as well. My office, twenty minutes."

Hell, he'd be lucky to get a taxi at this time on a Saturday night; he certainly couldn't drive. Grabbing his coat, mobile phone and keys, Tom was out the door and along the street in less than a minute. He increased his pace whilst trying a few taxi companies that he knew, all of whom could only promise a cab in an hour or so. No choice but to strike out for the main road and hope that either a bus or taxi came along that he could flag down. His legs waited for about five minutes before reminding him that they had been used a bit too much that day and despite the relaxant effect of the wine, they were going to hurt. Stiffening by the step, it was divine intervention that brought the black cab with blessed light on into his view.

Frank looked grey.

"Bloody awful night." He motioned a chair. "God knows what's got into the water but they've started early."

It was barely ten o'clock and Saturday night was still in its infancy. A man had been beaten and left for dead when a group of young lads stole his car near Old Trafford. He was now in the MRI and unlikely to survive. A young boy had been stabbed in Hulme and would not say a word through terror or misguided gang loyalty. Finally, and more worrying, a house fire in the Fallowfield area had killed two young children and their mother. There was no sign of the father and the fire service was talking arson.

"Sodding press were all over the place like a rash," Frank's love affair with the media clearly forgotten. "The wind caught the flames and managed to ignite one of the advertising banners hanging on the lamppost near the garden hedge. I can just see the headlines. 'Will Summit go up in Flames? Crime Rife in Host City'."

Tom inwardly thought this a bit of an exaggeration, but said nothing, rapidly thinking through cases and resources.

"I'll start with the young lad and then pick up on the fire. Dean can link with Rich on the mugging. We'll sort the other cases around them tomorrow." And that meant downgrading the Quays murder. Again. The drug dealer and shoplifting he would leave with Ryan and Elliott for the time being.

Frank stopped pacing and gave his hair a modest re-working. He nodded. "Good. Excellent. Keep me up to date. At least it's Sunday tomorrow and that gives us twenty-four hours before the briefing for the dailies."

Out of consideration to the nurses at the hospital, Tom took steps to clear the garlic and alcohol from his mouth. Three cups of water from the CID cooler, a black coffee and three extra

104 Boxing Clever

strong mints later, he showed his ID to the tired young uniformed officer standing guard outside the victim's room.

"Any trouble?" he asked.

"No sign, sir. Kid looks terrified."

"Not surprising given someone tried to kill him. Do we know him?"

"Name's Jordan Bell. Bit of petty crime, cars, that sort of thing. Wouldn't have marked him for the big league. Apparently he's lucky to be alive. Knife missed his heart by a whisker and he was left for dead."

Tom thanked him and went into the green and cream room that could have been in any hospital in the country. Monitors beeped cheerily signalling that the patient was still alive.

"I ain't saying nothin'." The irony was missed as the boy acknowledged his visitor as a figure of authority.

"Who did this to you, Jordan? I'm DI Tom Ashton, by the way."

"Fuck off," was the reply of the still-talking non-talker.

After ten minutes of his best fatherly approach, Tom admitted defeat. The boy suddenly remembered that saying nothing meant keeping his mouth shut and he refused to even meet Tom's eyes.

Fortunately there was more to go on at the scene of the fire. The chief fireman was a large garrulous man only too pleased to be able to involve others in the situation. The smell of charred metal, cloth and flesh lay heavily on the air as they spoke. The fact that the house was still smouldering and exuding heat showed that they had only just managed to kill the flames.

"Hear you think it's arson?" Tom wanted to establish as soon as possible whether this was a case for his team or not.

"Damn sure," the response was unequivocal. "Gut feeling when I got here, borne out by the petrol rag in the cellar being the source of the blaze. Reckon you guys will find that the husband has a nice fat insurance policy on his family somewhere."

"Reckon you're right. Looks like a straightforward one for a change."

Franklin liked Scotland. He'd watched the changing landscape on the journey north through slitted eyes, the woollen hat pulled low over his forehead. It scratched his skin but it suited his face. He liked the way that the clouds seemed to hang lower over the hilly ground as they approached Glasgow. He liked the grittiness of the buildings and the unhidden toughness of the men he met. And the women! Ballsy and direct. He had the number of a slender girl with impossible breasts, and as soon as Joe and Sam let him off the leash for a minute after the fight he would call her. Oh yes.

Martin had done well arranging this bout. There were bright yellow posters stuck on hoardings, bus stops and lampposts on the route from the hotel to the venue. Joe Murphy seemed to be known by the majority of older guys, their broken noses and tattoos testament to their past lives. The gym had all the equipment Franklin needed and there was a spotty lad in the corner who apparently wrote for the local newspaper. Franklin had heard Joe tell Sam that the *Evening News* might send someone up to cover it too.

"Fifteen more minutes, Franklin," Joe sounded like he was the big 'I am'. "Work on your footwork and that left jab to the trunk."

I'll fuckin' left jab you to the trunk, Franklin thought. He was unforgiving in his practice and the sparring partner, strung with a midriff padding like Michelin Man, began to grunt with the onslaught.

"Good, good!" Sam was grinning. "We'll make a champion of you yet." He was climbing into the ring as he spoke,

106   *Boxing Clever*

gesturing to Michelin Man to get out. Franklin was pouring with good, clean sweat. Cleansing. Purifying. He watched Joe flick open his phone, no doubt to report back to Martin, before closing his eyes as Sam released his headgear and then began to unfasten his gloves.

"He's looking great, training has gone absolutely to plan. Local journalist was here. Any nod from *The News*?" Joe said no more for quite awhile and Franklin thought, with eyes still closed, that Martin had passed on the required news and hung up.

"What the fuck did they want again?"

Franklin opened his eyes to observe Joe, standing stock still in front of him, face grim.

"No one is talking to him before this fight and not afterwards if I can help it. Was the journo there when they arrived?" An answer was delivered.

"Fuck." Pause. "Sort it." The phone was clicked shut and stuffed into the tweed jacket pocket.

"Okay, boss?" Franklin found the servile approach worked wonders.

"No worries – management issues, son. You did good today." Joe was trying hard to reach equilibrium and his face was twitching into an encouraging smile. "Now, let's say we eat and then you need to get some rest. Big day tomorrow."

Dean didn't appear until late Sunday morning. Tom was drinking his second cup of black coffee with a fat and delicious Danish pastry he'd picked up from the local bakery on the way in to work.

"What's happening?"

"What happened to you, more like. I was trying to get hold of you last night. All hell broke loose." He then proceeded to summarise the night's activity.

"Link up with Rich. He has been downstairs picking up the carjacking file. We might be looking at another murder here and the sooner we can get a lead the better."

While he was speaking, Tom moved across to the larger white board where, on his direction, Ryan had added the new cases, making room where she could. The Quays body and the shoplifting network had been relegated, for the time being, to single typed sheets of A4 paper, stuck on the metal frame of the board with magnetic clips. Each bore the heading: 'enquiries proceeding'. The death of Mel Chadwick had been moved to the bottom of the board.

Dean, now alongside Tom, took in the amendments.

"Fair enough," he commented. "I'll get started but remind me to tell you about the stuff I found out on Mr Franklin Raye. Reckon he might have been a bit of a Tyson in his past."

The rest of Sunday was a maelstrom of telephone calls, snatched briefings with colleagues and Frank Dawson handholding. The carjacking victim lost his fight just as Tom got the news that Jordan Bell had had an unwelcome visitor. No sooner had he put the phone down from the reporting officer, when a call came through from Mr Chadwick enquiring about how far they had got with his daughter's case. He tried to be sympathetic and diplomatic with the bereaved man at the same time as waving frantically at Elliott who seemed to be heading for the door. He needed him to get to the hospital and talk to the young lad ASAP.

By seven o'clock, Tom was beginning to see some light at the end of the tunnel. Dean had called in to let him know he and Rich had found a couple of eyewitnesses who were prepared to give statements. There was also the possibility of more coming forwards as Frank had agreed to contacting the local TV station

108   *Boxing Clever*

to have the incident reported the following morning. Seemed the boss was getting back his backbone; three cheers if they could now stuff the regional neuroses of bad press where the sun didn't shine.

The report was in from the house fire and the name in the frame was the husband. Not surprisingly, he was nowhere to be found, but his description was out and ports, airports and railway stations had been alerted. This tragedy would be covered on the evening news.

Elliott caught up with him in the corridor as he selected a black coffee, with sugar, from the vending machine. Elliott had a vague scent of antiseptic around him, mixed with building body odour.

"I bloody hate hospitals," the explanation of the sweat in that sentence. "Really give me the willies."

Tom donated his coffee and pressed the selection buttons again.

"Shouldn't think young Master Bell is having a ball either," he commented. "So who was the oink?"

"The nurse said that she had been with him when the officer asked if he could go to the loo. She got called next door for some emergency or other; Jordan was alone for barely five minutes. When our guy got back, he presumed the nurse was still in with him but, thank God for some intelligence, opened the door to let her know he was back. Sees this guy leaning over the bed, reckons he was going to smother him or something. Next thing he knows, the bloke is out the door, smashing our man against the wall and leaving Jordan with eyes like organ stops. The lad wouldn't say a word to me. He's obviously been told in no uncertain terms to keep schtum."

"He's not said anything anyway. Someone is very rattled at the possibility that he will." Tom sipped at the coffee that today had more than a passing resemblance to gravy. "Any idea who this visitor was?"

"Nope."

"Okay, file what you have, then tomorrow check the hospital CCTV and any other security. You'd best get off."

An hour or so later, Tom decided to do likewise, enjoying for the first time in ages that they were making some progress against the tide of human failure.

Jack wasn't in the house when he got home and he began to feel the first stirring of concern. He had been mildly puzzled by the cat's absence yesterday, but it was unprecedented for him to be out of sight for so long. A quick check in the kitchen told him that Jack, or some other creature, had finished the food he had put down, but there was no raising of the cat flap that often accompanied his return home. Admitting to himself that he was going soft, Tom thought he would pop round to the off-licence on the pretext of taking a detour to see Alice.

She looked surprised to see him. "Hello, Tom. Is there news?"

"Not really, I was just on my way to...erm...actually, wondered if you had seen anything of Jack over the weekend? His food has gone but he hadn't been around."

"Oh, yes!" Alice smiled with pleasure. "He's been here most of the time, such a lovely little companion."

As if on cue, Jack's lithe body appeared at the side of Alice's left leg, nudging her calf before he wandered out languidly to greet Tom.

"Good of you, bud," he bent to scratch the little black head. "It's not as if I don't feed you."

"Oh, I don't give him much," Alice was quick to reassure him. "Just some fresh chicken and fish now and again." Well, that explains it. Cat of refined tastes.

110   *Boxing Clever*

"Thanks, Alice, just wanted to check he was all right. All okay with you?"

"Hm," She was thoughtful. "I'm getting the sensation of something happening but I can't pin it down yet. Nothing to concern you, I'm sure."

"Well," Tom didn't need to be thinking of anything else, certainly nothing so vague, "you know where I am."

I can't believe I said that, he thought as he walked back home, never having made it to the off-licence. Anyone would think I'm looking for business. Maybe he should set up a 'crimes that will happen (possibly)' board, just like in that Tom Cruise film. Laughing to himself at the thought of Frank's reaction to such an idea, he decided to take himself off to his new club. Ellen would be impressed when he slipped his new squash hobby into conversation on Thursday, even if he hadn't actually picked up a racquet yet.

She was nowhere near his thoughts when the call came the following lunchtime.

"Tom Ashton." He carried on writing as he tuned in to the male voice on the other end of the line.

"Mr Ashton," the man spoke urgently. "This is George Barnett from Vanpharma. I'm hoping you may be able to tell me the whereabouts of Ellen Warner?"

CHAPTER 13

"I'm sorry?" he asked, almost immediately aware that he sounded incredibly stupid. "Ellen? Why on earth are you asking me? She came back from one of your company conferences yesterday and went straight off to a meeting in Birmingham. I spoke to her when she'd just landed at the airport."

"That's just it," the man replied. "She didn't arrive at the hotel last night and although colleagues tried her mobile they just assumed something had happened to delay her. I wasn't informed until a short while ago."

The name registered. This was the same man that Ellen had spoken to about the calls and the threatening letter. Head of security. What the fuck was going on? As he framed his next question he reached for his mobile phone and began to compose a text message, tapping in the characters with his right hand.

"I know no more than you do, Mr Barnett," he said, instructing the phone to 'send'. "I presume you've tried her home number? She could be ill."

"We think she would have let us know. She is very conscientious. She clearly hasn't contacted you...do you have a set of keys for her house?"

"I'm ahead of you." Tom was already on his feet, grabbing his car keys and phone. "I'll give you a ring when I get there."

"I rather think I should meet you there?" The cautious reply was of someone who knew and missed the form.

111

112   *Boxing Clever*

"Look, er - I'm sure there's a logical explanation for all this. Leave it to us. I'll be in touch."

He saw Dean's raised eyebrows.

"Ellen hasn't shown up for an important meeting. Going over to check her place."

Tom dutifully scribbled 'Out' on the movements board as he left. Seconds later, Dean was behind him, but he said nothing.

They took a quick detour to Tom's house, Dean turning the car round as Tom ran to his front door, in order to be facing the right direction for the quickest route to Ellen's house. He almost tripped over Jack who was sitting just inside the hallway as he came through and as he rushed through the house, the cat weaved in front of him, as if intent on slowing his progress.

"For fuck's sake, cat!" he yelled. "Get out of the bloody way."

Minutes later Dean was accelerating away, Tom with Ellen's keys in his left hand, issuing directions.

"Where was she meant to be?" said Dean when they were forced to stop at a red light.

"Can't remember. Leeds or London I think."

"Want me to check with Traffic?"

Tom felt his stomach clench, but shook his head.

"It's the third on the right," Tom said as they turned into the narrow, neat crescent. "Her car's still here." The smart blue Peugeot sports car was on the driveway, in front of the garage. Not in the garage. When he had called here on Friday, it was still in the garage.

"Car was in the garage when I came on Friday." He was beginning to feel alarmed. "She must have brought it out ready for her trip. What the hell is going on?"

Dean had pulled up in front of the driveway, effectively blocking in the car that was going nowhere.

Maureen Devlin   113

Tom at first couldn't see any signs of break-in or damage. Dark blue door closed, wheelie bin in position to the left of the garage door. It was only as he approached the house that he saw that one of the pots had been knocked over, just behind the car. The feathery plant spread its ferns like a fan giving the impression of a resting taffeta-clad diva. Within seconds he had the keys in the door and the house unlocked. As he gently pushed the door open, he was surprised to hear the greeting beep of the alarm. The alarm had clearly been set. She couldn't be here.

Tom moved through the house like a dervish, registering where she had dropped papers and files on the kitchen table, dirty laundry cascading out of the laundry bin in her bedroom and the discarded suitcase not quite empty in the little office. She had been here, got rid of the stuff she had taken to Spain and probably packed a smaller bag for the few days she planned to be away. In a hurry but no signs of a struggle. And there had been no text reply either.

"Where the bloody hell is she? This doesn't make sense."

"Could she have arranged to get a lift from someone and decided not to drive?" Dean offered. "Maybe we should try hospitals and such." He veiled his concern with a pragmatic tone.

Tom swallowed but recognised the sense. "You get on to that, I'll call the company back and let them know what we've found."

He dialled George Barnett's number as he walked back to the front door and stood looking at the car. And looked closely again. In his haste to get into the house, he hadn't noticed that the car was unlocked. He cut the connection just as the cheery telephonist was announcing the company name and wrenched open the boot. A briefcase and small suitcase with wheels sat snugly in the compact grey space. With heart sinking, Tom

114   *Boxing Clever*

opened the driver's door and reached under the seat to where Ellen normally wedged her handbag. She had chosen a black one, with two zips.

As he raised his head, he saw Dean standing by the open boot.

"She's been snatched." Tom's words were flat and definite. "There's no other explanation." He flicked open his mobile phone and recalled the number for George Barnett. "I'm going to alert the company, we'll have to work with them on this. You try and see if you can find a spare set of keys in the house to lock the car. We'll put her things in the house except her handbag. I'll take that; it's got her mobile in it. The scroats may try to contact us on that." As he spoke, Tom's eyes were scanning the quiet close. The area was deserted.

He stood in the modern chrome and glass lobby waiting for George Barnett to appear. Dean was reading the advertising posters that bedecked the plain white walls. The whirring and clicking of the turnstile was grating on Tom's ears – a stream of workers clutching folders and files were apparently going to the lecture theatre in an adjacent building. Time after time, they swiped their staff passes across the electronic eye and then pushed their way from the office area into the lobby. Tom began to rock on his heels. Where has this guy got to come from? Outer friggin' Mongolia? As he strode back to the front desk, a fifty-something, broad shouldered man appeared, hand outstretched in greeting. An intelligent gaze emanated from the craggy face and the voice, when it came, was deep and strong.

"Mr Ashton, I'm George Barnett. I'm sorry to keep you waiting, I'll explain when we go through." With that, he motioned for them to accompany him through the glass gate, which had been opened by the receptionist in anticipation.

Maureen Devlin 115

"This is my colleague, Dean Wilson," Tom explained as Dean's bulk moved alongside. More hand shaking.

The bright building was humming with the sounds of electrical equipment and muted human voices. A sense of quiet efficiency pervaded the open plan area in front of them, a corporate colossus. In spite of himself, Tom was grudgingly impressed. George guided them past a large restaurant and down a set of spiral stairs to the lower ground floor where, he explained, all the maintenance and security services for the Vanpharma buildings were housed. Tom, remembering Ellen's description, grew impatient with the man's guided tour. Subdued lighting and corporate grey/green carpet softened their arrival in front of a grey door marked helpfully 'Security'.

George pressed his pass onto the electronic pad on the wall to the left of the door. An answering click indicated that they were free to go through into a room dominated by technology. A bank of screens displayed images of the lobby, various corridors, the car park. Two men were sitting at a small round table to the edge of the room, coffee cups in hand, and another man was working at a computer console near the screens.

Introductions were made and drinks offered with Tom getting more and more impatient to be doing something constructive. He failed to see why Ellen's boss was here, although the HR director could be important. The man at the screens had been asked to leave.

"What does your policy say we do in these matters, George? As far as police procedure is concerned – as you know - we can only log Ellen as a missing person and can't justify pulling in resources from other cases. We've checked with the local hospitals. Nothing." He knew he sounded dispassionate, but it was the only way to help her.

"I'll be straight with you here. This situation makes me anxious as our initial searches after that note was delivered

116   *Boxing Clever*

didn't show any of the regular groups to be active in this area. Also, it's rare for a non-scientist to be targeted individually so there is the possibility that this is a new group or even," George paused in reflection, "a rogue player who's in over his depth and therefore totally unpredictable."

Tom declined one of the grey and chrome chairs and began to pace around the small area of uncluttered carpet.

"Similar experiences?"

The company men exchanged glances.

"We've never actually been in this situation before." George looked somehow diminished by the admission. "But we have got a massive database of information on other cases and can anticipate how these groups behave." As if to deflect the waves of scepticism radiating towards him, he quickly reached for the pile of folders on the grey table.

"This," he handed a copy to Tom, letting the others help themselves, "is a dossier of corporate kidnappings in the UK and the USA. These aren't confined to the pharmaceutical industry as I'm sure you'll appreciate." He drew their attention to the green coloured pages towards the rear of the dossier.

"We've collated a general profile of the type of individual that gets involved in this type of activity and here," he indicated the pale blue section, "is our procedural map."

"Meaning?"

"It shows, step by step, how the company will react to any demands or change in behaviour of the kidnappers. This approach has been found to be almost universally successful in known cases."

"Success rate?"

George eyed them both. "Good. In the order of ninety percent."

Tom pursed his lips. He wasn't even going to begin to think about the fate of the rest.

Maureen Devlin   117

They discussed their strategy for a further twenty minutes, to include talking to Ellen's colleagues at the conference, particularly given her cryptic comments to Tom. His mobile phone rang, interrupting the flow. Leaving Dean to negotiate the removal of one of the dossiers from the company premises, he moved towards the door to hear Rich's nasal tones.

"Tom? The Rodent's looking for you – wasn't impressed that Dean was out with you as well. Wants you both back here pronto. The guy who was mugged for his car? Only turns out to have been a leading light in prison reform. We've also got a possible sighting of the missing husband in the fire case. By the way," he added quickly, "is Ellen okay?"

"Am sure she is. Thanks. Back in fifteen."

He turned to find Dean already on his feet, clutching a folder under his arm.

"So, we wait until we hear anything? And you'll contact me on my mobile, day or night as soon as they make contact about what they want?"

George nodded and put forward his hand. Instead of shaking Tom's hand, he grabbed his arm in a gesture of support. Tom was impassive.

"I must just repeat, George, I'm unhappy about not contacting her parents. I can understand the media blackout..."

"Trust me on this, we can't risk anyone talking out of turn until we have had the first contact. Experience shows that it usually comes within twenty-four hours. We daren't spook them. This is not a simple missing person..."

No one disagreed with the statement and the words hung in the air. Tom fervently hoped that this likeable man in front of him wasn't completely out of his depth. He rang Frank.

The rest of the morning passed with no contact from George. Tom read through the complete dossier while the work of the

118   *Boxing Clever*

office played around him. Phone calls were made and answered, information on various cases shared and people coming and going.

Frank was understanding, but firm.

"There's nothing you can do at the moment, Tom." He had intercepted them in the corridor. Dean took the nodded hint and carried on towards the CID office.

When they were safely in his office, Frank continued. "As soon as I got your call, I got in touch with the National Crime Squad. They'll have someone here tomorrow. I've also spoken to a friend in the Met; they have built up a lot of competence in security cases because of Westminster and the City. They worked with Vanpharma to develop their policy. This guy Barnett used to be based there." He leaned towards him and lowered his voice.

"We'll support you all we can Tom, you know that - but you can't be on the investigating team. We've got a whole heap of other shit to sort out already. Get stuck in to that, I'm sure we'll know more soon."

By five o'clock, he couldn't wait. He rang George.

"Twenty-four hours have passed. Surely we need to move." He wasn't going to let George know he wasn't on the case.

"We've heard nothing and found nothing." George was clearly puzzled. "We can't jeopardise Ellen by acting too quickly. Look," he paused and took a deep breath. "There's something I didn't tell you earlier but it may have some bearing..."

Tom waited, twisting and twirling a pen between his fingers.

"This has to be confidential–"

"For God's sake, man!"

A sigh. "Vanpharma is about to announce that they are to go to court to protect their patent rights on a new life-saving drug for malaria. If they win, it will protect the price. However, it may make it almost unaffordable for poorer countries like Africa unless agencies such as the World Health Organisation step in to provide the funding."

"So, this could mean there are other aggrieved groups in the frame? Not just the animal rights lobby?"

"Exactly. And as a consequence, we can't even begin to second guess what they want. But just to reassure you – I have been talking with our legal and media teams and the agreement is to hold the announcement until next week."

Fucking big of you.

"And that means we wait for a little bit longer." George was apologetic.

That's your choice, Tom thought. Not mine.

CHAPTER 14

Ellen's house was quiet and unchanged. The answering machine was flashing so he hit the Play button and intruded on her life. The second to last message was a silent call, infuriatingly out of reach of the 'last caller' number retrieval system. He'd need the records. He went up to her office and switched on the laptop but could not get beyond the password request. He packed up the machine and carried it downstairs, flipping open his phone as he went.

"George?" Tom explained his laptop theory and was impressed to hear that they had already accessed her files through the main frame. Nothing. He tucked the padded bag out of sight on the floor and took a final look around the house. As he was leaving, alarm set, he saw Anne, the neighbour, arriving home. He knew everything looked as normal, the plant had been righted and Dean had moved the car back into the garage. She was obviously unconcerned and no longer on plant duty as she waved cheerily and went into her own house.

Thwack! Thwack! Tom grunted as his elbow hit the wall and his borrowed racquet ricocheted out of his hand. It was past nine o'clock in the evening and there had been no contact from the kidnappers. He had gone back to work from Ellen's but all he had managed to do was to get on everyone's nerves, demanding reports on anything and everything to keep a focus.

Maureen Devlin 121

When he decided that he needed to get away, there was an almost audible sigh of relief. What he needed, in fact, was to pulverise a small grey sphere against a whitewashed wall. Alone.

After going home to pick up his sports bag, again having to unravel himself from Jack who seemed to have sprouted eight legs, he was building up quite a sweat in competition with himself.

This one (*thwack!*) is for the bastards who have taken her. This one – an acceptable backhand shot – was for the faceless people at the top of her company who may in the end get her killed. And this one (*thwack!!*) for me being a useless git who can't do a sodding (*thwack!*), fucking (*thwack!!*) thing about it! Tom mentally roared in symphony with the sound of the ball bouncing from one wall to another.

He took a second to catch his breath and thankfully was able to hear the call of his mobile, nestling on his sweatshirt in the back right hand corner of the court. He snatched the tiny instrument to his ear, leaning against the wall, heart thudding and sweating profusely only to hear that the errant arsonist husband was en route from Portsmouth. Tom unclenched his jaw on hearing the message and instructed for the man to be held overnight. He would interview him in the morning. Tonight he felt in danger of punching him in the mouth for being a fucking irrelevance.

While he had the phone in his hand, he rang George. He was beginning to use the man as a security blanket but he at least felt like he was doing something.

"It's Tom Ashton," he announced, back in control.

"I'm sorry, Tom. No news here, but I have arranged for extra men to be on site tonight and we are having another crisis meeting tomorrow. You?"

122   *Boxing Clever*

Tom admitted that he had called Ellen's parents in Dorset but there had been no reply. Not surprisingly, he had not left a message. He had contacted the local police force and asked them to alert him as soon as there were signs of life. George didn't protest.

"I presume there is nothing from any of your other employees? No one else has been targeted in any other site?"

"No, and that's a good question. We are beginning to think it is a UK operator which tends to bring it more in line with the animal rights lobbyists." The phone went quiet for a moment. "Let's talk again early tomorrow unless things develop..."

Tom decided not to have a shower at the gym in case he missed the phone ringing. Instead, red, sweaty and dying of thirst, he drove home to find Alice standing on his doorstep. Jack was at her feet.

"Ah!" she exclaimed. "We thought you'd be back soon. I really need to talk with you." She looked at him closely. "Are you all right?"

He was bone weary and not in the mood for opaque conversations. On the other hand, he wasn't entirely looking forward to his own company so he gave her a weary smile and said, "Been to the gym."

He motioned her inside and apologetically pulled at his still damp and none too fragrant T-shirt.

"Please, make yourself at home, I'll down in a few minutes." He was up the stairs without waiting for a reply.

Alice had been brought up to be polite but she felt it would be discourteous to hover about in the hallway, so after closing the door, she followed her feline guide through to the kitchen, switching on the main light as she entered. Whilst this was not a man not brought up in her ways, there was a pleasing lack of take-away cartons and a disposable liner was clearly visible in the large chrome swing bin. She was quite taken by a fancy juicing machine (it took a few minutes to figure out what it was) and was just filling the shiny chrome kettle with water for tea when Tom appeared at the doorway.

"Leave that running for a minute," he said and pulled out a frosted blue glass from the cupboard near the window, filled it and drank the whole lot without stopping. He repeated the process before pulling out the two pine and chrome stools cleverly hidden under the work surface.

"I'm not sure I can do stools," she said, eyeing them warily. As he was already perched, and by the slump of his shoulders, she gamely hitched herself up and balanced, feeling quite comfortable. The kettle boiled as she had got settled.

Tom, realising her predicament, made the tea. He poured himself a cold beer and waited for her to speak.

"I know you believed me over Mel and I thank you for that," she rushed. "And I'm not even sure what it is that I'm seeing." She sipped at her tea as if to collect her thoughts. "Promise you'll hear me out before you ask me any questions?"

He nodded and drank. Whatever.

"I've been having sensations of being in a small, enclosed space. It gets warmer and warmer and I can smell petrol. My wrists ache like they've been tied. It's happened the same three times now and each time Jack has been there at first but when I've come round, he's gone. The last, that's the fourth time, was an hour or so ago, and when I came to, he was sitting on my chair with this," she held up a small beaded object, "stuck to his fur. Then he howled to be let out of the front door instead of going out through the kitchen window and I followed him. To here." She sat back gingerly and clutched the mug in both hands.

Tom's stomach lurched as he stared at the object, remembering how delicate it had looked in her ear and how she

124   *Boxing Clever*

had almost turned his house upside down to find it. She had been wearing the earrings on the night they went to the Underground Club – he said she must have lost it there or in the taxi home but she was adamant it must have dropped off in his bedroom. Trouble is, she'd been too drunk, and he too tired, to be sure. The ticking of the wall clock suddenly sounded like a bomb.

"It's Ellen's," he eventually explained quietly, turning the pink and crystal drop in his fingers. "She's my...she's a good friend and she's gone missing." He looked up into the kind eyes of his neighbour. "We have reason to believe she has been abducted." He focused again on the earring before adding to himself, "I don't know what the fuck this means."

There came a sharp little cough. He didn't apologise for his language.

"Alice – I'm clutching here at straws so small I can't even see them! Do you think you've been experiencing what has – is - happening to Ellen?"

She was definite. "Oh, yes. It's Jack you see. He has been trying to tell me something for days. Has he been odd with you?"

Tom remembered Ellen's observation just before she went away and how he had been tripping over the animal every time he came home during recent days. He sighed.

"To be honest, the whole world feels odd. I've got my hands tied by her employers and my boss, a million other cases to think about and here I am sitting talking with you the possibility that a cat is more in touch with Ellen's situation than I am." He took a long final swig of his beer. "However, I've got bugger all to go on, so why not?"

Alice clearly did not take offence easily. She put down her mug and folded her hands primly on the granite surface.

"Let me tell you what happened today. It felt different. Like I'd moved from a car or van to a room. The smell of petrol had gone but I could detect faint spices and sort of grubbiness. Not a

Maureen Devlin   125

clean place. Not as hot as before, but warm and stuffy and this time I'm sure I had something over my mouth. I didn't seem as frightened but I don't know why. There were voices in the background, male voices. Music, loud, not enjoyable. That's all."

"When was the first episode?"

"This last Saturday."

"Ellen was in Barcelona then, she can't have been taken until Sunday." Christ. He was actually beginning to believe that Alice's story meant something.

"Oh, that might explain it," came the response. "I came out from the dream – I had been asleep – but didn't feel any sense of urgency. As if the event was to come and may not happen at all."

Tom grunted. "Not an exact science then?"

Alice visibly bristled. "Well of course it isn't! But it's a start. I know you are under stress, but there is no need to be so rude." She levered herself forwards in preparation for a dismount.

Tom, contrite, raised his arm to persuade her to stay but she was down from the stool with surprising speed.

"Come on then," she said.

"Where?"

"To where she was taken from."

She insisted he bought a sandwich at the petrol station where he had to stop to fill the tank. He hadn't realised he was hungry until she mentioned it. He hadn't eaten since breakfast but hadn't wanted to. The selection in the fridge in the garage shop was even worse than at work so he opted for an alarmingly solid flapjack. He also bought a late edition *Evening News* and some mineral water.

His mind was working over what he knew about Ellen's disappearance as he turned the car into her road when suddenly Alice grabbed his arm. He was appalled to see her face a mask

126   *Boxing Clever*

of absolute terror, her eyes wide and mouth framing a silent scream. Her breathing was fast and shallow and she was pressed back into her seat as if in a high-speed jet. He slammed the car to a standstill in the middle of the road. She began to moan and tried to move her head.

"Alice? Alice!" There was no response.

Bloody hell, what was he supposed to do? Treat her like a sleep walker and wait until she comes to? Or do as Jack did when she was seeing Mel's collapse? He anguished for what seemed like hours as she struggled against an unseen adversary. She was seeing Ellen. Oh, fuck. He opened the window to allow in some fresh air and then tapped at her face to bring her round, she was still and silent. Shit.

A shuddering breath and she was back. She raised a trembling hand to her forehead and tried to rub it, succeeding only in patting it ineffectually. Her nostrils flared as she drew in the fresh air. He waited, desperate to know what she had seen, hating the thought that Ellen had gone through the same. Her eyes gradually opened, her gaze on the road ahead.

"Oh, Tom. I'm so sorry. She must have been terrified." She continued to stare forwards. He waited for more but she was silent.

"Alice," he pressed. No response. "I'll take you home." He was terse.

"No!" She grabbed at the wheel. "That would be the wrong direction. When the car they put me in (and I'm sure about that now) turned round, it turned left out of the crescent, not right."

He couldn't help the feeling of hopeful curiosity – and sod police training on evidence, evidence, evidence. This was personal. He turned the car in Ellen's driveway and followed the muttered directions. He drove slowly along the road, Alice's eyes closed as she tried to relive the experience. Left here, now right.

"There was a bumping sensation...either a bad bit of road or a railway line? And quite soon."

As they passed over the resurfacing works, Tom's appreciation of Alice grew. Maybe, just maybe... They drove on in silence.

"Where next?" He felt breathless with optimism.

There was no response. He eased off the accelerator, the car moving almost at a crawl. "Alice?"

She shook her head. "I'm sorry, Tom. I'm getting confused, as if they had gone round in circles. I'm not sure. But," she paused and then continued with a stronger voice, "we are right to here. I know."

He looked through the windscreen, sides and back window to get a better visual on where 'here' was. He had been more intent on what she said than concentrating on where they were. By the dim glow of the dirty street lights he could just make out a road sign a few yards up on the right near a T-junction. He crept forwards and read the name. Dear God. They had passed into Ardwick.

CHAPTER 15

Tom felt he had lost an ocean-going yacht and found a model car given away free with breakfast cereal. No more words passed between them until he pulled up outside Alice's house. Her eyes had dark circles under them and she looked ready to drop.

"I wish it could be more, I really do."

"No, I'm sorry." He patted her arm. "I was expecting too much. You've given me a really useful lead on where she might be, although," he paused thoughtfully, "I wouldn't have thought of Ardwick being a magnet for animal rights protesters."

"And why not? You are generalising and being judgmental. Maybe that's exactly why they chose it." She pulled at the door lever. "Call and see me tomorrow. We may be able to make more sense of it, that is, if you don't get news before then." She wished him goodnight.

Tom watched until she was safely inside and then drove home. Jack was waiting inside the hallway and he stroked him gratefully. All of a sudden, he hated living alone.

He lay in bed, arms under his head, trying to get his thoughts in some sort of order. He could not erase the image of Alice's reaction as they drew up outside Ellen's house. That she wouldn't talk about it made him more anxious. He began to accept that Ellen had been hurt in some way and she had been aware of it and wanted to spare him. By four o'clock in the morning, he gave up on the idea of sleep and got up to make a hot drink, taking an inventory of his spice cupboard as he waited for the kettle to boil. Order out of chaos. He needed paprika.

He sat in the darkened lounge, a nature documentary on the habits of prairie dogs flickering in the corner, the sound turned off. Jack's head and front legs lay heavy on his left thigh and the gentle rumble of his slumbering purr was amplified in the early morning quiet. Tom felt his eyes begin to droop and he leaned his head gratefully against the back of the sofa.

It was the phone, as ever, that disturbed him. The jarring sound made his body react before he was fully awake and his back gave an answering wrench as he twisted in the seat. Sunlight was glowing against his closed hessian curtains and a shoal of fish now glinted on the silent screen. He grabbed the phone, sending the mug holding chocolate dregs flying across the carpet.

"Yes?!" All his senses were on full alert and without registering the transition, Tom was on his feet.

"Thought you must be in need of a wake up call," Dean's voice was unhurried. "Your fire-loving errant husband is waiting for you in the interview room and Frank is on the prowl."

Tom rubbed at his face and let his eyes settle on the clock on the wall. Shit. Nearly ten o'clock.

"You okay, mate? Any developments?"

"No. Just had a crap night, fell asleep on the sofa in the end. And no, no news." He was now taking the stairs two at a time. "I'll be there in half an hour. Give the murdering sod some tea. Won't harm him to hang around and think on what's he's done. Oh, and–" he struggled out of his boxers with one hand ready to hit the shower, "– spin Frank a tale will you? Cheers."

130   *Boxing Clever*

"Hope you're not going to make this a habit, Tom," was Frank's greeting as passed him in the corridor. "I know you're having a hard time but let's keep it together, hmm?"

"Thanks for keeping The Rodent sweet, Dean," he remarked dryly as he threw last night's evening paper onto his desk. "He's just bloody had a go."

Dean raised his spare hand in supplication, the other clasping his phone to his ear. Tom sat heavily and did likewise.

"George?" He didn't expect anything from the man and he wasn't, at this stage, going to say what he had learned so far from Alice.

"I was about to call you as we waited for the morning postal delivery, just in case. Could we meet up later this morning at Ellen's house? There may be something there...it is a bit of an outside chance but..."

As he listened, Tom's eyes scanned the phone message notes on his desk, partially covered by the newspaper. One of them indicated that the Dorset police had called at eight-thirty that morning to report that Mrs and Mrs Warner had arrived home the previous night.

He passed this information on and then arranged to meet George at Ellen's house at noon, hoping that the arsonist (alleged) would do the decent thing and confess in time. He picked up his phone, an evidence bag and a single latex glove and went down to the allocated interview room, trying not to inhale the stale smoky air too deeply when he entered. The relief of all parties present was palpable but short lived as the duty solicitor puffed out his chest ready to deliver an outraged tirade.

"I'm so dreadfully sorry to keep you waiting, I do understand the inconvenience to you – I'm sure you appreciate how these things are unavoidable." Confusion rippled across the young lawyer's face unused to such a conciliatory tone.

Score one to me, thought Tom. Before the besuited youngster could respond he added, "Can we get you more tea?"

It may have been the waiting that seduced the man to try and deny starting the fire that wiped out his entire family. In response to the portfolio of evidence against him – the failing business, the insurance policy, the letter from the unhappy wife to her sister – he tried to concoct a story but his voice faltered as Tom, silent, twisted his pen repeatedly between his fingers. Slowly, deliberately and then quicker and quicker. This first-timer didn't have the experience to keep his mouth shut and the solicitor had clearly decided that this one was too embedded in the treacle to intervene.

The tape whirred on and the statement of admission was satisfactorily signed by eleven-forty-five.

"If anyone is looking for me, I'm out talking to some contacts for about an hour." He threw the remark to the desk sergeant as he passed on his way out, trusting the message would get up to CID just as he was arriving back.

George was waiting outside the house, blazing like a peacock in a bright blue Mercedes. Tom drove past him along the crescent and turned round at the top end to allow time to look for anybody watching. Who the hell he was looking for was a mute point. They didn't speak as Tom opened Ellen's door and tapped in the alarm code. The silent house felt critical, as if he was a very poor substitute for the missing owner.

"Well, no one has broken in." George stated the obvious.

"Unless they know the code."

They saw the white lined paper on the floor at the same time. Tom raised his hand in warning and bent down, repeating the movement of the post in the same way as he had done a week ago. The paper was pinned to the carpet beneath a couple of bills and had been exposed by the movement of the mail as

132   *Boxing Clever*

the door had been opened. From his back pocket he pulled out the latex glove and plastic bag. Suitably be-gloved, he picked up the single sheet and flicked it out so that both he and George could read it. Again, it was handwritten.

"Very clever. Now you know she's not here. Try and find us!!! You have until the 25th."

"Next Thursday," Tom breathed, his skin cold. "We've got one week and one and a half days." He slid the paper into the bag and sealed it. "This makes no bloody sense! What the fuck do they want?"

George licked his lips before he spoke, and then his voice was quiet; almost reverent. "That's the first day of the Summit. Maximum publicity." He swallowed. "Worldwide coverage in fact."

Tom's brain ran a series of short movies, pictures hitting his consciousness, turning his stomach. These people must be mad.

"But why Ellen? She's not a senior executive! What are they trying to prove?" Tom was waving the bag as he spoke and then stabbed it in front of George's pale face. "What does your bloody dossier say we do now?" George opened his mouth to speak, but Tom shook his head and spoke first. "No, George, we can't do this by the company book. It's got much wider implications than we thought. I need to alert my boss to this." Closing the still-open front door, he rang Frank.

For once, he was connected straight away. He wasted no time in hitting home with the implications of the latest development.

"You don't need to spell it out for me." The response was curt. "This is in our hands now and I'll be overseeing the case myself. Bring this George Barnett in with you and get back here ASAP. I'll look into what we can provide in terms of surveillance on the house although I suspect they won't be

Maureen Devlin   133

using that as a contact point again. And you," he concluded, "are in breach of orders. I'll deal with that later."

They were in Frank's office in less than thirty minutes. The mood in the room was sombre. Tom only recognised one of the three grave faces that turned to greet their arrival: a rising star from the regional office. Judging by Frank's demeanour, the other two were very senior figures. The introductions were duly made and Tom was impressed at how quickly the Head of Police Liaison for the G8 committee had reacted in order to be here. The second stranger was from the National Crime Squad ("we just refer to it as NCS," he generously provided). Fortunately both had been in Manchester anyway.

George, thanks to his time as a serving officer in the Metropolitan force, was clearly to be viewed as one of the team and not solely as a company representative. Tom reckoned that the Vanpharma man was thrilled to be back in the fold and as the reminiscing chit-chat carried on in anticipation of the arrival of coffee, he began to feel his bile rising in frustration. Without realising what he was doing, he took out the pen from his pocket and began to twirl it between his fingers, faster and faster. It was a trick he had learned at Sandhurst, and always resorted to it when he was compelled to be idle. It took about three minutes before the motion caught Frank's eye and a couple of seconds before he coughed and called the meeting to order.

"You have the note, Tom? And the previous one?"

Tom passed across the sealed evidence bag holding the second note. George advised the group that he had asked his colleagues to fax through a copy of the first note but he was able to recall the content and proceeded to recite it to the group. The NCS officer demanded an exhaustive account not just of what Vanpharma did and why they might be targeted, but also Ellen's role in the company and her background. Clearly Frank

134   Boxing Clever

had not told them that Tom was intimately acquainted with her and this piece of information caused a great deal of discussion.

By the end of the meeting, two hours later, Tom was exhausted and defeated. They had been over and over what they knew so far and the possible intentions of the kidnappers. That this was the work of a highly organised group, they had no doubt. The consensus was that it was a new or possibly a splinter group on the basis that George's initial search of the known activist groups had drawn a blank. The Head of Police Liaison had been emphatic that Tom should not be closely involved. He may jeopardise the investigation as he was understandably primarily concerned with Ellen's safety. Tom could not contain his fury at the glib comment.

"Of course I'm bloody concerned about her! Even if I didn't know her personally, this is a woman who is being held against her will, terrified and as far as we know, in danger of being seriously harmed!" He couldn't bear the confines of his chair and leapt to his feet, still protesting. "I know you have to protect the company's interests," this directed at George, "and that you all are petrified of any impact on the Summit and the image of Manchester, but for God's sake!"

"Tom." Frank's voice sounded unnaturally quiet. "You have just demonstrated exactly why it is best if you are not actively working on this case. And you know it is policy. I'll keep you up to date on what we are doing and if there is any way you can help to secure Ellen's release. You do us all a disservice by assuming we do not have her safety at heart."

George met his eyes in sympathy, but Tom knew that Frank would not be persuaded and certainly not in front of his superiors. As a final, meagre act of defiance he said, "I will speak to Ellen's parents. In person. It's the least that I can do." He waited for a reaction but none came. "By the way," he added finally as he stood by the door, hand on the handle, "for what it's worth, I think she's still being held in Manchester. They're obviously able to watch the house and they will want to be close by for the action next week."

Still too livid to go back to his desk, Tom strode out of the back of the building and walked down the service road towards the main road that led to the motorway. He stared over in the direction of Ardwick, to the west, to where he believed Ellen was being held. Agitation prevented him from standing still for long so he began to pace away from the office to nowhere in particular. If they thought he would let them just get on with it, well, they were very much mistaken.

He was talking to himself as he thumped along the pavement; luckily no one else passed by or they would have figured he was crazy. Well, there's more than one way of being on the investigation team and he had two things in his favour. First, whether they liked it or not, he was involved and was going to work all the hours he could to find her, and he was going to pester George to keep him in the loop; and second, in Alice he had an unorthodox and private ally. And he was going to keep it that way.

Realising his phone was on his desk and not wanting to be away from things for too long, he went back inside the police building, calmer and focused. He knew that the best way of keeping Frank reassured that he wasn't going to get in the way was to throw himself into other cases. On the surface, at least.

He saw Dean open his mouth to say something in greeting or support as he walked back to his desk, but he silenced his friend with a brisk, "Not now, mate, eh? Have to get in touch with Ellen's parents. And is that my paper?"

Retrieving his copy of yesterday's evening paper from Dean's grip as he passed, he reached his desk, grabbed up his mobile, and dialled the number for Mr and Mrs Warner in

Dorset. He walked across to the corner of the room as he waited for the phone to be answered, so he wouldn't be overheard.

Ellen's mother was very surprised to hear from him. It seemed her daughter confided little in the way of her personal life and she had only a vague idea that 'someone' was around. It was a delicate conversation. Tom had already decided he was going to see them in person and he told her just the basic facts in order to gain her agreement to a meeting later that day. It was going to take three or four hours to reach the village that Ellen grew up in but it clearly could not wait any longer.

Mrs Warner, intelligent like her offspring, had demanded to know Tom's full name and rank and the number of the switchboard to check that he was who he said he was. When he had been connected back with her via his desk phone, her voice was less sure and showing the signs of anxiety.

"I'll be leaving in the next hour." He wanted desperately to tell her that everything would be all right. "Please tell no one other than your husband. If Ellen gets in touch before I reach you, this is my mobile number." He waited as she read it correctly back to him, and then said a gentle goodbye.

When he had finished, it was to see Dean in front of him holding out a cup of coffee. He took it gratefully.

"You probably gathered I'm going down to talk to Ellen's parents. I'm not allowed on the team and it looks like it's getting political as well as mega dangerous for the company. Never mind that Ellen is somewhere, terrified, whilst they go through all the possible bloody scenarios without a hint of a ransom demand. They reckon I'm likely to worry more about Ellen, might skew my judgement. Bastards." His low voice could not disguise his anger and frustration.

"I'll ask if I can be assigned, Tom. They're going to need someone other than Frank to do the grunt work. I'm already in the picture and he knows I'll keep it tight."

Tom did not manage a verbal reply, just nodded in appreciation. He began to gather his things together for his trip. Trying to make conversation and ease the moment, Dean ran through a quick update of the other cases in progress.

"What were you saying the other day about our boxing boy?" Tom asked as they walked together down to the car park. Dean gave a low whistle.

"Well, he can fight, that's for sure. Put his opponent in hospital on Sunday and although the guy will probably pull through, he may not fight again. There was a piece in the *Evening News*. Just reading it you could tell that the reporter was clearly impressed – subtext in the article was that Mr Raye is fuckin' awesome. Comparisons with Mike Tyson, which from what I've been finding out, may be too close for comfort. There is a rumour that he was going to be up for the rape of a girlfriend but the trail suddenly went quiet."

"When was this? How long before he came up here?"

"About six months from what my mate said."

"Well I'm glad he's punching seven bells out of some bloke who was trying to do the same to him, rather than picking on a woman."

"Amen to that."

"I'll be back in tomorrow. Contactable at all times. Let me know if you get a sniff of any developments?"

"No worries. I'm concentrating on the death of the prison reformer, but I'll make sure I get five minutes with Frank about working on the team."

Making sure his mobile phone was connected to the charger that was plugged in to his car cigarette lighter, Tom headed south. He would call in to see Alice on the way, to let her know where he was going but also to give her his phone number in case anything happened whilst he was away. The analytical left

138   *Boxing Clever*

hand side of his brain was having a hard time coming to terms with the ease with which he was grabbing at psychic short straws. In any other circumstance...but for Ellen...

Alice looked brighter and rested. He knew he didn't reflect the same picture as he stood on her sparkling white doorstep. He was brief in his explanation and played down his lack of official involvement in the investigation.

"I'm going down to see Ellen's parents. I'm not intending staying there; I'll be heading straight back." He wasn't fazed about the prospect of hours in the car, any weariness was irrelevant. "I need to give you my phone number – in case? Erm," a thought struck him. "You do have a phone, don't you?"

"Tom," she admonished him. "I may be elderly and in touch with other dimensions but I'm not stupid. Let me get a pen and some paper."

"Don't worry, I've got a card with all the details on." He passed it over sheepishly. Alice squinted at the tiny type on the small, white card.

"Can you write it again on the back, a bit larger?"

CHAPTER 16

The drive was therapeutic. Once through the conurbation of the north and the midlands, he moved easily along the M5 towards the south west. It was as if a guardian angel moved ahead of him parting the traffic. No jams, no hold-ups. The radio chattered around him but he hardy registered the content, he just wanted to get there, turn round and get back to Manchester. He was feeling more and more impotent the further he went. As if he was going out of range.

He pulled in to a motorway service station to ring George. He needed a pee, but that could wait.

"Any news?"

"Tom, you have to trust us to get the result on this. I don't intend to lose Ellen. We're doing all we can to get a fix on whoever has taken her."

"I take it from that there's been no further contact."

There was a pause. "No."

"I'll be at Ellen's parents in about an hour. They may want a name at the company. I'll be giving them your number."

George agreed and hung up with the promise that he would let him know the minute anything changed even though Frank wouldn't like it. Tom didn't entirely believe him.

The tiny street leading from the post office past the church looked as if it had been virtually unchanged for hundreds of years. The houses that stood along the tree-lined stretch were

140   *Boxing Clever*

known by their numbers only, as the road was the only one that ran through the Domesday Village of Charlton Marshall, deep in the county of Dorset. Ellen's parents lived in the last house of the row.

He lifted the heavy brass knocker and rapped sharply on the door. Almost immediately, as if she had been waiting for the sound, the door opened to reveal a tall, elegant and clearly worried woman. A low 'whoof' echoed in the background.

"Mrs Warner? Tom Ashton."

She stood back and motioned him inside before he finished speaking. "Please, do come in. My husband is upstairs. He needs to keep occupied, you see." She was gabbling, words tumbling unnecessarily over each other to be heard.

She signalled him to follow as she crossed the open living/dining area, cosy with deep red carpet, a couple of squishy sofas and an elderly Labrador that was still struggling to its feet. She opened the white latched door that led off one corner of the dining area to reveal a narrow staircase that led to the surprisingly large upper floor. A number of rooms led off the oddly-shaped landing, and he stood politely as Ellen's mother called out to her husband at the same time as opening the second door on the right.

Tom was impressed as he passed through into the room. It was much bigger than he expected and easily large enough to accommodate a drawing table, two computers, a couple of old easy chairs and a filing cabinet. A series of framed cartoons on the walls gave Tom a clue as to the grey-haired man's occupation. He had swivelled round to face them as they entered.

"Thank you for coming, Tom." He stood, hand outstretched. "We appreciate you driving down, we've been in a nightmare since you rang. I take it there is no more news?"

Still standing, but happy to do so after the drive, Tom explained the situation as fully as he could. The couple looked

Maureen Devlin   141

at him, both sets of eyes locked on his face all the time he was speaking, drinking in his expressions as he delivered the words.

"You must be tired. Please forgive my rudeness – can I get you something to drink? Eat?"

Tom thanked her, accepting gratefully. He felt knackered now that she'd mentioned it. Not quite knowing why, but it seemed the natural thing to do, he sat in one of the chairs in the corner of the studio rather than follow Ellen's mother downstairs. This room seemed like a den, a haven. He felt close to Ellen.

"This studio is Ellen's favourite room," her father cut into his thoughts. "It was the main attraction for Ann and I when we first looked over the house, bought when Ellen was barely a toddler." He paused and when he next spoke, his voice was less certain. "Is there anything you haven't told us?"

Tom had decided on the journey down that he would not tell the Warners about the possible press issue with Vanpharma and how this might impact on Ellen's case. He needed them to believe that the company had her best interests at heart at all times. Nor was he going to tell them he was not formally involved in the investigation.

"I think she is still in Manchester. Other than that, as I said–" Tom jumped up to relieve Ellen's mother of a tray of steaming mugs and a plate of sandwiches. Setting the tray down on the floor for want of a better place, he continued, "We're going to have to wait until the real demands come in. We're only guessing at what they want." He looked in amazement at the mound of bread, ham and cheese that he was expected to eat.

"There are some here for us," Ellen's mother said, wearily in her husband's direction. "I realised we hadn't eaten either. I do hope that Ellen..." Her words dropped into the room and hung there as each mind there connected with the wish.

142   *Boxing Clever*

They wanted him to stay. Maybe they felt that because he had seen her last, keeping him in the house somehow brought Ellen in too. He recognised the same desire in himself but the need to be back in the thick of things was stronger. Being *useful*. He declined the invitation gently, passing on his and George's numbers with the promise to keep in touch. It was nearly midnight when he set off again, the moon bright in the sky and precious few other travellers on the road. His phone stayed mute as it had since he'd left earlier that day. Too cynical to pray, he knew he was going to have to concentrate on the facts and clues of the case to be truly effective. To try and disregard that it was Ellen.

It was Wednesday and Franklin was having a rare day without training. The win in Scotland was so very conclusive, and Sam and Joe were confident he would be at his peak in time for the big one in October that they had agreed to his request. He'd said that he was going to take a lie-in and then get some new clothes. Silly old fools believed him. Joe even slipped him an extra hundred like it was a big deal. He stretched his arms behind his neck, luxuriating in the sensation of latent power. The girl beside him murmured at the disturbance, then rolled over and looked at him, eyes desiring him, wary.

He stroked her tiny cheek with his massive thumb and then, just as she closed her eyes to cherish the caress, he squeezed her face in his hand and dragged her head down to where his throbbing cock demanded to be sucked. He held her there until he was finished, then pushed her away and rolled himself upright and to the edge of the bed.

"Be gone when I get back." He threw the words over his shoulder without looking at her, and headed for the shower.

He couldn't reach Col. Annoyed, he pulled up Otis' number and barked his instructions for the meeting.

"And get hold of that fuckin' Irishman."

He threw down the phone onto the crumpled and vacant bed and stood, drying off his dripping body. The stupid cow had left her phone number on the bedside table. She'd left him feeling edgy. He was going to need a better hit today. Fondling his cock as he dried his balls, he imagined the scene of supplication, could almost smell the animal fear. His eyes locked onto the distance, trees swaying in the breeze through the half-opened bedroom curtains. He brought himself to a shuddering, standing climax, turning in time to come all over the note left by the girl. He grunted in satisfaction.

It was early on the fourth day since Ellen had gone and still no word. Tom didn't understand it and he reckoned that for all his confident protestations, George didn't either. They must want *something*. What? Money? Political points? Maybe they wanted to leave it until it was too late for Vanpharma to deliver? Maybe it was too late already. He looked at himself in the mirror, razor in mid-stroke. She was just a pawn, a nobody to them. How the fuck was he supposed to second guess what these zealots were doing and why they were doing it? He was tired and his face showed the effects of a late night drive and three hours' non-nourishing sleep. It was barely seven o'clock.

Distracted, he poured breakfast cereal into Jack's dish instead of the dried kittymix that was stored next to the cornflakes. It was only after he poured the milk in that he realised what he had done. So much for clear thinking. Somewhat perplexed but game for anything new, the cat lowered his head and began to lick. Tom didn't prepare anything for himself, couldn't even face a cup of coffee.

144   *Boxing Clever*

He was at his desk, reading through some reports as Dean came in, sporting a new leather jacket and glowing with athletic good health. For once, there was no glib remark about Tom's pasty appearance.

"Okay, mate?"

"Yep." No more would be said on the matter. When there was news, it would be shared.

Apparently Lisa Waters had called to speak to him late yesterday afternoon. Not even noticing that it was just after eight o'clock in the morning, he dialled the number shown on the memo. A quiet and sleep-laden voice eventually answered the call.

"'Lo?"

"Could I speak to Lisa please?"

"Mm," the female said, obviously still grappling with the conscious state. "Yes, that's me."

"Lisa, it's Tom Ashton. You called yesterday? Did you have something else to tell me?"

"Oh, I'm sorry. I didn't want you to think...no, it's just that Mel's dad rang me on Sunday and wanted to know if we'd heard anything? I just wondered..."

Tom held his head in his free hand and momentarily closed his eyes. "I'm afraid there's nothing more I can tell you at this stage, but I'm still working hard to find Col." Liar. "Did he ever mention to you anything about playing in a band?"

Lisa couldn't help. Clearly there hadn't been too much conversation with this Col character – he had been looking for business after all, not looking for a soul mate. Tom finished the call, leaving Lisa with the impression that Mel's death was one of, if not the main, case he was working on. Walking across to look at the white board, he could see the true picture. Mel's death had been summarised on a sheet of A4 stuck to the frame in order to make room for the latest incident. Abduction of one

Maureen Devlin   145

female; lead officer, DCI Frank Dawson. Even though he knew why Ellen's name was not given, a ball of acid hit the back of Tom's throat and he swallowed furiously. He turned briskly on his heels, strode back to his desk and pulled off a folder from his desk. Within a minute, he was standing outside Frank Dawson's office door, idly flicking through the contents of the file. Margery appeared just before eight-thirty and warned him that the boss had a hellish diary that morning and he had been at a briefing meeting until late the night before. Not my problem, Tom thought as he smiled beatifically. He wasn't going to upset the boat. Not today.

Frank, arriving late looking ragged, was immediately on his guard. He motioned Tom to follow him into his office.

"Nothing has changed. You're too close to this. Unless there is something I need to know this morning, it will have to wait."

"Just wanted to say that I understand the situation, sir. I know you and George Barnett will keep me up to date and of course, if there is any way I can be of assistance... I'm hoping you'll take Dean on the team if you need extra manpower?"

Frank's eyes were looking for the catch but Tom knew his expression was rational, intelligent and calm.

"While there's enough to keep myself busy on the other cases we have outstanding, I came to see if there is anything else you want me to take on, to free up your time for Ellen's case? That's the only thing, sir." He remembered to vaguely straighten his shoulders as he spoke, giving an impression of standing to attention in front of a senior officer.

Frank's expression mellowed. "I never expected anything from you other than absolute professionalism, Tom. I told the rest of the team that after you left the meeting yesterday."

So the bastards thought he would mess it up did they? Arseholes.

146   *Boxing Clever*

Frank continued, relaxed, as he hung up his jacket and sat beneath the ghastly print. "Get me some results on the murders, and focus on Mr Do-gooder. It's thrown the prison reformers into a flat spin and rumour has it the Home Secretary has taken an interest. You break your butt on that – we'll be doing the same for Ellen. I'll think about bringing Dean across."

With that, the balding head dipped down as Frank began to assess the papers on his desk.

Tom called the rest of the team together when he got back to the office. He demanded updates from each of his colleagues, lines of enquiry, blocks to the investigation in question, looking for ideas that could be shared and maybe shed light on a case. He felt his internal battery dropping to the warning level but pulled out all the stops to create atmosphere of high energy and 'can do'. He could feel his senses reaching out, like the tube of a vacuum cleaner, trying to steal some of the energy in the room for himself.

If he could get them buzzing and out and about, then no one would notice where he was or what he was doing. When they thought about it, their memory would be that Tom was integral to each and every case but that he'd focused on the hunt for the drug dealer and the Quay's body. Blind alleys. He wanted to spend all of his time looking for Ellen. First things first, though.

"Did we get anything out of Jordan?" Eyes swivelled to where Elliott stood, leaning against the wall. At the question, his mouth twisted downwards, and he shook his head.

"Not a word. He's due to be discharged at the end of this week. We'll have to keep an eye on him, see who he talks to. His mother's getting hysterical, wants protection. Social services are involved now so will be liaising with them. He got in way over his head this time by all accounts. He's terrified."

More questions followed, with various suggestions of what the boy had been involved in. Other cases were flagged and discussed, Tom standing at the front of the room like a conductor and his orchestra. He saw Frank, pausing on his way to some meeting or other, looking through the glass in the upper part of the door. He didn't interrupt.

Resisting to urge to clap his hands to wrap the session up, he simply remarked drily, "Why the fuck are you lot still sitting around looking at me?" He felt charged by their laughter, better than if they had reacted to him with sympathy or curiosity. He didn't look directly at any of them, but walked straight across to the movements board and jotted down that he would be out most of the morning. Dean was quickly at his shoulder.

"Want some company?"

"Need to get my head clear, mate. Maybe meet for a beer later?"

"Deal. Just to let you know, Fiona is wondering why Ellen's not replying to any text messages? Saw her last night. Not getting suspicious, but just mentioned she thought Ellen worked too hard. Won't be long before she gets worried. Any luck with Frank earlier?"

"He's going to think about getting you on the team. No promises. Catch you later."

He didn't remember driving through the mid-morning streets. One minute he was getting into his car, the next he was pulling up outside Alice's house. He needed to know what she had seen or felt or whatever she called it when they were near to where Ellen had been snatched. Some little detail is often all it took.

It was a cloudy but warm day. He got out of the car in shirtsleeves and strode confidently to the door and rapped, hard. It took awhile to register that there was no answer. It had never occurred to him that she might be out. He paced for a moment, no doubt looking increasingly suspicious before deciding he would try around the back of the house. It was possible she was

148   *Boxing Clever*

ill or in a trance and lying there... 'being' where Ellen was... He practically sprinted round the corner of the terrace and to the gate of her back yard. He could see the kitchen door open and he shouted across the wall.

"Alice? Alice! Are you all right? Alice!"

"For goodness sake, Tom!" came the answering reply from somewhere beneath him. "You'll have the whole neighbourhood round here."

He peered over the wall to see the neat grey head rising up from inside a black wheelie bin.

"I was washing the inside with disinfectant. Smells horrid otherwise. Just a minute." She got carefully to her feet and unlocked the bolt on the gate to let him in to her small back yard. Her comforting face was flushed with the exertion and Tom realised in a rush just how much he was relying on her. He had been desperate at not being able to talk to her.

"You look dreadful," she observed kindly. "I take it you just needed a chat? I was expecting you a little later but let's have some tea. I could do with a break from the cleaning."

He watched as she propped the dustbin at an angle to drain and dry and then followed her into the kitchen. There was a cloud of bleach and cleaning fluids hanging in the air that made his nostrils wrinkle in alarm. Alice pulled off her bright yellow rubber gloves and rinsed her hands.

"I was worried that you'd collapsed or something when I couldn't get an answer at the front door," Tom admitted as she filled the kettle. Alice paused as she went to turn off the tap, leaving a gently cascade of water flowing.

"My," she said softly. "It's been a long time since someone was worried about me like that. Thank you, Tom."

He wriggled a little, uncomfortable at the exchange. In truth, his main concern was for what she could tell him more than anything personal. But he could live with it.

Maureen Devlin   149

He waited until she had made the tea and laid a tray to her satisfaction. Frighteningly delicate cups and saucers, milk jug (taken from the fridge), sugar bowl and a plate of ginger biscuits. She asked him to carry the tray as she picked up the freshly filled teapot and walked through to the front room. He sensed that niceties would have to be observed and he didn't want to rush her. He took the fragile cup and saucer, his hand wobbling with the effort of not dropping it, and accepted a biscuit.

They sat for a minute, making idle conversation until Tom could feel his jaw begin to ache with holding back the words.

"I need your help."

"I know," she said. "I'm ready now." She put down her cup and saucer and folded her hands rather primly in her lap. She waited for his request.

"I need you to tell me everything that you saw... felt... however you describe it. The situation is even more delicate than I thought and any, any small detail you can give me may just help us find who is holding her." He leaned forwards, resting his forearms on his knees. "This is not an official line of enquiry so anything you may give me will only be checked out by me. I'll protect you as my source."

"Well, until you told me that, I had no concerns of my own safety at all," she replied briskly. "Let's hear no more about that and get on to helping find your girl."

She sat back against the headrest of the chair. Her face relaxed in contemplation and her recollection was unhurried.

"So you understand, Tom – I don't see a whole reel of images like in a film or vivid dream. A lot of what I experience is sensations, smells, sounds, feelings. Occasionally I get a really clear picture, such as when my husband died but that was, well, that was because he was part of me. Ellen, well, my only link really to you both to date has been through Jack. The

150   *Boxing Clever*

images weren't clear." She stopped speaking in order to re-arrange the cushion at her back. "I may not give you anything."

"I understand. Please, tell me everything you can remember from the first time you knew something was happening."

He sat still and tense as she described again the feelings of being held somewhere small and warm. Smell of petrol in what she believed was a car. Could this mean an old car? Or one well maintained with a freshly filled emergency can or a recently filled tank? She described the awareness of movement and the changing smells from petrol to spices, and a background of music. He had heard all this when she had come with the lost earring. He waited patiently for her to tell him about the snatch. Her tone suddenly changed and he leant forwards to catch every word, murmur and nuance.

"There were a lot of hands; definitely more than one person and an unpleasant, unwashed smell. My cheek felt as if it was being squashed or rubbed against a rough fabric. I felt a sharp pain, as if I had either hit my head against something or been hit. I had the sensation of being dragged down into darkness and my eyes hurt and I could feel..." Her voiced tailed off for a moment, her face devoid of all colour at the memory. "There was... someone was touching me...I didn't like it." Two tiny spots of red glared out from the pale cheeks.

Tom swallowed as he realised the implications of what she was trying to say. He hated having to press her but he needed to know what he was dealing with. He drove the question through the taut silence that lay between them.

"I have to ask, Alice." He needed to know but dreaded the answer. "Were they touching your... chest or..."

No appropriate word would come into his brain so instead he gestured down towards his crotch. Alice mirrored his movement over her own lower body, her free arm clenched tightly around her waist.

His chest burned with rage. Fucking bastards. He clutched at the sides of the armchair, squeezing as if he would fall off into a void if he lost his hold for a second.

"Bastards." The word came out as a spit. There was no reaction from the other side of the room. He let his brain work and spin. Reason eventually pushed aside the red curtains of fury and questions formed in his clearing mind. He began to think out loud.

"What on earth do these people want? How could taking Ellen in the first place and then assaulting or raping her support their cause at all? This doesn't make any sense. This is not a political group, I'm damn sure of it. Must be money they're after." He focused on Alice who alarmingly looked like the small, elderly woman that she was.

Suddenly, Tom felt uncomfortable being a man in this gentle woman's home. He could not think of anything to say and he sure as hell couldn't touch her in a gesture of comfort. In an action reminiscent of his mother, he rose slowly, collected up the tea things and took them through to the kitchen. He refilled the kettle and made a single cup of fresh tea that he took through to the quiet front room.

"Thank you, Alice," he said. "I can see that was horrible for you to go through once and I'm really sorry that I asked you to go through it again. But it I think you have given me something important to work on."

Her face was still pale but her eyes had lost some of their distance.

"I hope so," she said. "I truly do hope so."

"I'll keep in touch," he said and let himself out, dialling up George's number before he had unlocked the car. There was no answer. Damn him. He was out through to an automated answering service.

152   *Boxing Clever*

"George, it's Tom. Frank took my Vanpharma dossier and I need to know if there is any reason to suggest Ellen will be raped?" Tom was banking on George responding quickly. Let him think he was just the jealous boyfriend.

He sat in the car deciding on his next move. He had barely covered the distance back to the office when George returned his call. Seeing the name identified on the little green screen, Tom pulled over into a side street and pressed a button to answer.

"Tom? Are you free to talk?"

"Yes."

George was effusive in his need to reassure. "There is no evidence to support your concern, Tom. Political groups have a code. I think we can safely assume that Ellen is unharmed."

"Have they made any demand? Or got in touch at all? We don't even know that she's still alive!"

"We have to assume that she is," George was firm. "To be brutal, they have nothing to gain by harming her. She is their bargaining chip."

Tom stayed silent waiting for the company man to speak again.

"In case you haven't heard yet," the voice came as Tom knew it would. "We have brought over the head of security from the American arm of the company. More expertise there."

Tom was sure he could hear the sound of fractured ego.

He decided to take a detour, a very long detour, back to the office. He spent an hour in the designer outlet shopping centre near the Quays. Clutching his purchases, he went to sit in a trendy cafe and ordered a toasted cheese and mushroom panini with a large black coffee. He needed to think. To use his brain. He could hardly engineer a house-to-house search of all the houses in Ardwick.

He had just accepted the offer of a refill to his coffee when the call came through. He heard beeps and a clonk of a pay phone and then a muffled voice.

"Why no news? The lady will be upset no one knows she's missing. We want £20,000."

With that, the line went dead.

Throwing down more than enough change for his lunch, Tom shot from his chair and out of the building to an area free of people. He called Frank. He called George. He then called the phone company to try and trace the number, knowing that Frank would think of instigating the same but only after being in touch with his superiors. He then dialled his own home number and tapped in the codes for remote access to the answering machine. No messages.

The cheese, bread and mushrooms had gathered together in an angry porridge in his stomach. He took a slow deep breath. £20,000. That wasn't a ransom. That was a test.

CHAPTER 17

George agreed. Tom had warned him that he was going to be calling to see him at Vanpharma's offices. He might not be part of the core team, but the kidnappers had contacted him directly and he wasn't going to be fobbed off. He was in the bright lobby twenty minutes after he had taken the ransom call.

The Rodent predicted his move and rang just as Tom was pulling into the visitor's car park.

"Tom, I have to ask you to leave this matter with us. Don't make me pull rank – I know how concerned you are but we must work this situation very carefully. We can't afford for you to go off half-cocked."

"I need to be here, sir. I need to talk to George. I am involved now. The ransom demand came to me; they may contact me again and I have to know what the company is planning to do."

Rational. Reasonable and delivered without emotion.

"If it was entirely up to me..." His boss was wriggling on a spike. "Get back here. I'll update you but you are not, and I repeat it, not to take any unauthorised actions."

Working out which fictional roadworks would be the cause of his delay back to the office, Tom ran up the steps of Vanpharma. The chirpy receptionist rang through to the security offices and within minutes George appeared, the beginnings of dark circles beneath his eyes. They maintained the pretence of normality through the open plan areas, the

154

routine offer of coffee made and declined. Tom resented that it was very much business as usual. People laughing and chatting, computers humming and phones ringing. He wanted to yell, to shock these corporate lemmings with the knowledge that one of their own was possibly in danger of losing her life because of who she worked for. Shit – he'd lay down his life for his country but not for a place like this.

Maybe George felt the same because as they reached his office, he said quietly, "We have kept this situation very tight. Only those you are aware of know. Silence is a tool to protect her."

"I haven't got long," Tom said when the two men working in the room had been asked to leave for ten minutes and had duly done so. "Is Vanpharma going to pay it?"

"They don't like being played but feel as you do that this is a test and the big one is going to come at a time that will hurt. We may get a better feel for what they want when they let us know how to pay the money. It may be a situation designed to embarrass. There have been cases of demands for the Chief Executive to pay the money in person, that sort of thing."

"And? How far is the company prepared to go to ensure Ellen's safe release?" Even as he asked the question, Tom reckoned he already knew the answer. George was cagey.

"Well, it's not all down to the company any more. Your boss and his colleagues are making it clear we have to consider the bigger picture given the chosen date of the 25th. I do believe, however," he puffed his chest in a show of loyalty, "that the company will do the right thing."

Tom gritted his teeth in disgust. George had just confirmed what he feared. Vanpharma was manoeuvring to absolve itself from blame should anything go wrong. Frank was in for a roasting if he let them get away with it.

156   *Boxing Clever*

Tom was walking through the back door of the headquarters just as Margery called his mobile to check on his whereabouts. He took the stairs two at a time and was outside Frank's office door in an impressive two minutes, only slightly out of breath. He rubbed at his face, trying to imprint an expression of professional detachment.

"Will the company pay the twenty grand?" He went straight to the point. "My concern is that they'll resent having their chain pulled without seeing what they get – aside from their employee." He paced across the carpet and then stopped, clutching the back of the chair facing Frank with both hands. "You said you would give me an update. I'm listening."

"I said I would, but for God's sake sit down. This is my office and I'm not going to be peered down at."

Tom sat, folding his arms across his chest and waited to be impressed. He heard nothing to reassure him. For all that Frank tried to fully explain the political and commercial sensitivities of the situation and the pros and cons of paying the ransom, Tom saw that he was thinking out loud, trying out the arguments for size. He cut across the lecture.

"Are you going to recommend that they pay up?" His question was an accusation. "Sir," he added.

"I think we have to wait until we get instructions for the drop, but in principle, yes." He was clearly uncomfortable at having to admit to not being the decision-maker. He was no more in control of the situation than Tom was.

"Appreciate your candour, sir. I feel a whole lot better." He was out of the room before Frank had time to register the sarcasm.

Elliott was staring despondently at the sandwich machine as Tom strode along the corridor back to his desk. He gave Elliott a cursory nod in response to the half-smile that was offered, then walked past him before turning round and joining his still undecided colleague.

"What's the latest on Jordan Bell?"

"Sweet F.A. He won't speak to me and apparently went ballistic when the local beat officer called in at his house to see if he could get through to him. In no way does he want to be seen talking to us. Doesn't want anybody charged. Usual nonsense. His mother wants the council to re-house them but that's going to take awhile."

"Any feel?"

"Only that he must have gotten in way over his head. Could be drugs. Want me to organise a search?"

"Where exactly was he found again?"

"On a side road near the new cinema complex in Ardwick. Looked like he'd dragged himself around a corner from the trail of blood."

Tom didn't register the second observation due to the resonance of the first. For a glorious split second he thought maybe he had found a witness to Ellen being transferred from the car, but then remembered that Jordan had been stabbed on the Saturday. The day before she was taken. Then again, maybe he had seen some arrangements being made?

"Let's go and talk to young Jordan."

Elliott looked up from finally making his choice, cheese and pickle on brown bread. If he was surprised at the sudden and vehement decision there was no sign as he replied, "I'll get a warrant."

While Elliott arranged the necessary paperwork, Tom reviewed the status of all his cases and jotted down next actions for all of them. He intended to beat Frank over the head with his efficiency and demand that he was taken onto the team. He needed to be close to the official line, he knew that information

158   *Boxing Clever*

was both power and ammunition. He sat back, the structure of his chair protesting, and read back over his notes.

1. Quays case. Re-check missing persons files for whole of UK
2. Shoplifting network. Elliott to arrange another meeting with all store detectives concerned. Be seen to be proactive
3. Murder of prison reformer. Chase Dean for update
4. Stabbing of Jordan Bell. Question re movements/search house for evidence of drugs
5. Mel Chadwick. Ring parents to pre-empt potential complaint. Col? Check search for guitarist fitting description

He didn't make any notes for Ellen. He didn't need to; his brain hardly allowed room for anything else. He was relying on Alice and he didn't like it. As soon as he had had time to think after the ransom call, he realised they had his number because Ellen must have told them. If they were as clever as everyone seemed to think, they probably knew exactly who he was. Tonight he was going to drive around the streets near where Alice had taken him, call into local shops and pubs, generally make himself seen. He was banking on it speeding up the action.

Elliott put Tom in mind of an eager terrier, straining to get out and on with the job. Tom let him drive. He wasn't surprised when they pulled in front of a narrow, drab house with dingy net curtains pulled any old way across the windows. They were within half a mile of the new city apartment developments. In reality it was a world away. No wonder the kids got themselves caught up in crap, Tom thought. This place doesn't exactly heave with hope and inspiration.

Elliott called through the letterbox to warn the occupants as he knocked on the slightly peeling door. They waited patiently while it was opened slightly, still held on a security chain as a woman looked at them carefully. Even though she must have recognised Elliott, she still asked to see some identification before she finally opened the door.

"Well, you'd better have come with some good news for me and my boy. We're living in fear of our lives here, I have a right to protection." Her chin was pushed forward and she had her arms folded across her substantial chest.

"Not entirely good news, Mrs Bell," said Elliott. "This is Detective Inspector Tom Ashton. We've got a warrant to search the house. We feel maybe Jordan has got involved with something and we want to try and find out what, and with who."

"Search my home!" She was blazing. "My boy nearly dies and you people come around here accusing him..."

"We're not accusing him of anything." Tom spoke quietly, but firmly. "Jordan has not given us anything that will help us find who did this to him. He can still do that today – we don't need to do the search if he talks to us."

Tom could see that she scented a trap but also that she did not want two police officers poking through her home. Store that.

"I'll go and talk to him. He's still very weak, mind, and I don't want him upset, d'ya hear?" She bustled off into the back of the house and soon her strident voice reverberated in response to a low, spasmodic murmur.

"God," Elliott muttered. "I'd turn to drugs if I had to live here, and with her."

"You're not paid to pass judgement," Tom replied, although thinking much the same.

160   *Boxing Clever*

Minutes passed. Elliott was jiggling coins in his pocket and Tom was just about to thump him when the woman's head appeared round a doorframe at the end of the hallway.

"You can have a word," she said imperiously. "But if he gets mithered, I'll be complaining to your boss." Good effort, thought Tom.

He let Elliott lead the way into the stuffy room at the back of the house, almost tripping over a tatty skateboard in the semi-gloom. Whilst there was a large TV/DVD player in one corner and a stereo system in the other, they did not look brand new and certainly were not expensive brands.

Jordan looked like the young, terrified teenager he was, lying incongruously on a blue leather sofa and covered with an Aztec patterned duvet. His face was ghostly, and the gaze, though aiming to be defiant, was fatigued and wary. Tom took the lead.

"I'm not going to mess you around Jordan," he opened, knowing that the fatherly approach wouldn't work. "Here's how it is. We know you've got involved in something serious, maybe by accident and we want to make sure that we catch whoever it was, and to prevent you – or your mum," who was hovering in the doorway, "getting hurt again. Now," he sat on the edge of a matching leather chair which squeaked on receipt of his backside, "let's see what you can do to help me."

Elliott stood near the fireplace, listening.

Jordan's mouth moved as if he was chewing the words before he said anything. He swallowed a couple of times before he offered, "I don't know nothin'."

"For Christ's sake!" His mother shouted and drew breath to say more.

Tom put up his hand to silence the flow. "Could you possibly make us some tea?"

Maureen Devlin   161

"I'm staying put," she responded, planting her feet even more firmly. "Not having you rough him up to get what you want."

"Be careful with your accusations, Mrs Bell." Tom spoke looking all the time at her son. "That your skateboard outside?"

"Yeah," Jordan must have seen no harm in the question. "What's that to you?"

"Used to have one myself once." Tom ignored the slight cough that came from Elliott's direction. "Funny that they've come back in again. Do you ride with any mates? Or on your own?"

The boy relaxed a little as he considered the question. "Mostly just me, mates do other stuff. Bikes."

"Ever hang around Joe Murphy's gym?"

Jordan's eyes narrowed.

"Impressive isn't he? Franklin Raye? See he won his bout in Scotland at the weekend. Word is he's going to hit the big time in a fight later this year."

Jordan made no comment, but his slight shoulders shrugged.

Tom pressed on. "Quite a few young lads work out with Joe. Any interest?"

Unable to help herself, his mother chipped in, "He's a bit young yet, but Mr Murphy doesn't mind him hanging around to watch."

"Mam! He's talkin' to me – shut the fuck up!"

"That's no way to talk to your mother! After all the trouble you give me!"

"You can talk, you fat slag!"

Oh, great. Tom did not intend to allow more of this mutual appreciation society. "Hold it, hold it. This is not helping anyone. Now, it's been a difficult time for both of you, let's just cool it down eh?"

162   *Boxing Clever*

After a mug of strong sugared tea, just the way he hated it, Tom felt he was getting somewhere. Jordan was a solitary boy, preferring to send his time alone, out and about on his skateboard. He betrayed a grudging admiration for the Murphys and from the answers dragged out over an hour or so, he clearly spent quite a lot of time in the vicinity of the gym.

On the night he was stabbed, Jordan admitted he'd spent some time at the gym but because Franklin and Joe weren't there, he had gone to use his board on the old steps near the bookies around the corner from where he'd been found. He said he couldn't remember getting stabbed and was adamant he had seen nothing and done nothing to warrant it.

Tom could see he was getting tired and was unwilling to press further, this time. But he was going to be having a good look at the area around those steps later. They'd done a search after Jordan was found and asked around for witnesses but Tom was sure they had been asking the wrong questions, about drugs or theft. No one knew that Ellen was going to be snatched the next day.

"Did you get anything there, sir?" Elliott was clearly relieved to get out into the fresh air, and to flex his legs from all that standing. Tom thought he was about to break out into lunges on the pavement next to the car.

"I'd like a few words with Mr Murphy. Maybe he's seen the kid hanging around with someone in the past, certainly spends a lot of time there. And," he warmed to his theme, "if the big man is there I'll ask him who he passed on his party tickets to. Kill two birds with one stone."

Their arrival was greeted with the same reception as a mother-in-law who arrives two days before she is due. Martin Murphy was by the wall talking to his father when they pushed through the steel-enforced door. It only took a fraction of a second to scan the gym and see that Franklin was not there and about the same to see the looks of annoyance on the faces of the two Murphy men. There was no sign of the rope-handler.

"You people are beginning to get on my nerves," started Joe.

"Dad," his son intervened. "Let me handle this, okay?"

"This is still my place and I want to know what they are hoping to achieve by this fuckin' harassment. I've already told you people," this directed at Tom, "that we don't know who Franklin gave his tickets to and it's nothing to do with anyone else here."

"I wanted to talk to you about a young lad called Jordan Bell. Name mean anything to you?"

Joe thought for a minute, still glowering. Martin, on the other hand was making some gestures or other to someone behind Tom and seemingly uninterested in the exchange.

"Why?"

"He's met with an accident," Tom said. "Lucky to be alive. He told me he liked to come and watch the training here. Thought you might have an idea about who he hangs out with, any reason he may have got caught up in a situation that ended with a knife an inch from his heart." There was a hesitation, the length of a heartbeat, before Joe spoke.

"Thin-ish boy? Always on a skateboard? Never would give me his second name. Wanted to take it up, too young yet but I said he could come back in a year or so when his muscles could be trained. No problem with him watching. Better than being on the streets. No idea what he gets up to if he's not in here, or who with."

Martin had nothing to add.

"As a matter of interest, do you charge the youngsters to train here?"

164   *Boxing Clever*

"What do you think we are? Sodding community centre? Course I do, but it's not cripplin' and they soon find the money if they're keen enough."

Tom waited for more. Martin eventually broke the silence.

"When did it happen?"

Tom told them.

"Can't help you there officer," said Joe with some satisfaction. "I was in Scotland."

Tom looked at the younger Murphy. He was either really thinking or making one hell of a pretence at it.

"Don't remember seeing him. We'd had the guy from the *Evening News* in and one of your people in *again* even though we'd already told you lot about the tickets. So can't help you. Pass on our best - hope he gets better soon."

The comment was delivered with an obvious lack of concern. Cold bastard.

"Thanks for your time." Tom straightened as if to move away. "By the way, congratulations on your new boy. Read that he had a successful fight at the weekend."

Joe Murphy's face glowed like a young girl getting her first real compliment. Martin looked as impassive as ever, watching.

"How did you find him? Not local I understand?" Tom adopted the easy stance of a mate chatting in the pub. Unfortunately, it seemed to be one question too many.

"We Murphys have an eye. Now if you don't mind?" The craggy face closed over like a clam and the interview, such as it was, was terminated.

Outside on the broken tarmac, Tom felt the same tickle of interest that he had experienced last time he was here. Probably had sod all to do with anything but it was enough to make him determined to dig. Just a little bit more.

CHAPTER 18

Alice settled into her favourite armchair with a generous glass of vodka and orange. She didn't often drink alone during the week, but it had been an exhausting day. After Tom's visit and the distressing revisiting of Ellen's kidnap, she had tackled the rest of her cleaning with renewed vigour. Like she needed to scrub away what she had seen and felt. She'd have to buy more bleach on Friday.

She looked through the TV pages and in the end settled on a documentary that covered the collection in the Hermitage Museum in St Petersburg. She was particularly taken with the soft cloth overshoes that visitors had to put on before they could enter the massive wooden floored halls. The commentator said it was to protect the surfaces, but it seemed to Alice that it was also a very clever way of getting the floor polished. Maybe she could rig something up for the soles of her slippers for when she was in the kitchen.

She sipped. The cool medicinal liquid stroked her throat and blazed a trail right down to her stomach. She closed her eyes as her muscles relaxed. Some minutes past and she checked her mind and her senses. She felt nothing untoward, which puzzled her a little. She could make no firm judgement but maybe this meant that there was no change in Ellen's situation. She held that thought.

She felt Jack's small feet tentatively ease across her stomach as he claimed her lap. She hadn't heard him arrive and he

166   *Boxing Clever*

moved so gently that the pressure of the first foot didn't even make her jump. He settled quickly, warm and quiet. She kept her eyes closed, stroking his fur and waiting for the purr. It soon came and she smiled.

She didn't feel sleepy but she kept her eyes closed anyway. She was desperate to tune in, to feel something, to understand more. She so wanted to help, knowing that Tom's girlfriend could be in the most dreadful situation. In truth, she couldn't understand why she had not seen any more. Certainly the last experience came because she had been in the place Ellen was taken. Did she need to be close to a person or significant place to absorb some sort of vibration?

Goodness, she thought. I'm sounding like one of those sniffer dogs. But maybe, maybe I could help by going back to where Tom had driven me on Monday. Need to do *something*.

"I'll call him and suggest it, Jack," she announced to the snoozing animal. "I could even suggest going in to her house to see if that brings anything, what do you think?"

Jack raised his head, and all of a sudden was off her lap and out of the room and the house, judging by the tapping sound of the kitchen blind.

"Well, I'll take that as a yes even though you probably just didn't like getting disturbed." She got up and walked through to the kitchen where she had pinned Tom's card onto her cork shopping reminder board. Taking it back into the front room, she picked up the phone and dialled the number Tom had written on the back of the card.

Tom's voice resounded in her ear and she was just about to interrupt him when she realised it was a recorded message. Flummoxed, she put the receiver down and stood for a moment, gathering her thoughts. She dialled again. Prepared this time, she waited for the message to finish before she spoke, slowly and carefully, as if to a small child. "Hello, Tom, this is Alice

Roberts. Would you give me a call please when you have time. It is not urgent. I have an idea. My number is–" She recited the numbers very slowly, forgetting that Tom had already made a note of it. "Thank you."

Satisfied, she replaced the handset and sat back down. The programme on St Petersburg had finished and the adverts soon gave way to the news. Checking the TV pages again, Alice spotted that there was a film with Morgan Freeman coming on in ten minutes. Oh good. She liked him.

Considering that his day had started so early, and after little sleep the night before, Tom was buzzing. He had been back in the office for a few hours after the visit to the Murphys, had pestered Frank to the point of insubordination and had cross-questioned Dean about Franklin Raye for so long that Dean accused him of losing his grip.

Tom knew that Frank was being squeezed both ways. He was no longer in the position of authority on Ellen's case and he was having to include Tom on the thinking of the team because he was the only point of contact that the kidnappers had used. They were all playing a waiting game and the strain was beginning to tell on the older man. He clearly hated not being able to take charge. He kept repeating that they would do the right thing, that they needed to hear what the kidnappers wanted and they would be ready to move. Tom was not to worry; strategies and contingency plans had been formulated.

"Which are?" Tom had demanded. "Presumably some of them will need to involve me?"

"If and when," came the infuriating response. "I know you will do all that is needed if and when the time comes."

Dean was considerably more forthcoming as they sat in the canteen with tea and a slab each of plastic-wrapped fruitcake.

168   *Boxing Clever*

Tom ran his tongue over the glue that had formed over his teeth from the first bite of the heavy fruit mixture and gulped at his tea. Black, weak, no sugar.

"How's Fiona?" he asked.

"Yeah, good. Probably see her at the weekend. What do you want me to tell her... if..."

"Just say for now, if she asks that, apart from being mega busy, Ellen had her phone nicked from a hotel lobby and she's using one of her colleague's as and when. That should hold for a week or so."

Both men chewed, rinsed and swallowed. "Tell me a bit more about our Mr Raye. The Murphys got a bit twitchy when I asked about his background. I don't suppose it's got anything to do with anything. I was there about young Jordan – the big man wasn't around. Can you get in some time and ask him directly about the club tickets?"

"You know we haven't got anything there. Last thing we want is charges of harassment."

"We've got to be seen to be doing all we can on the drugs death. The girl's father has been on to me and to Lisa Waters. The last thing we need is a complaint." Tom's retort was quick. "Besides which, it's keeping me occupied."

He sat and listened as Dean outlined what he had found. He had spoken a number of times with the local sports journalist and also to one of his old mates in the London Metropolitan Police force. Franklin Raye's route into the boxing world had been predictable. Problematic at school but by no means stupid, his potential had been spotted early by an enthusiastic PE teacher who was still optimistic after many years in an inner-city school. Joe Murphy's cousin ran a similar outfit to Joe in South London nearby and he had taken the young Franklin on.

It seemed that the local police force and his frantic mother breathed a collective sigh of relief that the boy was being

Maureen Devlin 169

trained to use his fists in a focused way. Apart from the teacher, up until then the only person Franklin listened to was his grandmother. First got into trouble with local gangs when she died. It was all going swimmingly, Dean reported, until Franklin allegedly raped the sister of one of his friends.

"There was a massive hoo-ha, with the charges eventually being dropped by the girl. Franklin disappears and then pops up some months later in Manchester. Our boys reckoned she was either leaned on or paid off, and the brother went ballistic. Trail ends there, no case to answer."

"What happened to the brother?" Tom asked, a thought forming in his brain.

"Got into a lot of bother, had never been in trouble before. A caution for drunk and disorderly; mouthing off Franklin in a pub got him a beating, arm broken. Kept going into the station demanding that they arrest Franklin. Must have been persuaded otherwise – he's not been in trouble since."

"Since when exactly?"

"Not sure. Why? Want me to find out?"

"Yes. And see if he has been listed as missing."

Dean choked on an errant currant. "Tom! Talk about clutching at straws!" he protested. "The guy's about to hit the big time, no one in their right mind would risk it!"

"That body in the Quays has got to be somebody. Just make a few enquiries?"

Dean breathed out loudly, shaking his head. He changed the subject quickly, probably to prevent Tom from linking the boxer to every other crime on the patch.

Tom wasn't really listening. He was aware of Dean's voice and most of the words he issued but the talk of rape had reminded him of what Alice had suggested might have happened to Ellen. He could understand the brother's rage. Oh Jesus. Got to get out.

170   *Boxing Clever*

Dean caught up with him by the door, grabbed his arm and whispered earnestly in his ear, given that a couple of WPCs were on their way past. "Take some advice, mate, and get some rest. You're not with it and you're going to need to be."

You've no bloody idea. Tom nodded and rubbed his face. "I am knackered," he admitted. "I'll see you tomorrow. Cheers." With that he wrestled back his arm and left the building. It was early evening.

In his car, he rang Alice's number to find that it was engaged. He pulled out of the car park and headed towards home. He needed something to eat before he went off on his tour of the streets of Ardwick. He had barely gone half a mile when his phone beeped to let him know he had had a message. It was Alice. He listened to her careful speech and laughed for the first time in days. She sounded as if she was about to be shot. He called her number.

"Hello, Alice," he said, still smiling.

"Tom, I wondered...I presume there's been no news but maybe it would be worth me going back to where the trail went cold? Or maybe into Ellen's house to see if anything...I know this sounds ridiculous..." She was losing confidence. "But I thought it would be worth a go?"

"I'm planning on going over to Ardwick later anyway," he informed her. "Leave me to do that but if you still want to go to Ellen's?"

She did. He arranged to call for her in an hour. By the time he had got home, changed, fed and patted Jack, and defrosted, heated and eaten one of his green curries, it was time to leave again. He was outside Alice's house only a few minutes later than he had promised.

As they drove to Ellen's house, he recognised the familiar burning bile reach up into his throat. The curry was not sitting comfortably and without warning a massive belch rushed out of his mouth. He was mortified.

"Apologies," he murmured. "Ate in a bit of a rush."

"Spicy food is probably not good if you're a bit upside down," was the only comment. He didn't say anything more until they were outside Ellen's house for fear of opening his mouth and being surprised again.

"Okay?"

Alice merely nodded and was out of the car at a speed that belied her age. She was at the front door as he locked the car and retrieved Ellen's house keys from his pocket.

The beeping of the alarm sounded unnaturally loud in the quiet house as if to amplify her absence.

"Will it be all right with you if I wander around the house?"

Tom nodded but put up his hand to stop her from coming over the threshold. He checked the post. No note. He motioned for Alice to follow him through. He flicked on the answering machine to hear a message from Fiona and another girl called Anne. Alice had pushed past him and was standing in the door of the living room.

She mustn't try too hard. The gift would come if there was anything to see but her back was damp with the desire for knowledge. She looked around the pretty room. It was obvious that this was a woman's home. Alice touched a few of the books on the shelves and a framed photo of an older, handsome couple. No tingles. No warmth. She moved through into the kitchen and then upstairs to the bathroom, study and bedroom. She was aware of Tom maintaining a distance behind her.

It came in the bedroom. She had been expecting something, if it happened at all, would come in the study where Ellen kept all her work things. She had walked from the study, losing heart, when, as she crossed the threshold of the lovely lilac

172   *Boxing Clever*

room, she had a flash of Ellen and Tom together. Here, in this bed, happy. Pretty girl. Then she saw just Tom. In front of her, smiling even though she knew he was behind her. Her flesh began to itch, as if her clothes were suddenly made of cheap wool and she could smell stale clothes and dirty feet. Her hair felt matted and she knew the smell was coming from her. She touched the top of the duvet and was filled with the most unbearable longing. Her eyes filled and she sank onto the edge of the bed.

Tom had been getting anxious to leave the house as Alice walked into the bedroom, the last room. He suddenly felt stupid, counting on the paranormal. He didn't know what he had been expecting – a sudden wail and then a gentle swoon as the trance hit? He was about to tell her that they should go when she turned and sat on the bed and lifted her face. She was crying.

He ran forwards and sank to his knees, gently taking hold of the old, cold and trembling hands in his. She coughed a little, swallowed and then began to speak. Her voice grew stronger as she explained what she had felt.

"She's not in a clean place, that's for sure. She is missing her own things but I also think, Tom, that she is missing you." She paused for a moment. "I didn't have any head pains, or anywhere else for that matter. Let's hope that means she hasn't been harmed any further."

He waited. "Was there anything else?"

"This is odd. I saw you both, in here." She tapped the bed and Tom felt the sudden warmth of an erotic memory. "But then, I saw just you, right in front of me and smiling. You're obviously playing on her mind."

"She must think I'm going to get her out of there. God, I hope I can. Alice, we must go."

She didn't protest as he bundled her downstairs and into the car. He reset the alarm, locked the door and was soon driving back to Chorlton. He thanked Alice and watched as she opened her front door and went inside. Then he sped off to the Ardwick, hoping that some of Alice's sight had rubbed off on him. He sure as hell needed all the help he could get.

Franklin was not pleased. He sat glaring at Otis across the table in a noisy bar in the city centre. You could hardly hear yourself think in here, let alone eavesdrop on anyone else's conversation and that suited him just fine.

"Whaddya mean, ya can't find him? When did you see him last?"

While Col and Otis worked different areas of the city, they generally knew each other's whereabouts in case of trouble.

"Last Friday," Otis replied. "We met in the Atlantis Bar for an hour or so because I was running short of E and you weren't around. He arranged a drop for me, which was cool, and that was it. Mobile's not answering. Tried him as soon as you called earlier and few times since. Want me to go round to his place? Check it out?"

Franklin thought. He'd rather keep any knowledge about Col to himself for the time being. Control. He needed to keep control but he didn't like this situation one fuckin' bit.

"Nah," he said, eventually. "Leave it with me. I'll sort it." He had other people he could use. He had other eyes and ears he could call on. Stupid Irish bastard.

Tom drove until his eyes blurred and each street looked exactly like the next. He'd stopped at two tiny shops selling all and nothing from behind reinforced glass and now had two bottles of whisky clinking on the floor behind him. The first pub he had gone into was punishingly bright, and the half pint of lager

174   *Boxing Clever*

that he'd ordered had been delivered with a sneer by the sallow-faced bar man.

"Pushin' the boat out then," he muttered.

Tom shrugged. He could hardly claim poverty with his car nestling the kerb outside. He would be remembered just as well by saying nothing.

The second pub was more like it. Older, grubby and with a game of darts going on in the corner. A real local pub. He knew he was being observed and this time he decided to go mad.

"Pint," he grunted and pointed at one of the taps on the top of the bar. He took his time. The beer was cold and tasted fine but he was beginning to feel the effects of the last twenty-four hours. He bought a packet of crisps to try and soak up the alcohol, finally finishing the glass at nearly ten-thirty. He pushed himself away from the bar, having spoken to no one.

By the time he got home, he was ready to drop. He desperately hoped they would get in touch with him soon. Tomorrow was Thursday. One week left.

CHAPTER 19

He was back in the office before eight o'clock the next morning. There had been no word from the kidnappers and no word from George. He had called Ellen's parents on the way in to work, apologising for the early hour, to let them know there was no further news. He reckoned they'd already been up for some time.

He felt he was living in a parallel universe. He could see the reality in front of him and all around him but it was all out of kilter. No one would be able to guess what was happening in his life if they just caught a glimpse of him driving by. What else was going on in other people's lives behind the masks you had to wear to face the world? He would never take anything for granted again.

He stopped at a small pharmacy near the university and bought some antacid tablets, plus a bottle of the same thing in liquid form. The last time he'd bought this stuff was before his father's funeral when all the grief had centred in his guts. Just as the assistant was ringing up the total, he asked for some painkillers as well. His back was playing up again, and there was a low suggestion of a headache behind his eyes.

He took a swig from the bottle as soon as he got back into the car. Urgh. Aniseed.

Each minute seemed like an hour as he stole repeated glances towards his phone on the seat next to him. He kept checking it was switched on, checking that no sudden text

175

176   *Boxing Clever*

message had appeared while he had maybe gone momentarily deaf. By the time he got to his desk, he had convinced himself he was in the wrong place, that he should be out there, somewhere, trying to find her. He didn't even sit down but instead turned on his heel and strode along the corridor to Frank's office. He rapped on the door.

"Come."

Tom said nothing as he pushed his head around the door, instead merely locking his gaze with that of his superior officer. Frank didn't look well. He tightened his lips and shook his head. He sighed.

"We need instructions. They've got us primed ready to move but we don't know where. The NCS officer is back in London talking to experts here and in the States. We have plans in place. We need the call." There was barely concealed fury beneath the tired tones.

"Will the company pay?" Tom asked quietly, as he had the day before.

Frank averted his gaze and considered the papers on his desk. "We will recommend it."

Dean had been busy. His eyes were bright with excitement and curiosity when he passed on his news, along with a cup of decent coffee he'd bought for Tom on the way in. Even though he was sure the caffeine would do nothing to soothe help his burning guts, Tom sipped at the fragrant liquid gratefully.

"Good hunch, Tom," he reported. "The girl's brother hasn't been seen since just after Christmas. Local guys figured he must have got the message and decided to keep his head down after the arm breaking episode. Not reported as missing though."

"Any description?"

"Could fit our guy – but it's still vague. Above-average height, white, brown hair but guess he could have dyed it."

"Let's get hold of the hospital records for the broken arm. Maybe... hang on." Tom riffled through the pile of files on his desk. He found the one he wanted and flicked through the papers. "Thought I'd seen something. Our guy in the Quays had had his tonsils taken out. See if the hospital made a note. If not, try and get hold of GP records. And a photo. What's the guy's name?"

"Andy Harris."

Tom looked over at the white board at where the A4 sheet outlining the case of the Quays body showed signs of curling round the edges. He rocked back in his chair, then leaned forwards and scribbled the name on the file, in pencil. Dean was already on the phone.

George called just before eleven. A kindness, nothing more.

"Hello, Tom, I just wanted to see how you were doing."

"Appreciate it, George," Tom sat back and began to twirl his pen between his fingers. "Are you making any progress with your people on paying the ransom as soon as we hear?"

"Yes. Notwithstanding the political implications of the situation, we are of the mind that Ellen is our concern and twenty thousand is a small price to pay even if is the start of the game." Ah. This was the real reason behind the call.

And Vanpharma don't want to have any finger of blame pointed at them, Tom thought cynically, but he was relieved none the same.

"Cheers, George. That really is great news. And by the way," he added. "I went round to Ellen's house just to check all was as we left it. Nothing there." He hung up.

"Yo?" Dean called across the office just as Tom's phone began to ring again. He flicked the handset open and pressed the button to answer, at the same time nodding at Dean to indicate that he was listening.

The two pieces of information merged into one.

178   *Boxing Clever*

"Andy Harris had his tonsils out when..."

"You'd better listen carefully. I'm not repeating–"

Tom's brain began to hit overdrive. He jumped to his feet, waving frantically at Dean to shut him up. It was a young voice. Male. Tom had the impression of a script being read out carefully. A call box.

"–this. We want the money in cash. We want it at exactly five o'clock tonight. You, Mr Ashton, are to take it to Piccadilly railway station. In a brown envelope. You will walk to the end of Platform One and push it under the metal barrier leaving one corner showing. You will then get lost. You will come on your own and no one must be watching. Do you understand and agree." The speech ended with a statement, not a question.

"Is she unharmed?" Cold unseen fingers drummed on his back.

"Yes or no."

"Yes." Tom was definite and brief. Fuck procedure. The line went dead and he snapped his phone shut. And ran.

Seeing that Frank was on the phone, he merely waved his mobile and nodded. The message got through.

"Well?" Frank barked. Tom told him.

"Shit." Frank ran his hands over his head. "Don't like this. Busy place. Pulling you in. Get George Warner." As he issued the instruction, he pressed through to Margery on the internal phone and demanded that she get hold of the other three team members, pronto. "Arrange a conference call on a secure line, Margery. It will be quicker."

Tom sat down at the circular conference table, where, in central pride of place, was a conference speaker phone. He called Vanpharma and told George the developments.

"Can you hold on, George?" Tom could imagine him getting ready to shoot out of his office to the police HQ. "We're arranging a teleconference. I'll give you the number to call."

Maureen Devlin   179

Less than five minutes after he had burst into Frank's office, they were both sitting at the table, hearing the voices of George, and the three other police officers coming through the large black triangle on the desk. It was just before eleven-thirty. As time went on, Tom picked up from the questions asked and the general discussion that the NCS guy was impressed with the simplicity of the request and the choice of location for the drop. Almost a grudging respect. Bastard.

By twelve o'clock, Tom's stomach acid was gathering strength. Frustration with Frank, fury with the NCS officer and anger at the collective criticism of his response to the kidnappers' call.

"What the hell was I supposed to say to them?!" he eventually shouted at the phone. "Who knows what might have happened to her if I'd refused to commit?"

"All right, Tom, don't lose it. But we must make sure that this is a negotiation situation, not a straight ransom payment. We are going to make sure we get something in return for this cash." This came from the Head of Games Liaison. "My suggestion is that we pay ten thousand pounds, with a promise to drop the second ten grand at a place of their choosing when and only when we have evidence that Ellen is alive and unharmed. And Tom should have some sort of back-up."

"For heaven's sake," Tom said. "We're not complying with their demand as it is. We can't have it all our own way. I'll be perfectly safe and they're bound to get in touch again, surely? For the rest?"

The discussion lasted for quite some time before it was agreed that Tom go alone as the man had demanded, as there were security cameras in the station that could be used to observe the scene. Ten thousand, in cash, would be delivered by George to the Police HQ no later than four-thirty with a typed note on plain paper. The final wording of the note had taken

180   *Boxing Clever*

awhile but now, just after one o'clock, agreement had been reached. Frank ended the conference call with obvious relief.

He eyed Tom cautiously. "You are one hundred percent behind this? Play it as we agreed and no trying to hang around or follow anyone?"

"Give me some credit." Tom was pissed off. "Sir." He was already planning how he wouldn't be there alone.

A quiet knock sounded on the door. It opened slightly and Margery popped her head around the varnished wood to remind Frank that he had a meeting at the Town Hall at one-thirty. Tom was glad of the opportunity to leave.

"I'll be back before you go," was Frank's parting comment. "And keep this on a need-to-know basis."

I will never, ever want that job, Tom decided as he walked out of Frank's office and in the opposite direction of his own desk. He needed some fresh air and to think.

Well away from eavesdroppers, standing near the brick and metal fence marking the perimeter of the car park, he rang Alice.

Less than fifteen minutes later, he was entering the CID offices, clutching a sandwich and a cup of coffee. The noise levels were considerably higher than when he'd left and he saw that someone had written 'Andy Harris?' on the paper sheet describing the Quays case. Dean rose to his feet when he saw Tom and waved a slip of paper at him.

"You were right," he announced gleefully. "Andy Harris had his tonsils removed when he was a teenager. He would be about twenty-six now, which doesn't chime with what we know about our guy. I want to get on to the local CID and get them to have a word with the family. Find out if they have heard from him before we take it further."

Maureen Devlin   181

"Good. Give them the details as we have them. Arrange for a DNA sample to be taken from the body, though what we'll match it against I'm not sure. The father if there is one, or any of Andy's stuff that is still around after all this time."

Alice had almost finished dusting her porcelain figures when Tom called. She checked the clock and was reassured she would have time to get them all done before she needed to leave for the station. She was neither excited nor afraid at his request. If anything, she was reassured that he still thought she could help.

Her routine carried on as normal. She had already taken out all the figurines from her glass-fronted dresser in the back room and put them carefully on the drop-leaf table. She polished each of the empty shelves whilst enjoying the conversation supplied by Radio Four. By the time the figurines were wiped and replaced, it was time for her lunch. The ornaments on the mantelpiece and window ledge would be done in the afternoon.

She prepared a ham and tomato sandwich, and shook out a packet of salt and vinegar crisps onto the plate with it. One of the blessings of still having most of her own teeth. As if on a piece of elastic, Jack appeared just as she was ripping open the packet of ham.

"You must have the best nose and ears in the world," she said to him affectionately as she pulled off a small bit of the fat surrounding the meat and offered it to the cat. She then brought him up to date with the situation as she flicked the switch and waited for the kettle to boil.

When all her work was done, she went upstairs and got ready for her appointment. Face washed and hair combed, she chose a brown and pink floral dress that she would wear with some flat brown shoes and her beige mac. Her large beige shopping bag would complete the inconspicuous outfit nicely. She was still a little early but decided to leave for her bus

182   *Boxing Clever*

anyway and use the spare time to have a look at the new gardens near the station.

It was nearly four o'clock. Tom chewed on an antacid tablet as he reviewed the case of Andy Harris. If the body did turn out to be him, then Franklin Raye had to be the first port of call. Bit too much of a coincidence that a man should turn up in a Manchester canal a short time after a guy he had a serious problem with had also arrived in the city. Franklin Raye, let's be honest, would be able to beat someone to death without breaking sweat and there was certainly a motive there if he was getting hassled. On the other hand, Tom thought as he swallowed the chalky remnants, would he want to risk his boxing career and...he leaned forwards and shouted across to Dean.

"Any evidence that he got into serious fights after he turned to boxing?"

"Nope. Used to use his fists quite a bit when he was at school. Boxing club seems to have focused that aggression. Certainly that's the approach Joe Murphy takes with his boys and I reckon his cousin would have been the same. No guarantees though."

"Right. When we get back the info from the family we go and pay Mr Franklin Raye another call. Get your snouts to keep an eye out over at the gym, okay?"

He carried on looking over files and trying not to look at his watch. His phone rang at twenty past four with the message that a Mr George Barnett was waiting for him in reception. He felt the calm anticipation of action descend. Now it starts.

George looked wistful as he waited on one of the new blue benches in the reception waiting area. Tom had requested for one of the interview rooms be available for him. Once inside and before George could inhale the air and get nostalgic for his past career, Tom put out his hand. George passed over an A4 sized brown envelope that looked surprisingly flat.

"Ten thousand? And the note, as we agreed?"

"Of course." George confirmed. "As they didn't stipulate denomination we got fifties – I figured the thinner the package the better. We've written that we expect you to receive a call from Ellen tonight to show that she is unharmed. We will deliver the second ten thousand to wherever they want. It's ready. We've also asked in the note for them to tell us what they really want and who they are working for."

"Jesus, George." Tom checked his watch. "Do you think this will work?"

"Yes. You're going alone. They will see we mean business."

He decided against taking his own car given the problems with parking near the station. Instead, he asked George to drive him. Frank was in the reception area as they came through and he walked with them to the car. For once, he said nothing, merely slapped Tom on the shoulder in a welcome gesture of moral support.

Piccadilly was a mess. Cheerful banners around the place announced the extent of further investment in the modernisation of the station and the fact that the work was on time. Not in time for the Summit though. Dust was everywhere. George dropped him in an area at the bottom of the station and after riding a couple of escalators, he was met with a wall of corrugated steel embracing the concourse. Scrappy notices hinted at which way the platforms lay and Tom had to squeeze himself through a tide of weary workers all going in the opposite direction to get himself in front of Platform One.

Tom was filled with increasing unease. This is crazy, he thought. How the hell is this going to come off? The plan felt worse than thin; it was practically invisible. He was being

184   *Boxing Clever*

constantly jostled by people eager to get home and the envelope now felt as fat as a brick.

He slowed to a snail's pace and ran his eyes carefully over the solid barrier that protected the public from the work being undertaken on the other side. Sure enough there was a gap under the barrier, just near where it bent round towards the platform. His sight of the drop point was momentarily blocked by a large woman in a black linen trouser suit as she began her manoeuvre past him, tutting. He swerved slightly to avoid her and glanced at his watch. Four-fifty-six. Time for action.

He strode purposefully past the point and onto the platform. Then, as if he had just forgotten to buy an evening paper, he stopped dead and spun on his heels to face back the way that he had come.

"Sorry, sorry," he exclaimed to the startled couple behind him. "Do excuse me."

He was within a metre of the spot when he felt a push to his back and the weight of somebody leaning heavily against him.

"Oh, oh..." The voice, so familiar, tailed off weakly.

He turned slightly to one side and caught Alice as she fell into an Oscar-winning swoon, carefully placing her on the ground in a half-seated position because of the crush and so that his knees became pressed against the metal barrier. He flapped his free hand across her face and raised his head hoping to catch the eye of a passerby whom he could persuade to run for help. Alice, he noticed, clutched her bag to her as if her life depended on it. She did manage to look pale, he thought. Very impressive.

"Can someone get some help?" he called to no one in particular. "And some water?" He put the envelope on the floor next to his right knee and then with both hands adjusted Alice's position to that she was more upright and blocking the right side of his body.

Alice gave a groan and knowing that any eyes turned their way would be drawn down to her face, Tom slid the envelope – thank God it fitted – under the barrier leaving a corner sticking out. Safe from passing feet but evident to someone looking for it.

A pretty young woman with glorious blue eyes crouched down in front of them and held out her bottle of mineral water.

"Take a sip of this," she said gently. Alice fluttered her eyes and did as she was instructed.

"Thank you, my dear," she whispered then seemed to gather sense of her situation. "Oh, I'm so sorry!" She tried to get up, embarrassment evident on her face. "I don't know what happened..."

Halleluiah, thought Tom as he saw the uniform of a station employee pushing through the small knot of onlookers protecting Alice from the passing feet. We need to get the hell out of the way. He gave Alice a nudge in the rib.

"I'm feeling much better," she said, in a strong voice. "Please, will you help me get up and find somewhere quiet to sit? And maybe a cup of tea?"

The station employee went into overdrive and practically hoisted Alice into a fireman's lift before proclaiming to the crowd, "Excuse me please! Please make way, thank you!" Tom thought he sounded rather thrilled by the whole thing.

He got to his feet, dusted off his trousers and checked his watch. Five seconds before five o'clock. He kept his eyes to the ground and sped towards the exit. He could just hear Alice's voice across the general rumble of conversation and machinery. "Oh, oh - I'll just have to stop here for a moment young man. Could you maybe find me a chair?"

As agreed, they met on the tram. Alice told him that she had been placed with great delicacy on the five-thirty departure after convincing her helper that she was well enough to go

186   *Boxing Clever*

home. The helper had even taken her change and put it in the ticket machine for her. Tom had waited at the tram stop in Market Street until he saw her bright face peering out from the nearside window and they were now sitting squashed together, rocking slightly from side to side as the tram made its way south, giving a cheerful 'toot' as it passed the circular Central Library. They got off at the next stop and walked slowly back towards the main road where Tom knew they could pick up a taxi outside a nearby large hotel.

"You okay?" he ventured.

"Never better," she replied. "When can we talk?"

"As soon as we get to HQ," he replied. He called through to reception and asked for the use of an interview room in ten minutes. He wanted to hear what Alice had to say as quickly as possible and in a safe place.

He paid for the taxi as it arrived outside the main front entrance and explained to her that he would go in at the back and meet her in a few minutes when he had been contacted by the check-in officer. On the way through the building, he called up to Rich and asked him to get hold of any CCTV tapes from Piccadilly Railway Station, near Platform One, for that afternoon and to pass on to Frank that he would be back in about fifteen minutes.

A few minutes later, he was sitting with Alice in Interview Room Two. She had declined the offer of tea.

"Anything?"

"I think so," she began. "After you left, I pretended I felt a little woozy and stopped by the barrier on the other side of the concourse so I could see where you had asked me to faint, and the corner of the envelope. The nice young man went off to get me a chair and by then I might as well have been the invisible woman. I kept my eyes fractionally closed until some thug tried to snatch my bag." She pursed her mouth in disapproval. "Must have thought I was a soft touch. Anyway," she continued, "I shouted something to scare him off and that must have created a useful diversion because I could just see out of the corner of my eye, a group of young boys, seemingly jostling each other and one looked as though he had dropped something. He bent down but because he was surrounded by the others I couldn't see if he had actually picked the envelope up. It certainly wasn't there when he stood up and he was messing around with his jacket."

Tom interrupted her account in order to get a full description of the clothes he was wearing and any other details that she could give to him about height, age, race.

"I'd say he was half-caste," she declared. Tom winced but he didn't correct her, mentally logging 'mixed-race', young, late teens maybe, slim.

"They all went passed me but about five minutes later, the boy who'd picked up the envelope came back up on his own. I got sense of an almost overpowering smell of spices, but sweeter than curry. I can't quite explain it but it was really fragrant."

"It could be Thai food, "Tom said. "Ellen's favourite – maybe you could smell it because of that link. Maybe..." He thought for a second. "This boy, he couldn't have been part Thai or Malaysian could he?"

Alice opened her mouth to speak and the closed it again. Her face sagged. "I can't pretend, Tom, I don't know. He wasn't very dark, though." She paused and then asked with excitement, "You didn't see a Thai restaurant or smell that type of food when you drove around last night?"

"Hardly," Tom's reply was scathing. His route hadn't exactly taken him to the heights of culinary sophistication. He stood and began to pace around the room, pen dancing between his fingers.

188   *Boxing Clever*

"We may be being too literal here, Alice," he stated. "I wonder if we really should be looking to the Far East?"

Unwilling to say any more, he thanked her again and promised to keep in touch. She was horrified at the thought of being driven home in a police car so he left her waiting in the reception area for the taxi summoned for her by the reception clerk.

CHAPTER 20

"Your mind's not on it, boy!" Sam Jones stood with his hands on his hips. "What the hell did you do with your day off? Friggin' disagreed with yer, whatever it was. Now," he ordered, "get the hell in front of that punchbag and get some work in. Your timing's crap."

"I'm knackered!" Franklin roared back. He had been in the gym since late morning and as the day moved into evening he was losing his enthusiasm. Besides which, he had other things on his mind.

"Now you listen to me." Sam's voice dropped to a whisper and he edged close to Franklin's right ear. "You may be a friggin' star in the makin' and you had a good result on Sunday. That's one fight, boy. One fight. And we've told you a hundred times that you've got to have your head as well as your fists right. Don't let me get anxious about your attitude. Now!" he roared at Franklin's semi-bowed head. "Fifteen minutes on the bag and then fuck off. And make sure you're back here at seven in the morning. You've already missed one run this week."

Less than an hour later, Franklin was in his car in a multi-storey car park, the music turned down low as he tried one number after another. The answer was always the same. Col hadn't been seen. All his usual haunts had been visited, and there had been no sign of him at the flat he rented in Fallowfield. He rang Otis. His number was engaged. Franklin could feel the pulse throbbing in his forehead.

190   *Boxing Clever*

"Get the hell off the phone, motherfucker!" he shouted, slamming the palm of his right hand against the steering wheel. "Don't play games with me!" He sat, drumming the massive fingers of his right hand against his thigh, rocking backwards and forwards as much as the cramped interior would allow. He worked to regain control of his breathing, like he'd been taught. His phone rang. It was Otis.

"Saw you'd tried to call," he began quickly.

"Meet me in fifteen. Usual place." He made one final call before setting off to meet Otis. Just to say he was going to sort it.

The bar was quiet for the time of evening and Franklin was on his guard. He chose a table in the corner and sat with his back to the wall so that he could see all angles. Otis was dead on time, his sallow skin looking a bit paler than usual. He bought a drink and pulled out the chair opposite Franklin.

"I don' like this. You brought this guy to me and now he's fucked off. What you goin' to tell me?"

Otis took a breath. "There's something." He played with the beer mat in front of him. He took a sip of his drink. "I've been asking around, seems a friend of the girl that died met someone in the Underground Club, police getting pushy trying to trace all the tickets issued. Col was there. Maybe he was at that party where the girl died and he's layin' low."

"Why now? She snuffed it days ago." Franklin wasn't convinced.

"But say, I don't know..." Otis was staring at the table with the intent of a lover. "What if he had been trying to steal my patch and got cold feet when she croaked and did a runner with your stuff? He'd be terrified to come back."

"You told me you'd seen him on Friday. How come he was still around then?"

"Maybe because you weren't," Otis ventured.

Maureen Devlin   191

Franklin glared at him, his brain mulling over the idea, unwilling to accept that he may have been shafted. He leaned forwards and moved Otis' half full glass away from his reach. Otis took the hint.

Once alone, he flicked open his phone and searched the memory for a number. He would make sure that Otis wouldn't try the same thing. A little warning. The negotiation was swift but before he finished he mentioned, casually, that there was a flat in Fallowfield he needed someone to look over. He made sure the listener knew that he expected a neat job and a call back before the end of the night.

Frank was clearly waiting for him. He nodded intermittently as Tom regaled the non-Alice version of the trip to the station. His self-satisfaction evaporated as soon as he had finished speaking. His mission may have been accomplished but the consequences for Ellen could be disastrous.

"I'm getting really unhappy about this, sir," he said. "We might well have seriously pissed them off."

Frank said nothing in response because the black phone on the table began to beep. He jumped out of his chair and across to the table and pressed a button, releasing George's voice into the room.

"Did the drop go to plan?" he asked.

"Yes," Tom replied. "But it still stinks."

"They'll be in touch soon, we're sure of it."

And I'm sure you people are hiding something, Tom thought and before he knew it had said, "Does Vanpharma have any interests in the Far East?"

Frank looked at him as if he had just pressed the fast forward on a video and had made him completely lose the plot. Even without the benefit of a visual link, he reckoned George would have exactly the same expression.

192   *Boxing Clever*

"Where the hell did that come from?" Frank did not sound pleased. "Do you have information you haven't shared with us?"

He thought quickly. Shit. Inspiration from Ellen's living room. "I read something recently in the *Economist* about pharmaceutical companies exploiting natural remedies and resources? Nothing directly about your company and more in South America... but... now the Far East..." He trailed off as he thought he had better quit while he was ahead. Where did he dig that up from? She must have mentioned it to him. Awesome retention, Ashton.

"We have interests in many parts of the world, Tom." George had become cooler and defensive. "All the big companies are global players. Anyway," he added with a triumphant note, "there's only Japan represented at the Summit so it'd be an unlikely arena for that debate."

Frank was still looking at Tom with incredulity, as if he had grown a second head. "You will be contactable at all times, George?" he said to the phone.

"Of course," came the reply, followed by the sound of disconnection.

"Leave me to update the others, Tom. I have to attend a meeting tonight but I will keep my phone on at all times. And for God's sake, keep your phone line clear."

What a stupid bloody comment.

Tom rubbed his eyes and looked at his watch for the umpteenth time. Seven-thirty and still no word. He took the bottle of thick aniseed gloop out of his desk drawer and swallowed a generous gulp. He didn't dare dwell on how Ellen was feeling.

By eight-thirty, he could stand it no longer; the need to be doing something physical was overpowering. For the second time in recent days, he knew solace would not be found in the kitchen. He felt like a spring at the limits of its tension. He rang through to the gym but was told that there were no squash courts available that night but with a determination that would have amazed Dean, he got into his car and drove there anyway. One tip he had picked up from Dean was to keep a sports bag in the boot; it was only when he got to the gym that he discovered he had no clean socks or t-shirt.

He waited until the changing room was relatively clear before he gave the kit in his bag a tentative sniff. Dear God. Fortunately he had a spray deodorant that he applied liberally to his socks and t-shirt. He dressed quickly and went through to the main gym area, filled with earnest individuals on a variety of machines. He watched for a moment as a pretty but very plump girl lying directly in his line of sight used a cushioned device to help her do a series of sit-ups. Her face got pinker with each jerk and Tom felt himself getting warm just by watching.

He noticed that a cross-trainer was free over in the far corner. He moved quickly to claim it, carefully placing his phone in the holder designed for a bottle of mineral water. He began to pump his legs, hoping that his rising whiff was sufficiently far away from everyone else. He got into quite a rhythm and before long sweat was dripping from the edge of his nose and down from his chin. Fifteen minutes, then twenty minutes passed. His head began to feel clearer and lighter, whether through a need for food or just as a reaction from the exercise but he felt his mood begin to lift. They would hear soon. By this time next week it would all be over. He was sure of it.

He didn't bother with a shower. He couldn't risk being out of earshot of his phone even for a minute, so no doubt to the disgust of those he passed on the way out, he drove home still in his sports stuff. He opened the door, dropped the kit bag in the hallway and feverishly checked his post before he had even closed the door. Two messages on the answering machine. Both from people he did not want to hear from. He deleted them. He

194   *Boxing Clever*

ripped off his clothes and threw them in the direction of the kitchen to be put into the washing machine before running upstairs for the quickest shower on record.

Jack was waiting outside the bathroom door as he came out.

"Hello, buddy! You've been a bit of a tart haven't you? Always slipping off to see Alice. Rascal." He was stroking Jack's head all the time he was speaking and the cat showed his pleasure at the touch by arching his back and rubbing against Tom's still damp calf, leaving a slight but unmistakable trail of black hairs.

"Come on you. Food." Tom trotted down the stairs, Jack in close pursuit.

The washing machine sloshed gently as Tom vigorously beat the eggs in the pan. Scrambled eggs were the only thing he thought he could face when he had looked through the contents of his fridge and his cupboards. Jack clearly wasn't in a fussy mood and accepted the out of date ham with gusto.

Tom added a knob of butter, rock salt and fresh black pepper to the mix and slotted two slices of granary bread into the toaster. No booze tonight. He needed his wits about him.

By ten o'clock he couldn't bear it. Leaving his mobile phone free and recharging, he picked up his cordless phone.

"George?"

"Go, Tom," came the swift reply.

"No, no," he said apologetically. "No news – I just couldn't sit here. What do your colleagues say? Have we blown it?"

"We don't believe so," George reassured him. "There was a very similar start to an incident in Venezuela last year. Ended well. The view is that each party needs to know the other is serious. It's like playing chess. Tactical."

It was all he needed to hear. That people with the experience were looking at all the angles.

He went up to bed just before midnight, unwilling to sleep but recognising that he needed to be as alert as he could be and a snooze on the sofa was not going to be enough. He made sure his phone ring tone was switched to its highest volume. As he lay on his side in the darkness, watching the green glow of the phone display and thinking of Ellen he felt a slight movement as Jack jumped up onto the bottom of the bed. He also felt the stirring of something more worrying. It wasn't all a natural reaction to someone you cared for being kidnapped and in danger. He was beginning to realise he was falling in love with her.

"Whu?!" the sound escaped from his mouth as his brain reacted to the jarring sound in his ear. He shot out his hand and grabbed the phone, blinking frantically so that he could focus on the keypad and press a button to answer the call.

"Yes!" His heart was thudding more than when he had been at the gym and the sweat began to prickle on his back.

"Tom?" Her familiar voice was less than a whisper. "They are angry. Please get the rest of the money. They both want it in the same place at eight-thirty tomorrow morning."

He spoke quickly and earnestly. "Are you okay? We'll get you out of there. Can you help me find you?" But the line was dead.

He switched on the bedside lamp and his head resounded with the force of the light hitting his eyes. He looked at the clock; it showed four-twenty-six.

Rubbing at his temple, he called Frank. It took a few minutes for the phone to be picked up, by which time Tom was out of bed and pacing across his bedroom floor. They arranged to meet at seven o'clock. He then rang George. He agreed to meet Tom at HQ at seven-thirty with the money.

He sat back down on the bed, relief washing over him that she was still alive but every nerve ending screaming that they

196   *Boxing Clever*

may have got it all wrong. Jack's head nudged at his hand and he began to stroke him, and with each movement he could feel his pulse slow and his breathing ease.

He ran over the call again. Both. That's what she'd said. Both of them wanted the money... there were only two of them? Or only two of them that she had seen. Was she trying to tell him that there were only two of them holding her – but where?

He pulled across the notepad he kept by his bed and began to make some notes.

1. She is still alive, able to speak calmly. No hysterics
2. They are currently within maximum four hours travelling time of Piccadilly Railway station
3. They know the station well, either locals or have been watching it carefully as a useful public place
4. They are still in the game
5. There are two people (not necessarily men) with Ellen
6. Those picking up the money may/may not be the above

He looked over his notes and the burning question was still there. What did they *really* want?

He couldn't begin to think about going back to sleep so he had a long soak in a warm bath followed by an ice-cold shower. He then sat in front of the TV with a mug of tea, his skin tingling. The world news washed round him as he tried to get into the minds of the kidnappers. By six o'clock, none the wiser, he was at his desk.

He met with Frank at seven o'clock as arranged. The three other men joined them by phone; George was on his way in.

"Will we hear today what they really want?" asked Tom. Frank had told him before the disembodied voices of the others had boomed into the office that he had already managed to speak to the NCS officer. It was his view that they would. His was the first voice in reply.

"Yes, Tom I believe that we will. We have now established that we are willing to play the game and there is less than a week to go. The weekend should cause us little problem, but of course, if significant sums are involved we will need to activate lawyers, financiers, et cetera." Mutterings of assent came from the other two members of the team.

Tom sat feeling like he was caught up in a TV drama. He was here, looking at the phone and at Frank but he felt strangely disconnected. He started to repeat silently, "I am here with a crack team because Ellen has been kidnapped. It could be global and political. I am here..."

The intercom buzzed to announce George's arrival. He bustled in to Frank's office behind the duty sergeant; Tom thought he was almost rubbing his hands with excitement. Git.

"Tom, Frank." He nodded in greeting and waited for the door to close behind him. "All set?"

"I've asked for the station cameras to be positioned properly on Platform One – we got nothing useful from yesterday's film," Frank reported.

Tom watched as George took out an unsealed A4 envelope and passed it across the table.

"Anything else in here?"

"A note to ask them to get in touch with you ASAP with their real demands. You can read it. It is non-confrontational, as I discussed with Frank earlier."

You didn't mention that conversation, Tom thought but kept quiet as he peered into the envelope and pulled out a single sheet of company-headed paper. He read it quickly. Okay. He re-inserted the sheet, pulled away the protective strip and pressed the flap down. He looked up at the two men.

198   *Boxing Clever*

"I'm going to quickly let Ellen's parents know that I have spoken with her before I go." A warning came from one of the regional officers. "I'll do it here, now," he said, anger rising, "so you can all hear."

The call was brief. He gave his name and then said that he had heard from Ellen last night and she was well. He could say no more but would be in touch. Frank nodded at him in approval.

"George?" Tom was on his feet. "Drop me at the station?"

"We're a bit early," George looked at his watch.

"Traffic may be bad. Besides, I need a coffee." Army training. Always do a reccie.

The station was even busier than it had been the day before. The mood was different too; you could see in people's faces that it was nearly the weekend. Some were even smiling.

He bought himself a large cup of black coffee and an almond croissant on the lower level of the station and watched the time tick round until it reached twenty past eight. Clutching a newspaper that had been discarded by a previous visitor to the café, he walked briskly in the direction of Platform One. His eyes scanned the faces of the crowd in front of him, desperate for a glint of recognition from a mixed-race boy. The area near the drop was heaving – oh bugger - a young mother suddenly stopped and bent down to comfort a crying toddler, just where he needed to be. It was eight-twenty-nine.

The child decided it was going to be sick and promptly vomited on the floor near a mess of belongings that the woman had dropped. She looked around wildly for help and before he knew it, Tom was elbowed out of the way by a well-meaning matronly woman who bore down on the hapless child like a steamship. Both women glared at him as he moved to stand in the way of their chosen route. He muttered an apology and edged to one side and watched in frustration as the various bags and a striped buggy were gathered by the larger lady who created a pathway through the crowds for the mother and child. He checked his watch. It was eight-thirty-three.

Tom pushed his way back to the barrier and after making sure he was past the pool of vomit, he dropped his paper and in one movement bent down and pushed the envelope into the gap.

"Pillock," somebody commented as they barged into his shoulder. The contact hit his balance and he wobbled on his haunches, hitting the barrier so that it sounded like a call to arms. He put his left hand out to stop himself from falling, straight into the cold, clammy mess behind him. He thought he heard a laugh, but he didn't dare look around. It was eight-thirty-five.

His face burned as he pushed back through the station and into the gents' on the lower floor. He washed his hands repeatedly and tried to calm himself but all he could hear in his head was, "I've blown it, I've blown it. Fuck, fuck."

He needed to know. He ran back up to the place and could see that the envelope was gone. Thank Christ for that.

He took a taxi back to the office and reported to Frank.

Dean caught up with him as he was walking along the corridor back to the CID office.

"Well?" he asked urgently. "Frank won't say shit."

"She's still alive, Dean, we know that much," Tom smiled wearily. "Watch and wait, eh?"

His friend absorbed his mood and continued in silence. As they approached the office door, Dean remarked, "Nothing more on Andy Harris yet but I'll give the local CID another call later."

"Cheers. Let me know?" Tom stopped by the white board as they came into the room. "Did you get anything from your snouts?"

200   *Boxing Clever*

"Only that the Murphys need this new guy to bring in some cash. They've been in a tight spot for awhile and there is a rumour they owe big time."

He got his files up to date. He called Mr Chadwick again to reassure him they were doing all they could to find the man who had sold Mel the drug that killed her. He sat with Elliott and discussed the shoplifting spate that seemed to have gone up a gear. Elliott grabbed the idea of a workshop with the store detectives and got ready to organise it as soon as Tom had finished outlining the idea.

"And for God's sake," he said before things could get any worse, "make sure they keep their absence quiet or get cover for when they're with you. Last thing we need is us giving the gang a free shot."

He managed nearly four hours at his desk before he had to get out. He walked as quickly as he could without breaking into a trot, out of the front of the building and down onto the canal towpath. He had bought a bar of chocolate from the machine on his way out and he stood for a minute, feeling the warm air on his face, and took a large bite. The glorious caramel and chocolate swirled in his mouth and before he knew it, he had an empty wrapper in his hand. The sugar lift came quickly and he turned to make his way back inside. His phone rang as he was just passing an elderly man walking an equally ancient dog.

The words boomed in his head. His vision swam and he felt his legs buckle. A long stream of brown fluid shot from his mouth as he vomited onto the patchy grass with the words echoing in his head.

"They've found a body on Moreton Moss."

CHAPTER 21

The elderly man hovered for a moment, clearly unsure of whether to offer assistance. The little dog took the chance to sit down and rest its legs.

Tom couldn't speak so he waved one hand ineffectually, and gave the man a weak smile as if to say he would be okay. As the man turned away and dragged the dog into the standing position to continue their journey, Tom swallowed hard and ran his tongue around his mouth.

"Male? Female?"

"Call's just been picked up from Air Support," Dean replied. "Thought you should know ASAP - we're waiting for more details."

Tom's stomach was doing somersaults and he thought he was going to throw up again. He took a deep breath.

"Get onto Air Support. I want to hitch a ride there now. I'm coming back to the office – meet me in the car park in five minutes. Your car."

He started to run, his heart already thumping. Thoughts jumped in and out of his brain with each step. It can't be Ellen – Alice would have seen it. Don't be stupid, she's not the bloody oracle – you just want to believe her. Why the hell would they kill her for twenty grand? No, it can't be Ellen. His legs seemed to be borrowed from someone else as he ran into the car park. He was heartened to see Dean's bulk already in the driving seat.

202   *Boxing Clever*

He yanked open the passenger door and was still pulling on his seat belt as they shot off in the direction of the air field.

"What do we know?"

"Fuck all." Dean didn't look at him. "Ryan knows to call me or you if anything comes in."

"Frank?"

"Pacing the carpet."

As if linked in by radar, Tom's phone rang. It was Frank.

"Where are you?"

"On my way to pick up the chopper. This could be Ellen." He needed to point the finger.

"We have no reason to believe that, Tom." The tone was defensive and placatory.

He couldn't be bothered to reply and sat in silence for the rest of the journey, his brain drawing images he didn't want to see but couldn't stop exploring and revisiting. It just didn't make sense. His stomach began to burn and he realised he had left his tablets in his drawer. He turned his head and watched as the motorway railings flickered past the car, and the houses grew fewer and fewer. Dean turned into the driveway leading to the airfield, flashing his identification as they approached the police helicopter.

The navy and yellow machine was rocking gently as the rotors turned in ever slowing circles. It must have just got back from its flight over The Moss to map the co-ordinates of the body. The engine was idling ready for a quick take-off, the pilot visible in the front right seat. The radio crackled into life as Tom got out of the car. He leant back in through the open door to hear what was said. Patrol cars were on their way to secure the scene. The pathologist and photographer had been alerted and would be arriving in the next sixty minutes. The transmission ended.

"I'll follow by road," Dean held Tom's gaze. Unable to find anything else suitable to say, he gave a slight nod reached across to close the passenger door. He crunched the car into reverse gear and drove away.

Tom ran to the helicopter, clambered into the front left hand seat and put the headset snugly over his ears. The whoop, whoop of the blades began to get louder and faster, and the helicopter began to rock dangerously on the ground as if it was a tethered dragon struggling to escape. Tom felt sick. This was the first time he'd been in a chopper since Greg had died. Shamed, he realised he'd not dreamt or thought of his friend since Ellen was taken. Sorry, mate. Please God, don't let me lose her too.

A sudden lurch of the aircraft shocked him back to reality.

"How was the body found?" Tom yelled into his mouthpiece, trying to control his fluttering guts.

The pilot winced as the sound hit his ears. "From what we know, a group of Venture Scouts training for their Duke of Edinburgh Award were on the Moss. A couple of them got the map co-ordinates a bit wrong and had split from the group. Literally tripped over a foot."

Tom was about to ask more questions when the navigator seated behind him broke across the communication channel and issued directions to the pilot. They were within two minutes of the site.

The ground below had turned to a patchwork of muted greens and browns. No trees. Even in the summer daylight, it was a bleak place. Although the motorways linking north to south and east to west were less than twenty miles away, it looked desolate and remote. Moreton Moss was an area of peat bog remaining after industrialists in the mid-nineteenth century had drained and cultivated a large acreage to supply vegetables to the growing city of Manchester. In Tom's view, nobody with

204   *Boxing Clever*

any sense spent any time there unless they had something to prove (like the scouts) or to hide.

The pilot's hands and feet were working in a complicated dance as the helicopter sank towards the patch of ground indicated by the navigator. A flash of blue and red showed the presence of the scout leader who had agreed to stay near the scene until the police arrived. Tom was glad to see he was alone.

He removed his headphones before they hopped to a halt on the ground and was out of the helicopter as soon as the pilot gave him the signal. He crouched low as he ran towards the scout, but even then his shirt felt it was going to be ripped from his back.

"DI Tom Ashton." He introduced himself quickly to the man whose pale face belied his calm posture. "Thank you for your prompt action. Can you show me...?"

The man nodded and took a few paces to the left and pointed over a small rise in the ground. He visibly swallowed and then cleared his throat. "Can I join my group now?"

Tom assured him that he could head back to his group, but that some of his colleagues would need to talk to him and the rest of the party soon. As the man waited, Tom rang Dean and asked him to arrange for a patrol car to collect the scouts who had found the body, yelling to be heard over the sound of the departing helicopter.

The sudden silence of the place was deafening.

Tom walked carefully towards the body, his eyes scanning the ground for any items or traces that could be important. He reached the top of the rise, and looked down into the soft curve of rich earth. As he stepped tentatively down towards the shoe poking out from the brown earth, a rich earthy smell escaped the ground with each spongy footstep.

It was a small foot, if the bit of the shoe that he could see was a guide. Black, unless that was staining from the peat. He sank onto his haunches and stared at the clumsy mound. Please, no.

He began to smooth away the earth from around the foot, as gently as a caress. The rest of the world had retreated and there was no sound other than his shallow breathing and the soft scrape of the peat as it gave beneath his probing fingers. It broke off in clumps and he threw them behind him as he worked. Black fabric trousers, lightweight, not as heavy as denim. He pushed them away from the leg, no socks, flesh mottled with dirt. There were dark coarse hairs matted with the grime. Probably not a woman's leg. And certainly not Ellen's.

Dean arrived just before the patrol cars, the strain of wanting to learn what Tom had found etched on his face. He stood and listened as Tom passed on the news to Frank and by the time the next five colleagues had arrived, they had eased away much of the peat surrounding the lower part of the victim's body. As soon as Tom pulled away the clump that was covering the guy's left hand he knew who he was looking at. The long nails on the slim hand. He reckoned this was the dealer in the Reyka and unless he was losing his touch, this was the mysterious Col.

Within the hour, the scene had been cordoned off and the entire body exposed. Still fully clothed and the face badly beaten but recognisable as the man described by Lisa.

"Well, well." Tom's relief and elation had long given way to welcome curiosity. "We know what you've been getting mixed up in but why should you end up here?" He looked at Dean. "Did you get anywhere looking for a left-handed guitar player?"

Dean shook his head. "Got overtaken by other stuff but I did put the word around. At least now we can ask if anyone missed a gig or whatever."

206   *Boxing Clever*

"Get Ryan on to it – don't rely on your snouts. I'm going to go and call in to a few places now; I'll take your car – you can get a lift back?"

He held out his hands for the keys and set off for the city. He parked the car near China Town and began his tour of the pubs. A few people almost laughed in his face at the vagueness of his query but he carried on regardless. Someone would know who this guy was. He got his first lead in a Seventies retro bar near UMIST. The barman was smearing the bar top with a grimy cloth, moving the grease and dust around in a gesture of cleaning. He paused for a moment to reflect on the question and after a short interruption to serve a pint of bitter to a thin young man, he offered a name.

"He's only played here occasionally in the past but from what I've heard, he knows all the bands and session musicians. Fiddle player, goes by the name of Bearded Pat. His most regular spot is the pub near the Aquatic Centre."

Ten minutes later, Tom was there and learning that Bearded Pat was due in later that day.

Tom wrote up the case on the white board and drew a red line from the section for Col's murder across to the death of Mel Chadwick. He was pretty sure that her parents wouldn't be at all distressed to hear the news. He read over the information they knew so far. The initial pathologist report at the scene was that he had been strangled; the beatings on the face had occurred prior to death. He'd been in the peat for less than a week. And was probably aged in his early to mid-twenties.

The rest of the afternoon passed with no word from Ellen's kidnappers and Tom was increasingly grateful for the demise of Mr Col Whoever because it meant it wasn't her. He called Mel's parents to let them know that they'd found the man he believed had sold their daughter the fatal tablet. He hoped it

Maureen Devlin   207

would help them to get on with their grieving. He also rang Lisa in Cumbria, although he wasn't sure the news would have the same therapeutic effect. She thanked him in a small quiet voice before saying goodbye.

Dean agreed to go with him to meet Bearded Pat. They were at the pub in time to see the large and very bearded man arrive, clutching a battered violin case and a plastic carrier bag.

"Could we have a word?" Tom asked, intercepting the man before he could reach the bar.

"If you get me in a pint of Guinness, then I don't see why not," was the affable reply. Tom left Dean to go to the bar, and followed the other man to a table in the corner of the pub.

By the time Dean had made his way to join them cradling three pints of Guinness in his massive hands, Tom had discovered that Pat had a good grasp of the bands who played the city pubs.

"Have you come across guy named Col? Irish or Scottish, plays guitar?"

A shadow crossed the man's face. "That young git. Let me down at a big do last Saturday. Why?"

Tom thought he looked genuinely saddened to hear exactly why the young man had let him down. He drained his glass and shook his head a couple of times before he answered the questions that came at the end of the explanation of Col's absence.

"Col Mawhinney. Good little player. Came over from near Belfast a couple of years ago to go to uni. But dropped out from what I can gather. I know he had a flat in Fallowfield somewhere." He raised his finger across towards the bar in what must have been a well-known gesture, for a replacement pint was put in front of him within minutes. He couldn't think of any more to tell them, so Tom left him with a card in case he remembered something at a later date.

208   *Boxing Clever*

Dean was on the phone as soon as they got out of the pub to try and get an address. Tom called his answering machine at home, just in case. No messages. He hoped that the silence was good news and that the next demand would go straight to Vanpharma so that they could get it sorted and bring her home. He was glad of Dean's offer of a curry. He hadn't looked forward to spending this particular Friday night alone.

They parked in the patrolled car park behind one of the restaurants. As they walked round to the main road, Tom sniffed the aromatic night air and his stomach let out an audible whimper. The shops and restaurants were lit up like a strip in Las Vegas – a neon competition lasting about a mile along one of the main arterial roads into the city. Rusholme. The curry capital of the North West, home to a multitude of restaurants boldly proclaiming on banners hanging outside that their chef was the "Manchester Curry Chef" of this year, last year, some other year.

They strolled towards Dean's favourite eatery, ignoring the calls of the waiters standing on the pavement trying to entice people in. They ordered their meals and as they munched on spicy popadoms, ran over the facts of the case.

"It was all very neat," Tom observed. "One minute we have a young girl dead from drugs and before long the dealer ends up murdered. It's like some sort of divine justice. If we can find who he is working for, that will give us the reason he died."

"How much effort do we want to put into this?" Dean piled onions and raitha onto a massive piece of the crispy snack. Mouth full, he continued, "Good result all round, I reckon."

Inwardly Tom agreed but merely said, "Have to be seen to do the job – besides which, even though he was a low-life, there is a bigger low-life around who put him in the bog."

They munched through a vast array of red and orange dishes, fragrant rice and naan bread without much conversation.

Maureen Devlin   209

Tom devoured his meal with the gusto of a starving man. It seemed an age since he had eaten, and discarded, the chocolate bar on the towpath. Relief at the discovery of Col rather than Ellen had somehow steadied his equilibrium, and the acid calmed as it found something to work on other than the lining of his stomach. He even tried to find a dessert that appealed, but the laminated card of pre-formed ice creams did not tempt him and he sat back, satisfied and eyed his friend.

"Has Fiona asked any more?"

Dean shook his head. "She will be soon though. I've said you've heard from her and that she's really caught up with stuff. Fuckin' nightmare." His voice hardened. "Wish I could do more."

"So do I, mate. So do I."

Saturday morning. Nearly a week after she had been taken. George called to say that they were having a meeting at the company that lunchtime to go over all the plans that they had put in place. They would be ready to act quickly, Tom must feel reassured.

For the sake of something to do, he went over to her house just to sit amongst her things and feel her existence. The little place was quiet and watchful and after an hour lying on her bed, eyes closed, he felt recharged. He decided to visit Alice.

He nearly missed her. She was at the bus stop waiting to catch the number 42 into town. He tried to persuade her to let him drive her there, but could find no argument to override her insistence that she could use her travel pass for nothing, and his fare would be cheaper than parking. For the first time in years, he found himself pressed against the grubby window of a double-decker bus.

"You seem quite bright today," she said cautiously as they jerked to yet another stop. She checked the faces around her and

210   *Boxing Clever*

carried on. "I've seen nothing more. Shall we find somewhere for elevenses when we get into town?"

She surprised him by ordering a large cappuccino and a slice of pecan pie. He would have said she was a tea-and-scone person. He joined her in the pie, but with a large black coffee. As he waited to pay for the order, he watched as she bustled across to where a young couple was about to leave a cosy area with a small sofa and easy chair. How she managed to nudge aside the two young women ahead of her aiming for the same seats he wasn't sure, but claim them she did.

He carried the tray carefully through the busy café and they sat, heads together like a pair of lovers.

"I feel surprisingly calm," she said. "It's like we're in a freeze-frame."

He knew exactly what she meant. As she sipped her coffee, he told her the outline details of the previous day and as he spoke, she began to shake her head.

"What a dreadful world we are living in. How people can hurt one another." Then she added suddenly and with certainty, "She is okay, you know."

He felt his eyes prickle. "You will call me anytime, with anything...?" he knew he was looking at her with desperation. She patted his hand and pushed his plate a little nearer to him.

"Of course, now eat. You are a busy man under a great deal of stress. Enjoying a slice of pecan pie does not mean that you are uncaring."

In the face of such wisdom, he ate.

He left Alice to her shopping and caught a taxi back to police HQ. He tried to reach Dean to find out if they had any result on Col Mawhinney's address, but on getting the engaged signal, he switched on his computer and began to run through the files to see if there was any record of him. Although there was nothing there, that didn't mean he'd led a blameless life – just that he hadn't been caught.

Not expecting anything to be so simple, he rang through to directory enquiries to see if there was a telephone number listed for Mr C Mawhinney in Fallowfield. He nearly laughed out loud when the lady flicked him through to an automated system that gave the details. He wrote down the number out of habit. Mr Mawhinney may have a flatmate for all he knew. He dialled the number at the same time as he tapped in the details into his computer to bring up the address. No one answered.

Dean was technically on leave even though Frank had instructed people to be available for duty the week prior and all during the Summit, so Tom left a message on Ryan's desk telling her where he was going and with instructions to follow him. He wrote the same on the white board – the thing had been his idea after all.

He drove through Rusholme and along the same road for a few miles to Fallowfield. Many students who had tired of the university accommodation way of life rented flats and houses here, as they were affordable and on the most well-served bus route in the city.

He parked in front of the house. It was a modest two-storey semi-detached property, with weeds the height of a man's thigh in the front. He walked up to the door, and without much hope, rang the doorbell for Flat 2. He waited for a few seconds and then pressed the bell for Flats 1 and 3, and for good measure, banged heavily on the door.

"Okay for fuck's sake, keep your hair on." The door opened to reveal a less-than-alert face topping a rather grubby blue t-shirt. "Well?"

Tom held up his ID card and allowed the man to squint his eyes and focus on the content. It took a moment for the

212   *Boxing Clever*

realisation to move from his eyes to his brain and then his mouth. He was clearly puzzled.

"Why you lookin' for me?" The dark brows gathered across his forehead, but the tone was not aggressive.

"I'm trying to reach Mr Col Mawhinney. Flat 2. There was no answer."

The relieved neighbour explained that he hadn't seen him around for a few days but they weren't really friends, so he wouldn't really expect to know where he was. He could see no reason not to let Tom come in and take a look at the place, but he didn't have a key for anyone else's flat. Tom reassured him that was not a problem.

He followed the man through the stale air of the house to a brown varnished door with a number two painted on it in white gloss paint, and a single Yale lock.

"Could you contact your landlord, please? I need to gain entry."

"Why?" He was getting suspicious. "Don't you need a warrant or something? What the fuck's going on?"

At that moment Ryan arrived, rushing through the house like the cavalry. "Need another shoulder?" She looked past Tom at the door.

"Mr Mawhinney's neighbour here is going to call the landlord for a set of keys. Give him five minutes and if we're still waiting then you can do the business."

He left Ryan outside Flat 2 while the call was made and walked towards the front door for some fresh air. He could hear the excited tones but not all the conversation. Clearly urgency had translated to the landlord as a yell came through from Ryan that the keys would be along in ten minutes.

"Find out what you can about Mr Mawhinney from our friend here," he instructed, his eyes locking on to the slim young mixed-race man on the opposite side of the road. He

Maureen Devlin   213

paused for barely a second as he walked by, but he lifted and turned his head to look directly at the house. Even with the bruising around his mouth and right eye, and without the rope in his hands, Tom recognised him. And he reckoned the recognition was mutual.

The woman was flustered and angry in equal measure. "Never had any trouble with my houses," she kept muttering as she pushed past Tom towards the locked flat. "Don't want to know what he's done, not my business."

Tom decided it was her business and as she put the key in the lock told her not to expect any more rent from this particular tenant. She was visibly shaken by the news, enough to accept a cup of tea from the open-mouthed neighbour.

Ryan issued a low whistle over Tom's shoulder as they took in the scene. The living room had been comprehensively trashed. Shelves had been swept clear and the resulting pile of books, CDs and magazines were spread haphazardly where they had fallen. The sofa cushions had been slashed and the stuffing spilled out onto the floor like the guts of a freshly caught fish. Tom moved carefully through the mess into the kitchen where cupboard doors gaped and the contents of various packets gathered in heaps across the floor. The small fridge stood open, a solitary undamaged egg on the middle shelf. Its companions had oozed artistically down onto the glass lid covering the salad box at the bottom of the fridge and the door of the tiny freezer compartment was hanging askew.

Still not speaking, Tom edged back out of the kitchen and through the second door off the living room into the bedroom. A large Irish flag draped across one wall, and a couple of framed photographs showed the dead man with a round-faced smiling older woman. Whatever they had been looking for, they

214   *Boxing Clever*

had left nothing to chance. The place was a mess. A guitar, its neck broken, lay crookedly on the floor.

"Wonder if they found what they were after," Ryan commented.

"Not going to matter too much to Mr Mawhinney. See if you can find any details of family. Would guess that the woman in the photo in the bedroom is his mother. I don't think we're likely to find anything else, but look for mobile phone, bills, anything that would give us an idea of who he mixed with. Whoever paid him a visit had the keys – get the fingerprint guys over and secure the place." He thought for a moment. "You stay here. I've got a visit to make."

CHAPTER 22

F or the first time in nearly a week, Tom switched on the radio as he drove towards Joe Murphy's gym. Opinionated voices discussing the arts was a welcome reminder that the world was still turning as it should and he let the voices wash over and around him like a salve. He had just pulled up at the last set of traffic lights before his destination when his idle reverie was interrupted.

"Hello?"

"Tom, it's George. We've had contact. They want your boss to go to Old Trafford. Tonight. To get the next instructions."

Tom's brain went from nought to top gear as he took off from the lights, mounting the kerb as he turned into the next road on the left and stopped the car.

"How did the contact come?" He really wanted to know why it hadn't come to him. He listened as George explained how the call had been taken by Vanpharma security. The caller had been brief and, in the opinion of the security guard who had taken the call, young and smug – apparently he had laughed before hanging up.

"Is she okay?" Tom asked. "What's the feeling with your guys?"

"We'd just finished a planning meeting when the call came in. I've spoken to Frank, he wants to talk to your people. We feel he should go. You can count me in as the company representative tonight."

216   *Boxing Clever*

Yeah, and I bet you're gagging to be in on the action. "Whatever. Not my call. Talk to you later." He cut the line and dialled Frank's number to tell him he was on the way back in to the office. The Murphys could wait.

Tom couldn't decide if The Rodent was really as livid as he was making out or just relishing the chance of getting out from behind his desk. He was pacing the carpet in his office, his hands clasped behind his back rather than running them over his head. Tom sat with great deliberation, silently demanding that his boss stop and look at him.

"I am going to cancel all leave," Frank announced eventually. "We will need to have secure back-up for this op."

Tom gritted his teeth. "What are the details, sir?"

There was no explicit demand for Frank to be unaccompanied but the team had decided that he should appear to be alone. He had to be at the front gates of Old Trafford football ground at nine o'clock and, Tom sat up at this, he had to wear a Manchester City scarf.

"They're laughing at us!" he exclaimed. "It's all to make you look stupid, that's if you don't get beaten up by a United fan in the meantime. What the hell has that got to do with Ellen or Vanpharma?"

"It's all about control." Frank spoke patiently as if Tom was dense. "Don't forget the whole reputation of the city is at stake as well as Ellen. We are taking this as a clear reminder of what could happen next week if it isn't sorted to their satisfaction. The experts believe that the set of instructions they deliver to me tonight will be the last and the definitive ones."

"I'll be there." It was a statement, not a request.

Frank nodded. "I expected as much, but we'll have to play this very carefully to maintain security."

Maureen Devlin   217

They arranged to meet again at five pm. The regional officer, George and the Head of Summit Liaison were coming in to meet with Frank at four o'clock to fine tune the plans and would then be in place when Tom returned. The guy from NCS would be advising them by secure phone.

"I'm presuming we are going to have air support? And request that the football club has its cameras working on our behalf?"

"We will certainly discuss all the options." Frank was cautious. "We have to weigh up all the risks but I will recommend that we have aerial back-up, yes."

"We don't know if she's still alive though, do we, sir?" Tom felt the need to remind his boss that this was not some practice operation. "Are you going to demand some evidence that she is unharmed?"

"Ellen is our priority, Tom," he replied. "Trust me."

At least something was happening, Tom thought as he walked back to his desk, but he couldn't shake off the underlying anxiety that Ellen was at risk from the people attempting to secure her release almost as much as from those holding her.

Ryan was at her desk, munching on a steaming pasty that tainted the room with a greasy, meaty and vaguely unpleasant aroma. Tom thumped her on the back while she was mid-chew and indicated that she should grab her stuff and follow. Tom scribbled on the movements board and waited at the door as Ryan scrambled from her chair, stuffing the last of the savoury concoction into her mouth. She had hardly finished it as she asked, "Where are we going?"

Wiping away the crumbs that had sprayed on his shoulder, Tom merely replied, "Old Trafford."

As they drove, Ryan filled him in with the details she had learned about Col Mawhinney from the neighbour and the

218   *Boxing Clever*

initial search of the flat. They had found a letter with an address near Belfast that could be the parents (Ryan was just about to check it out when Tom had disturbed her). Other than that, the place had been cleaned out of anything that would shed light on the man's life. No bank statements, no building society books, no mobile phone or address book. No drugs other than painkillers and tablets for hayfever.

Clearly the man had something to hide, or at least those who had trashed the place thought so.

"Anything else from the landlady or neighbour?"

"Not much. All of a sudden they were both talking about him as if he was some sort of martyr. Lovely bloke, never late with his rent, always willing to lend milk, that sort of thing. By the time I left, I could see that they'd both rallied enough to be getting ready to go out and spread the news."

"Any friends?"

"Not that they knew of. Kept himself pretty much to himself. Often went out with a guitar case at weekends; reckoned he'd played in pubs."

"That much we do know. Get onto that address as soon as we get back, okay?"

"Where did you leap off to?" Ryan flicked the indicator and pulled the car to a stop outside the fabulously maintained Manchester United Football Ground.

"Saw someone outside the flat. Recognised him from Joe Murphy's place. Might just be a coincidence but I wanted to check it out."

The next hour passed quickly as they explored the area for the best lookout positions when The Rodent was in place. Dean had agreed to be available to support the operation, Elliott and Rich were also on standby. Tom knew that negotiations would be underway to have officers in civilian clothes either on foot or in

Maureen Devlin   219

passing cars around the time of the exchange. Frank would make sure he was in no danger.

"Do me a favour, Ryan?" he asked as they pulled into the HQ car park. "Pay a visit to Joe Murphy's place. See if you can find out who the guy is that hangs around Franklin Raye - was holding a rope for him last time I was there with Dean. Slim, mixed race. Maybe you can find out how he got his black eye? And if you can get Franklin to say he gave his tickets to Col Mawhinney for the launch of the Underground Club, I'll make you a decent lunch instead of that reconstituted crap you stink the place out with."

Ryan gave Tom a feigned look of hurt, but waved a hand as she reversed the car and headed back out towards the Murphys' gym.

Frank's office was humming with a suppressed air of excitement. Someone had secured a map of both the football ground and the surrounding area and it was laid in pride of place on the conference table. There were various coloured dots already stuck onto the map, indicating some strategic positions that Tom was in the dark about. He didn't speak, but walked around the table, avoiding the feet and legs of the other men, carefully overlaying his recent sighting of the area with the paper replica. He had to admit the dots were in useful places where people could watch but not be seen. The dot showing where Frank would stand was larger than the others and in red.

He looked up and made eye contact with the Summit Liaison Officer.

"Looks good from what I can see," he reported. "Only thing is that I would add another two vantage points, here," he pointed with his pen, "and here. There is also a container lorry parked here," another jab, "which is off its wheels and I reckon going nowhere tonight. It offers good shielding and you, sir,"

220   *Boxing Clever*

he looked at Frank's serious face, "will be directly in the line of sight."

The men nodded and the regional officer gravely added three more blue dots to the map.

"How will we find out if Ellen is okay?" Tom demanded. "We can't just wait to be given another demand without knowing how she is."

George leant forwards and clasped his hands together, as if in prayer.

"Frank is in the best position to take this forwards," he intoned. "The experience shows that by playing the game this far, he will either be able to ask a kidnapper or representative directly tonight, or," he paused to gain eye contact, "we request evidence before adhering to their next demand. The stakes are rising, and we believe we will get the real reason for the kidnap tonight."

"What's our total resource?"

"All in all, with some support from Liverpool and Sheffield," Frank glanced at the regional officer, "forty. Plus the helicopter."

Tom's forehead ached with the upward pressure of his eyebrows. "We'll have to work hard at keeping that lot invisible. Am I right in assuming there will be no attempt to arrest anyone? Not until we know Ellen is safe?"

"Absolutely."

"What if they try to grab you, sir?" he asked.

They went over the plans a number of times before they felt they'd exhausted all of the potential pitfalls. Tom reckoned he had an hour or so before he needed to be getting ready for the operation, so he decided to follow Frank's lead and head home to change and eat. Next rendezvous: HQ at eight pm.

Franklin could spot a cop from a hundred yards even if they were female and in jeans and a denim jacket. She couldn't be anything else. He watched as Joe and Martin edged in towards the woman, Joe looking curious and Martin with a hard look on his face, impatient as ever. He tried to hear what was being said, but the noise of grunts and thumps bouncing off the walls in the gym made it hard for him to pick anything up. He decided to play the innocent.

"Who's that, Sam?" He peered down at the trainer, who had also noticed the visitor. "Journo?"

"Dunno, son." Franklin could see that the man was puzzled. "Not seen her before, but don't reckon the boss is too pleased to see her, whoever she is. You best get back to your work, we'll find out soon enough if it's anything to do with us."

The older man had been around long enough to know when to mind his own business, but Franklin was desperate to know what was going on. Otis had told him that people had been nosing round Col's flat. Franklin knew the boys would have done a good job at cleaning the place, but there was stuff going on that he couldn't figure. He needed to get back into control.

The woman looked away from Joe towards him and started to walk in his direction.

"I said no," Martin's voice was harsh. "He's in training. It'll have to wait."

She was clearly made of sterner stuff and carried on regardless. Franklin heard her utter something about obstruction and within a few steps was leaning on the ropes of the ring.

"Just a couple of questions, Mr Raye," she looked at Franklin and then smiled at the trainer. "You may be able to help too. My name's Ryan, Manchester CID. Friend of yours, works out here, understand his name's Otis. Can you give me a surname? Address?"

Franklin stared at the woman, working hard to mask the rage that began to burn through his body. He felt his world shift, as if forces he couldn't see were trying to unbalance him.

222   *Boxing Clever*

He breathed in and out slowly as he had been taught all those years ago and was able to meet the woman's gaze. He began to speak just as Sam opened his mouth and replied, "Ain't no friend. He just likes to hang around. Don't know his name, not important, never asked."

Franklin shrugged as if to say, "you know how it is." He began to flex his shoulder muscles, trying to keep them relaxed and loose.

Sam picked up the hint. "Don't get cold, son." He looked at the woman. "That it?"

"Heard you had a couple of tickets for the launch of the Underground Club some weeks back. Who did you give them too? Was it a guy called Col Mawhinney?"

Ryan ignored Sam and kept her gaze firmly on Franklin.

Fuck. What's goin' on? Franklin's brain was doing somersaults and his stomach was fusing into a ball as he struggled to keep his cool. He blessed his counsellor as he mentally counted slowly to ten while asking Sam to get him his sweatshirt. As the older man moved away to get the shirt, Franklin eyed the woman and shook his head as if confused.

"Who's that?" he asked. "Don't know the name. Afraid I can't help. Lots of people come around here - must have passed them on to one of those guys. I wasn't interested. Training."

How he managed the goofy grin of the dedicated athlete to go with the last statement, he'd never know. He counted in his head, keeping the panic fluttering but in place just under his breastbone.

She looked at him for a moment longer, then thanked him and walked towards the door. Martin gave her a brief nod and turned away to go back to the small office. Joe exchanged a few words and then, worryingly, looked over to where Franklin was swinging his arms in a half-hearted attempt to warm up the muscles.

Franklin thought the old man looked perplexed, as if he had got back from looking for food and found a magpie in his nest.

Tom wrinkled his nose as he pushed open his front door. There was a strange and unpleasant smell somewhere and he went off in search of the cause of it before he took a shower and changed. There was nothing untoward in the fridge or the bin in the kitchen, but he saw the little black and brown pile as soon as he walked into the living room. Jack was feigning sleep on the window ledge and barely acknowledged Tom's shout of disgust at the mix of furball and cat food on the carpet.

"For fuck's sake, cat." He stomped off in search of some old paper and a cloth. "Why can't you chuck this stuff up outside?"

He grabbed the free newspaper that was sitting on the kitchen worktop ready for the recycling bin and pulled a double sheet out to use as a scoop. As he laid the scrunched sheet on top of the mess, a headline caught his eye. "*Thugs taunt police.*" The story told of how a local station had been the focus of a campaign of graffiti, urination and, the reason for the story, a crude petrol bomb.

Tom stopped what he was doing for a second to read the report. How bloody depressing. He hadn't heard about it at work, another example of demarcation. How they were supposed to do their job with such little respect for the law? Sometimes he wondered why he bothered. He managed to get most of the stain out with warm soapy water and in no uncertain terms told Jack he could go and beg for food from Alice because he was a little sod. Jack purred and by the time Tom was drying himself down from his shower, he had gone.

He had run out of time to make a meal, so he slapped some smoked cheese and tuna onto a frozen pitta bread and popped it in the microwave for a minute. He was munching at the surprisingly adequate snack when a knock sounded at his door.

224   *Boxing Clever*

He debated on whether to open it as time was getting short. He pulled on his jacket, grabbed his phone, keys and sandwich and opened the door, clearly on the way out. It was Alice.

"Tom." She was breathless and her eyes looked bright. "It may be something and nothing but I knew you were here because of Jack... Can I come in for a moment?" Without waiting for a reply as on the first time he met her, she pushed past him into the hallway.

"I keep hearing laughing," she explained. "Young voices. Boys really. Not malicious. And then I get a sense of quietness, and a smell of alcohol. I think it's to do with Ellen." She paused for a minute and then asked, uncertainly. "Does she support Manchester United?"

Tom stared at her. "Why do you ask?"

"I saw a football shirt when I dozed off this afternoon, and then heard the laughing." Her eyes were transfixed on his face. He realised he must be gawping.

"This is weird, Alice," he said eventually. "I've been getting the feeling that whoever has taken Ellen is laughing at us and now you tell me this. We have to be at Old Trafford tonight for more instructions. I'm worried it's a blind alley..." He rubbed at his face and saw his watch. "I have to get back to work. Can you do something for me?"

He drove in to work, his eyes looking forwards but barely aware of the road. His brain ticked through all the things he knew about Ellen's situation. How they had found who she was, where she lived and who she worked for. He wasn't convinced that George knew what they were dealing with any more than his police colleagues were. For a split second a thought came into his head – surely not?

The beep behind him told him the lights had changed, and for the first time in years, he stalled the car. The beep gave way to a furious hooting. By the time he got the car going again, only one other car was able to follow him through the lights. How embarrassing. He stored the thought, letting his subconscious consider it as he concentrated on getting to work in one piece. He'd talk to George first.

Ryan was standing on the back steps smoking as he pulled into the car park. She crushed the half-smoked cigarette on the concrete and dropped into step beside Tom as he strode down the corridor. She gave him the rundown of her visit to the gym.

"They're as tight as a gnat's chuff there," she moaned. "The guy you're interested in is called Otis but Franklin Raye claims not to know his surname or him, for that matter. He really clammed up when he heard the name Col Mawhinney. He worked hard at it but I reckon he was thrown by the mention of him. Joe Murphy's son is a hard bastard, made it clear I was very unwelcome. There's something there, sir, I'm sure of it."

"You and me both," Tom could feel the vibration of retribution gathering, every instinct telling him he was on the right track. "We're going to be paying them another visit just as soon as we've got tonight out of the way. And," he paused as the cogs turned. "We'll pay another visit to Jordan Bell. He was always hanging around the place."

He pushed open the office door, causing a number of heads to turn expectantly in his direction. A wave of support, almost sympathy, hit him. The word must be out but he knew no one would refer to Ellen explicitly. He gave a quick nod and picked up a red pen to write on the white board. Next to 'Col Mawhinney' he wrote 'Otis X?' and linked them both to 'Franklin Raye?' Dean was by his side as he finished writing and gave a low sigh of exclamation. "Bloody hell."

CHAPTER 23

The Rodent was barely recognisable in casual gear. He was one of the older generation who insisted on pressing jeans, so he was resplendent in smooth blue denim, with a hint of a crease down the front of each trouser leg. He wore a grey polo shirt and had a lightweight sports jacket over his shoulder as the evening was overcast and threatening rain. His trainers looked in pristine condition and Tom was desperate to scuff them up a bit. Funnily enough, the Manchester City blue and white scarf set off the ensemble rather nicely.

He was fitted with a small microphone piece connecting him directly to a surveillance van parked about two hundred yards from where he was to stand. Tom wanted to be somewhere near the massive wrought-iron gates of the club so he'd be able to see what was going on but had accepted that he was probably known to the kidnappers and his blatant presence might be counter-productive. He admitted defeat and agreed to join George in the van.

The virtual convoy began to leave from vantage points around the region in time to be in position at eight-forty-five. Just after eight-fifteen, Tom drove to a nearby pub on the canal side, left his BWM in the car park and walked through to where the van was parked. George and the driver were already inside. Tom knew he would have to switch off his mobile phone when Frank began to transmit and he was already beginning to feel the pains of amputation. He had about twenty minutes before then so he made full use of them.

"I won't be able to speak to you until after nine o'clock," he apologised when Alice answered. "Are you still happy to go?"

Alice said she was and was just at that moment getting on her coat. She reassured him that she would be fine and would leave him a message when she got home.

He dialled again. He didn't speak. He didn't need to. He knew there would be no answer; he just wanted to hear Ellen's voice.

George was watching him. Tom didn't enlighten him as to the nature of his conversations, and George, well-trained, didn't ask.

The interior of the windowless van began to warm up as the three inhabitants waited. A couple of green lights on the console flashed occasionally, showing that the equipment was ready and willing. Each man put on a set of headphones and waited. When Frank's voice eventually came through, it sounded unnaturally loud and Tom saw George jump and then try to hide the fact. Even though he knew The Rodent wouldn't come up with a quote to rival Neil Armstrong, Tom did think that the "I'm here" effort was a bit wet. It was seven minutes to nine.

Tom could feel the hastily eaten sandwich lying heavily in his stomach and the beginnings of an attack of reflux. He belched, trying to hide the noise with his hand. George wiped his brow with a single forefinger, clearly unwilling to draw attention to the beads of sweat that had formed there. The electronic connection with Frank was almost silent; there was a residual hissing noise confirming that the link was still live and transmitting.

By nine o'clock, Tom was ready to punch his way out of the van with his fists, so desperate was he to see what was happening on the street outside. A small cough echoed in his ears, followed by a whisper.

228   *Boxing Clever*

"No one here yet, am going to stroll towards the roundabout and then back again. Helicopter sighted."

Three more minutes passed. Silence. He looked at George, whose eyes were staring down intently at the fabric of his trousers. Tom nudged his foot to gain his attention and mouthed at him.

"Still convinced?"

George nodded, breathed in deeply and sat up ramrod straight, holding Tom's gaze. He held up one hand and made a patting motion in the air as if to say "calm down". He nearly got a punch for that. There was something wrong here. They had shown up dead on time before, what was going on tonight?

Another cough and Frank came through again. "Still nothing. I'm giving it until nine-thirty. No later. Ah." He paused. The silence lasted a lifetime until Frank came back through to quash the hopes.

"Still waiting."

She wasn't too sure of the buses so she had been glad when Tom had suggested she took a taxi. The car, when it came, was clean enough and with a strong smell of air-freshener. She sat primly on the back seat clutching her second best handbag on her lap, fairly confident that the brown striped upholstery would not mark her beige raincoat.

The journey took a little over fifteen minutes and Alice could feel her shoulders stiffen as she approached her destination. She was glad that it was still quite bright even with the cloud cover although she noticed how the quality of the daylight flattened amongst the mean streets of the sprawling housing estate. She asked the man to stop and opened her window, looking, smelling and listening to the world outside. Her three other senses were idle, idle and on alert, respectively. She asked the man to drive on a little, slowly.

She could see him stealing glances at her in his rear view mirror – so what if he thought she was a batty old woman? There was something here now, without question, but it was too far away. Tom had told her to stay in the car but the glass and metal were acting as a shield. She needed to be on the other side. She instructed the driver to pull over.

"I'll just be a few minutes. Will you wait here for me, please?" Without waiting for an answer and sure that he would do as she asked as no money had changed hands, she walked slowly along the road for a few yards towards a house with a bright yellow door and an ether of vibration emanating from the upper floor. She breathed evenly and without haste as she obeyed the call. Her hand held the wrought-iron gate for a second before she pushed it open and walked up to the front door. She had no idea what she was intending to do.

"What the fuck do you want?"

The words thrown at her came from behind and she twirled round to face a young boy, suspicion pouring from his eyes.

"I..." Her brain shot through available responses and she swallowed to gain some time. "I'm sorry. Do you live here?"

"Who the fuck are you to ask? Sod off."

"I used to live here," she lied. "I'm going into a nursing home tomorrow and I just wanted to have one last look..." She let the words trail away. "I'll go now."

She began to edge past him towards the road and the haven of the taxi but his quick hands suddenly reached forwards and grabbed at her bag. She tried to hold onto it but he was too strong for her; she could smell his last meal as he invaded her space and pushed her away. It may have been a bit of uneven path or her shoe that gave way but before she knew it she was falling backwards towards the unforgiving ground. Her vision began to mist over as the shaft of pain thrust through her head – but not before she had seen the shadow of a face at an upstairs window.

230   *Boxing Clever*

He was out of the van within seconds after the decision came to abort the operation. Frank was pulling off the woollen scarf from around his neck in obvious disgust as Tom reached him.

"A friggin' wind-up. Get on the phone. Find out if any contact has been made. Where's George? We need a de-brief. This stinks."

Tom ran back to his car, dialling his home number as he ran. The answering machine clicked in and he pressed in his access code to retrieve any messages. He wrenched open the door and was midway to sitting in the driver's seat when the first message came through. Laughter. Gleeful laughter. They didn't speak, just laughed for a few seconds and then hung up. Second message. Silence. Third message – for fuck's sake. His mother.

By the time he got back to office, he was certain that the gang were determined to stretch them to the limits. These games were beyond him. He knew where he was with straightforward murderers, robbers, thugs. He pushed open Frank's door without bothering to knock and was met with four glum faces.

"Just how sure are we that this is about Vanpharma? Seems to me these guys are getting their rocks off wasting police time."

He told them about the message on his answering machine. The Head of Summit Liaison shook his head, but without much conviction.

"It's about challenging authority and keeping control. I have to agree with you that it must be about more than Vanpharma and that makes me worried that we have other lobby groups involved that are the real reason behind this. They have made the company jump by paying out a modest sum of money, and they have now seen the city's security agencies do the same. Have you checked with your office?" The question was directed at George.

The discussion went round in circles. There had been no demand or further instructions. The debate raged again about releasing the story to the media and again the vote was stacked against even though there were only five days remaining before the start of the Summit.

"Do we know where the call boxes are that have been used in the calls to you, Tom?"

"Not tonight's call, but the last one was from outside Piccadilly Station."

Coffee appeared as if by magic as the group revisited the plans and contingencies developed over the recent week. Trying to do something useful, he stood and excused himself to call Alice. She should be home by now.

The relentless ringing of an unanswered phone had to be one of the most infuriating sounds in the world. He tried his home number again in case she had left a message but there was no cheery voice to ease him. He looked at his watch. It was nearly ten-thirty. Not good. Where was she?

She would have rung him if she could. She had tried, with a frail and flailing hand to tell the ambulance man that she needed to call someone, but then the soft velvet of oblivion stilled her arm and her mind.

By midnight, they had exhausted the options. No one was happy with the decision to wait but there was nothing else that they could do. Frank's face was grey as he called the meeting to a close. Tom knew the colour had left his own face some hours before. He had tried Alice's number again three times but without success and in the dying moments of the meeting had elected to try her house before trying to retrace her steps. There could be a million and one reasons for her absence. She may have had no success on her excursion and then met up with a

232 *Boxing Clever*

friend or... he struggled to think of any other reasons apart from the fact that she might be in trouble. And it was down to him.

Her house was in darkness. He shouted through her letterbox without much hope. As he turned back towards his car, he tripped over Jack who had crept up behind him. "Shit, cat!"

The cat yowled, a deep and throaty cry that sounded incredibly loud at this late hour and with a quality that set Tom's teeth on edge. He crouched to stroke his pet but Jack continued to yowl.

"I don't know where she is," he said, feeling stupid but adding. "Any ideas?" He thought out loud, hoping his voice would calm the almost frantic animal. "I'll try the taxi firms and then drive over to Ardwick." Jack's cry got louder. "I'll try the office as well, see if there have been any accidents..."

As he said this, Jack stopped howling and sat at his feet, purring. Not allowing himself to dwell on what he was doing, he dialled the main switchboard.

"Tom Ashton, CID." His number and identification was verified before he continued. "Can you tell me if there have been any reports of an elderly woman in an accident, possibly in a taxi, anywhere between Chorlton and Ardwick? Name Alice Roberts?"

He explained to the nurse on night duty that he was a friend as well as an investigating officer. They both spoke in a whisper, even though the majority of the patients in the crowded ward were either sedated and didn't care, or glad of the diversion of a visitor in the heavy early morning hours.

"She's had a bad fall – there may be concussion and we need to look at her ankle again tomorrow when the swelling has gone down. She needs to rest now; you'll have to come back in the morning."

After a little persuasion, and his promise not to wake her, the nurse guided him to a bed towards the end of the ward, on the left hand side. Alice was absolutely still, the bedding swaddling her tiny body, a small mound at the foot of the bed protecting her leg. She looked old. He stood by the bed for only a few minutes, hating the battle of guilt and frustration playing out in his tired head. Had she seen anything? Was her accident a coincidence or a message? He knew from the sketchy incident report that her bag was missing and that she had been identified by the name she'd given when booking the taxi.

Without speaking or even touching her hand, he turned away towards the exit. Maybe the anxiety showed in his face because the nurse's voice was kind when she told him to call after nine in the morning. There might be some news for him then.

The early hours of Sunday morning had a surreal feeling. Tom was exhausted but wide awake. Reluctant to go home, he drove into the city centre to China Town. He parked the car and walked, stealing energy from the crowds milling around the vibrant, fragrant streets. He crossed through into the Village and found a bar still open for business. He ordered a glass of red wine and an espresso and sat in a vile green chair, watching. His eyes locked on to some distant horizon, and he felt he was existing outside of himself. A woman came up to him and asked if he had a light. She was pretty, and drunk, and smiling. He shook his head.

"I don't smoke anyway," she said. "You just look like you need some company. Just got dumped?"

He winced. If only. "Something like that," he volunteered. He must have been giving off the vibes of a starving puppy because her face softened and she put one hand on his thigh. Jesus, that felt good. He was almost overwhelmed by the desire to sink his head into her soft breasts and sleep.

234   *Boxing Clever*

"Forget the bitch," she said. "She's not worth it."

He shot out of his chair so fast that the woman rocked backwards and almost fell. As he pushed past her to the door, her face became ugly as she snarled, "Seems like she had the right idea, weirdo."

He took in as much air in one breath as he could outside on the pavement. He needed to go home.

He was back at his desk at six-thirty am. Work would be his therapy. He had to keep busy until the next call came and until he could speak to Alice. He looked at the white board and checked his notes. He was letting things slip.

He walked over to Dean's desk to look for the file on Andy Harris. The DNA results were still outstanding but he was convinced that this was the identity of the bashed body in the morgue. The link to Franklin Raye was tenuous, but he planned to pay the big man another visit. He agreed with Ryan that the lack of information provided by Raye and the Murphys on this Otis character was interesting. He stopped at Ryan's desk. The file on Col Mawhinney was in the second tier of a blue plastic desk tidy marked 'Action'. Tom was impressed with the organisation.

He took out the file and whilst looking at the computerised image of the dead man, found the address in Belfast. He tapped the particulars into his computer and after a few minutes got the confirmation he needed. Mrs M Mawhinney. He noted the telephone number and then rang the switchboard.

"Can you get connect me to our main contact in CID, Belfast?"

"Police Service in Northern Ireland," the operator confirmed. "Hold on."

He was connected to a duty officer. Tom gave the details of Mrs M Mawhinney and the fact that he believed the body of her son, Col, was now lying in the morgue of the Manchester Royal Infirmary. He was advised that someone would call him back. Poor Mrs Mawhinney, thought Tom as he scribbled a note for the file. She was probably still asleep, blissfully unaware that she was about to get the triple whammy of not only hearing that her son was dead, but that he was murdered and probably because he was a drug dealer.

The morning sun was casting a waking glow on the room. Tom stood for a moment to look out at the city, windows beginning to twinkle with the strengthening sunlight. It was still barely after seven o'clock and he was quite alone. Suddenly desperate for company, he dragged open the door and strode through towards the front desk, stopping on the way to get his second cup of coffee of the day. As he stood at the vending machine he realised he was still holding the paper version of Col's face. He folded it and shoved it into his back pocket.

The night duty sergeant was yawning as Tom came into the glass-fronted room at the front of the building. A second uniformed colleague was transfixed to the computer screen, tapping in details and speaking quietly into his headset.

"Morning," said Tom brightly. "How's it going?"

"I'm just grateful I'm off duty at eight," the sergeant replied, rubbing her face wearily. "There must have been a full moon or something last night. Seemed like every juvenile we know was in action. Might be a coincidence with whatever operation was going on..." She looked at him for more information, then carried on when none was forthcoming. "But the switchboard was jammed with reports of car theft, muggings and ram raids. We had sod all resource to deal with it. Today is going to be a blaze of complaints and if the press doesn't pay a visit at some point, I'll be very surprised."

This was too much of a bloody coincidence.

"Where are we talking?"

236   *Boxing Clever*

The sergeant pointed behind Tom to a city map stuck onto the wall. She traced out a circle that touched on the city centre. He had been convinced that the activity would centre on Ardwick but it didn't even figure. All the action had taken place to the south-west of the city, miles away. Damn.

Dean was the first one in at eight-thirty. Tom was anxious to get to the hospital so he updated him on the call he was expecting from Belfast. Ideally they wanted someone to come and identify the body today, and in the process find out any more details on the dead man. Dean didn't ask where he was going, merely nodded when Tom announced he would be back in an hour or so and waved his mobile to show he could be reached. As he reached the door he said, "See if you can chase up Andy Harris. I want to use him when we talk with Mr Raye. In fact, I think we should pay another visit to the Murphys today. Let's rattle the tree and see what falls."

He didn't wait to hear Dean's opinion.

It was a different nurse who greeted him as he pushed through the blue wooden door to the ward, ignoring the notice stating visiting hours. She held up one hand to stop his progress, but he had whipped out his identification card before she could speak.

"I'm here to see Alice Roberts. She was brought in last night." He pointed down towards the bed he had stood beside a few hours ago. It was empty. He looked quickly back at the nurse, dreading what she might say.

"She has been taken down for a scan. We had hoped she would come round this morning but she is still unconscious."

"Do you normally scan so quickly?" Please don't lose your memory Alice.

The nurse replied that in all cases they liked to check for any evidence of haemorrhage so that they could treat it right away.

Maureen Devlin   237

She added that Alice was booked for an X-ray on her ankle while she was away from the ward and suggested he might like to come back in an hour. He gave her his mobile number just in case anything happened before his return and thanked her.

An hour wasn't really long enough to go anywhere and as the notice on the restaurant door stated that it didn't open until nine-thirty, he bought a bottle of mineral water and a bag of crisps from the shop in the hospital foyer and went to sit outside. He savoured the salt on his tongue and the cool liquid that washed it away and thought about Ellen.

After five minutes, he stirred himself into action. Thank God for mobile phones.

"Any progress?"

It seemed that the Belfast police were a model of efficiency. Within ten minutes of Dean's call to them soon after Tom had left, they had dispatched an officer to the house of Mrs M Mawhinney and confirmed that she had a son called Col who was living at the Manchester address. They advised that she and another son were booked onto a flight later that day and would need to be met at the airport. Dean assured Tom that he would sort everything out.

"I presume you want to talk to the mother?"

"Yep, but I'll leave you to escort them to the morgue. What about Andy Harris?"

"I've rung the Met. They've been a bit snowed under but they did confirm they got a sample of hair from an old comb in Andy Harris' bedroom. Seems from the family he often did a wandering trick so a lot of his stuff is still there. They've promised to push on the DNA match with our sample. Hopefully by tomorrow."

As good as sorted. He didn't commit to Dean when he would be back in the office or available to call on Franklin Raye and he appreciated that his friend didn't push it. He

238   *Boxing Clever*

checked his watch, stood from the iron bench and, leaning on the railings by the main entrance, rang George.

"Tom?!" The question was loaded with anticipation.

"You've heard nothing either, then? George, just how long does your protocol suggest that we wait and do nothing?"

"It's not just us now. In fact," Tom could hear the indignation, "Frank Dawson gave me the distinct impression last night that this was completely a police matter now. But I want you to know that I'm sitting in my office right now re-reading all the material we have collected here on any case of corporate ransom and blackmail. Ellen is one of ours. I don't intend to lose her."

Tom almost confided in him. He had to talk to Alice.

The hospital was much busier as he negotiated the corridors back to the ward. Two elderly men shuffled past him, unembarrassed in their dressing gown and slippers. A bent and yellow-skinned middle-aged woman was being pushed towards him in a wheelchair so he stopped and pressed himself against the wall to allow them to pass. He saw her skinny hand clutching a packet of cigarettes. She was obviously one of the army of ill people who clustered around the front door to smoke. Tragic.

The nurse gave him a smile of recognition as he came back to the ward but then shook her head in response to his raised eyebrows.

"You're welcome to sit with her. Familiar voices often help."

He pulled out a chair and took hold of her hand.

"I'm sorry, Alice," he leant forward and whispered directly into her ear. "I didn't want you to be hurt. I'm so sorry." He leant back and then forwards again to add, "Forgive me, but please, please open your eyes and talk to me. I need to know what you saw. I need to know what happened. Alice! For pity's sake!"

"Inspector!" The nurse was clearly horrified. His voice must have risen without him realising and he was mortified as he saw the expression on the nurse's face. "I think you should go now. I will contact you if anything changes." She waited protectively by the foot of the bed as he stood, shame-faced.

"I'm sorry," he muttered. "That was unforgivable. I'm hoping she may be able to help me with other enquiries." He met her disapproving gaze. "I can't impress on you how important it is that I speak with her the moment she wakes up. The moment." He squeezed Alice's hand in goodbye and looked at her again before he left just in case the scene had had an effect. It hadn't.

CHAPTER 24

It was only when he got back into his car and heard the slight crackle from the sheet of paper in his back pocket that he decided to pay a visit to Jordan Bell. If the boy hung around the gym as often as he suspected, he may have seen something to explain why Otis had been near Col Mawhinney's flat. He called Dean to tell him where he was going and to arrange to meet him at the Murphys' place in an hour.

Mrs Bell glared at him when she saw who had knocked on her door. Before she could use the huge intake of breath that she had taken, he put one foot in the door and said quickly, "I think Jordan may be able to help me, Mrs Bell. And I have to let you know that I have some good friends in the housing department and I intend to speak to them about your situation. Tomorrow. Personally."

He ignored the folded arms across the ample bosom and motioned towards the back room.

"In the back, is he?"

"He's not up yet," she replied. "You'll have to come back when it's more convenient." A flash of the small triumph shone in her eyes.

"You misunderstand me, Mrs Bell. I will not forget to call the housing department tomorrow. But I may let it slip that you are quite happy where you are. And," he paused for added gravitas, "we don't want Jordan getting hurt again, do we? Somebody wanted to teach him a lesson and I want to know who."

240

She flared her nostrils and said nothing. Tom stared back at her until suddenly she announced, "Stay here. And don't touch anything." She turned and thumped up the stairs.

By the sound of things above, Jordan was unimpressed by the disturbance and Tom had to endure a good five minutes in the grubby hallway until at last the young boy appeared. He was still pale and in obvious pain as he limped his way carefully down each stair. He shuffled into the back room, Mrs Bell bustling behind him, making sure Tom had to wait that little bit longer.

When the boy was comfortable on the sofa, Tom passed him the paper. He looked at it for a minute and then up, a question in his eyes.

"Have you ever seen this guy before?"

"Might have," came the sullen reply. "What's it worth?"

"This guy has just been pulled out of Moreton Moss. Not nice. I think he knew someone who hangs around at the Murphys' gym. What can you tell me?" He kept his tone neutral so the boy would feel no threat of accusation.

Jordan shrugged, trying to look like he was unfazed by the news but the pallid face had turned ashen.

"Seen him a couple of times." The mouth clamped shut.

God, this was going to be like pulling teeth.

"With?"

Again the shrug. "Guy called Otis."

Tom sat back as if he was in no hurry and could give all day to this chat.

"Any surname?"

Jordan looked at his mother and demanded coffee and toast.

"Now!" He shouted when she took her time to move away from her position by the door. She didn't offer anything to Tom.

242   *Boxing Clever*

He waited until she was out of earshot before leaning forwards and saying quietly, "Don't play games, Jordan. You know as well as I do that you're scared shitless about this guy getting murdered, so cut the crap and tell me what you know. Otis who? Seen him with anyone else?"

The boy's eyes darted nervously at the door.

"King. He hangs round with Franklin Raye, you know, the new boxer the Murphys have got."

"And this guy? Col?" Tom pointed at the sheet. "Where did you see him with Otis? Ever seen him at the gym?"

Jordan gave a jerk as if he had been lanced. His mouth began to work rapidly as he formed the words.

"In bars. Cafes. In Didsbury and town." The swallowing was frantic and Tom knew he had hit a nerve.

"Just the two of them? Otis and Col?"

Mrs Bell arrived with a tray, sighing like a martyr.

"Jordan?"

There was no reply. The shutters had come down and Tom wished with all his heart that the fat cow had given him just another minute.

"Can't you see he's exhausted?" She put the tray down on the table in front of the sofa and tried to touch her son's forehead, playing the earth mother. He waved her hand away, but with little aggression.

Tom sat with his hands on his thighs for awhile longer, watching Jordan as he tried to chew the thick white bread, gulping frequently from a large striped mug.

"Jordan has been very helpful, Mrs Bell," he said as he stood. "I may have to talk with him again but not today. And I will have a word for you."

It was as if she had sensed that some seismic shift had occurred when she had been out of the room. There was no sarcasm or bluster. She merely nodded at him and looked back at her pale and quiet son.

"I'm sure you can see yourself out," was all she said.

He called the hospital as soon as he got outside. The ringing tone lasted until he had reached his car, unlocked it and sat behind the wheel, seat belt fastened. The nurse who answered was slightly out of breath and not very helpful. There had been no change. Yes, they knew he wanted to be contacted as soon as there was any news. She must have practically dropped the phone back into its cradle from the sound. His stomach began to growl and he realised he had eaten nothing all day. He popped an antacid tablet into his mouth and chewed, hoping it would calm his guts.

Dean was waiting outside the steel-shuttered building, about as inconspicuous as a monk in a beauty parlour. He looked even wider today, thought Tom as he drove onto the broken tarmac. It must be the T-shirt, tight around the arms and chest.

"How ya doin', mate?" Dean asked.

"Crap. Last night freaked me out. Those bastards aren't playing the game, I just know it. And our bloody superiors," he spat the word, "have got no fucking clue and won't admit it. Honestly Dean," he confided, "I think she is in real danger, and not just from the gang. I wonder if it came to it... with the politics and stuff..."

"Don't even think it!" Dean was adamant. "No way!"

They stared at each other, Tom unwilling to voice any more of the thoughts crowding his brain. A teenage boy pushed past them to the door of the gym, glaring at them as he opened the door.

"Well, at least we'll be expected now," Tom said, changing the subject. "Jordan told me this morning that the guy I saw outside Col Mawhinney's flat is an Otis King. Friend or

244 *Boxing Clever*

follower of Franklin Raye – contrary to what he told Ryan yesterday. He and Col know each other. Now, I reckon we can be sure Franklin gave his club launch tickets to Col. What we want to know is, what else have they all got in common?"

Franklin's training had not been going well for the past few days and today wasn't much better. Sam was getting meaner by the hour and wasn't going to allow him to have his usual Sunday afternoon off this week. He flexed his neck in an attempt to free the tightening muscles. He wanted to lose himself in his body and his power, to switch off the fluttering and clicking in his head. He closed his eyes and tried to count his breathing. He tried to recall his grandmother's voice telling him he was her best boy. One, two. In, out. Best boy. Best boy.

"We need to ask Franklin a few more questions, Mr Murphy."

The words cut across the noises in the gym; his ears - rendered more sensitive by his sightlessness - were finely tuned to the danger in the request.

No, no! Best boy, best boy. One, two. In, out.

"This is harassment, Mr Wilson, Mr..."

"DI Ashton," the voice said. "A man has been found murdered. He had been seen in the company of an Otis King who hangs around here sometimes. We think your Mr Raye also gave the dead man some tickets for a party that ultimately led to the death of a young girl. We are working on the assumption that you are a sensible man. Maybe you would prefer us to ask our questions in your office? Or maybe at ours?"

Franklin's chest was hurting as if he had swallowed acid. The breathing wasn't working; his fists were locked in two tight balls and he couldn't open his eyes. He didn't want to open his eyes. They couldn't make him. No one could make him. That's what

Gramps had said. *No one can make you do anything, but you can do anything you want to. That's why you're my best boy.*

The jarring of the phone ricocheted around the walls and battered at Franklin's ears. He opened his eyes and saw Joe staring at him but was heartened to register the sly wink that came when they made eye contact. Sam came bustling over from the ring with a towel and began to rub away the sweat from his cold and clammy back.

"Of course we will help gentlemen. But I think, given that Franklin needs a shower, we should chat in my office? No need to go all the way into town for a few minutes' chat." Joe was courtesy itself, although one of the men was not listening; he was by the door with his phone clamped to his head.

Franklin found he had the courage to speak.

"Be out in five, boss. Need a shower. Muscles tight."

The facilities at the gym left a lot to be desired and Franklin rarely used them, preferring to go home to his own bathroom. There was a nasty smell of old wood and ancient grime but today the little room, with its broken blue tiles, was a sanctuary. His head almost touched the plastic shower head that spluttered out warm water through the build-up of scale, but it felt like a waterfall in paradise. Use the time, he said to himself. Use your head and use the time. He stroked the water over and around his body, relishing the contours that rose and fell under his hands. In, out. In, out.

"Please tell her I'll be there as soon as I can." Tom's stomach wriggled with the news. He so wanted to talk to her now and discuss the message that the nurse had given to him from her, but he knew he had to talk to Franklin first. Dean was looking at him expectantly. Tom didn't explain.

246   *Boxing Clever*

"What do you reckon?" Dean asked as they left the gym twenty minutes later. The Mawhinney's plane was not due to land for another forty-five minutes and he strolled infuriatingly in Tom's way.

"Well, we've certainly rattled their cages." Tom was anxious to get to the hospital and slipped past his colleague. "I'm still not sure I believe the sudden memory surge from Franklin that he may have given his tickets to Otis who then passed them on to Col but there's nothing to say he didn't. Joe Murphy looked like he'd swallowed a wasp when you casually mentioned a missing Andy Harris. Franklin was slick with that, though. Acting the Mr Contrite. Get onto that DNA test; once we've confirmed it's him then we'll pull the bastard in." He stopped by his car door. "See you later."

"I don't understand," He knew he sounded plaintive but he didn't care. The nurse looked at him and then tried to explain.

"It is quite common for head injury patients to be lucid one minute and unconscious the next. We are fairly confident that she will come round properly soon but as you can see," they both looked down at the little figure, "she is not aware of us now and we must leave her to rest."

"Tell me again what she said. Exactly." It was crumbs but he needed to hear it.

The nurse sighed. "She said, 'Tell Tom that it's all wrong. Tell Tom I know...' That was it."

"Are you sure?" He couldn't let this go. "Maybe someone else heard something?"

"I am sure, Inspector." She wasn't smiling now. "I do realise that this is important and I called you just as soon as she spoke."

He had to confide in her, to tell somebody.

"A woman is in danger. We think Alice may have some vital information. Please can you make sure there is someone with her in case she speaks again?"

The nurse shook her head regretfully. "You can see how it is. I'll do the best I can but we are short-staffed and just can't have one person sitting by her bed. Surely you can get a police officer to do it?"

Hardly.

"Same problem, really," he replied with a matching wry smile. As he was leaving, having pushed the nurse to the point of irritation by reminding her to contact him as soon as Alice woke, he saw the light. Or rather, he spotted a TV on the wall in the corner of the ward showing a church service taking place. It was Sunday after all. And didn't God help those who helped themselves?

The hospital minister was clearly delighted to be needed even without knowing too much of the detail. Tom wasn't sure what Alice would make of the earnest young man praying over her bed when she opened her eyes, but he left knowing that at least this way both her physical and spiritual needs were being well taken care of.

That the building was the same house was quite clear, but the doorway looked too large and the walls seemed to be swaying slightly. A young woman was approaching the door – to go in? She was crying. There was a sound of boys laughing which suddenly faded away to leave only the thump of a heart and the wheeze of elderly breathing.

Alice's eyelids ached as she struggled to reach the light that sat heavily on her skin. The sounds around her were unfamiliar and she tried to moisten her mouth. The effort of opening her eyes was rewarded by a dagger of florescence and the tears created rolled down her cheeks. She wanted to talk to Tom.

248   *Boxing Clever*

Turning her head in response to a voice, she saw a man walking away from her bed, talking in an urgent murmur to a nurse. She tried to utter a plea for help, but the blackness was gathering again at the corners of her mind. She heard a small cry that may have come from her, before she sank once more into oblivion.

It was a week since she had been taken and what was he doing about it? Sitting in an interview room, trying to sort out why a young man was murdered and waiting to get some sense out of a mother who had just identified her dead son. Sometimes the odds just seemed inevitably to be stacked against them. Tom didn't want to be here and he could feel little sympathy for her grief. He was wasting time.

"I appreciate that this is incredibly difficult for you, Mrs Mawhinney. Would you like some more tea?" He just wanted a five-minute break. To make another call.

The woman sniffed loudly and shook her head, her eyes still cast down at the table. Her thin hand shook as she reached across to grab that of her other son, sitting on her right side. Gaining some strength from the contact, she looked up, the blue eyes washed out and red-rimmed from the tears.

"I want you to find out who killed my son." Her voice was surprisingly strong, the accent rich. "He was a good boy."

They always are. "Did Col talk to you about his friends here? What he did in his spare time?"

"He didn't have much time, with his studies and all," she started. Interesting, thought Tom, but not surprising that he hadn't told her he'd been thrown off his course. "He used to play his guitar some nights," she continued. "To earn a wee bit of cash. He sometimes sent me some, to help, like. He was–" the sob was sudden and choking.

Tom, suppressing the desire to fiddle with his pen, pressed on.

Maureen Devlin   249

"How did he send it? A cheque or cash?"

"Why?" The brother suddenly found his voice. "What's that got to do with anything? He wasn't fuckin' topped for his money! He was skint half the time!"

Yeah, right. "His flat was cleared out just after he went missing. All his personal papers were taken. If he sent a cheque, that would tell us which bank he used. We need all the information we can get to help with our investigation."

"I have one." She fumbled to open the zip on the brown bag on her knee. She retrieved an envelope, opened it and passed across a folded slip. A cheque. Made out for fifty pounds, hardly Mr Generous. He jotted down the bank details and account number and passed it back to Mrs Mawhinney. She probably would never see the money, but then, that would be the least of her worries.

One last effort and then he really did have to make another call to the hospital.

"Did he ever mention somebody called Otis King or Franklin Raye?"

Her face clouded a little. "Is that his name now? He only ever mentioned a lad called Frank. Col seemed to admire him – said he did a lot for the local youngsters. A good boxer too by all accounts."

That was enough. Tom looked at his watch and explained that he had to make some calls but that he would keep in touch and he was very sorry for their loss. Blah, blah. Let them find out some other way what a little shit he really was. He left the family in Dean's capable hands; they had asked to see Col's flat and he would stay with them before ensuring they got safely to their hotel.

He called George first but there had been no contact made with the company. Tom gained no reassurance from the short conversation and he ran upstairs to see if The Rodent was

250   *Boxing Clever*

around. The gleam of hope in his eyes as Tom came through the door was a clear enough message. He was just as clueless.

"Sir, I'm going mental here!" He couldn't stop the shout. "We should be doing something! What do the others say?"

"I know, Tom." Frank sounded weary and didn't even bother with the expected reprimand. "Sit down."

He waited until Tom had perched on the edge of the chair facing across the large mahogany desk.

"I'm trying to persuade the others to allow me to try and talk to the kidnappers via the media. Probably TV, although we may need to use the national left-wing press. Apparently Number 10 has been advised of the situation and we are expecting some word from them. I can't tell you just how delicate all this is." He shook his head in time with his words. "They are sure to want no press coverage for the kidnappers and we may jeopardise Ellen's safety but this do-nothing strategy is beginning to really piss me off."

For the first time since Ellen went missing, he felt that The Rodent was on their side. Frank's final remark was a welcome flash of the real man and Tom was so grateful for it, his eyes began to burn. He coughed. All he could manage in response was a quiet, "Thank you, sir."

He gave Frank an update on their other cases, both men relieved to be able to focus on other things for awhile.

"We've got enough to bring Franklin Raye in for questioning, sir. He knew the dead dealer and there has to be a reason he denied all knowledge. There's also a strong possibility that he is linked to the Quays case and if we can get a DNA match to confirm that it is this Andy Harris then we can hold him for a little longer."

The Rodent nodded. "Good work, Tom, particularly given the circumstances. Do it and keep me in the picture."

The nurse said there had been no change. He let her know he would be in to visit shortly to give the vicar a break and then put his phone down and looked around the office. Ryan and Elliott had just disappeared off to interrogate the main suspect in the carjacking murder, brought to ground after pleas for help in the local press. Tom was in no doubt as to the power of the media but they would need to be so, so careful for Ellen's sake. But even talking about the idea with Frank had lifted his spirits and he began to allow himself to believe it would be okay. He moved across to the white board. He rubbed out the question marks by his last scribbles with satisfaction so that the link between Col Mawhinney, Otis King (he wrote in the second name) and Franklin Raye was now a definite line. Next to Franklin he penned 'Joe and Martin Murphy?'

He rang Dean who sounded vaguely distracted. There was a wailing sound in the background and Tom realised that the sight of her dead son's belongings must have reduced the mother to a state of absolute despair.

"Get someone to cover you," Tom ordered. "We're going to bring the big man in."

CHAPTER 25

The metal shutters were down. Why they should close it on a Sunday evening, Tom had no idea. He wouldn't have called them card-carrying church-goers, the Murphy clan. Maybe they couldn't afford to keep the lights on.

He munched on a banana as he waited for Dean to get hold of an address for Franklin. The sharp glance in his direction and shake of the head wasn't entirely unexpected, more irritating.

"It'll have to be the house, then. You know where they live?"

"That I do know. Followed Joe there last year to talk to him about a post office job and he was fuckin' livid." Dean laughed. "We might well get a replay."

"Do me a favour, Joe!" Dean was exasperated. "Wasting our time is going to get him into worse shit. I don't care if you can't reach your son; he can wait. Address. Now."

"We'll wait for your solicitor to arrive before we start questioning Franklin, Mr Murphy," Tom added. "Honest."

The old fighter seemed smaller amongst the floral walls of his hallway, the noise of a TV playing in a distant room. A woman opened a door behind Joe and that seemed to spur him into action. He held up his chin and met Tom's scrutiny, back in the role of defender.

"I'll show you."

Maureen Devlin   253

The black BMW stood out like an advert on the road outside the modern block of flats.

"That his car? How did he afford it?" Tom asked.

"Sponsorship deal." The reply was so slick that Tom laughed out loud.

"If you say so."

It was a stroke of luck that another resident was coming out of the electronically protected front door as they approached it. Dean showed his ID card but his size alone probably would have done the trick. They ran up to the first floor and banged on Franklin's door.

It was a full five minutes before any sound was heard from inside the flat, Joe Murphy adding weight to the sound of the knocks.

"Need to speak with you, son. Open up now."

Franklin looked startled and then angry when he saw his manager was not alone. The fact that he was wearing only tight jersey boxer shorts gave a hint that he might not be alone either but Joe either did not register this or cared even less. He stepped across the threshold, pushing against Franklin's bare shoulder.

"Get yourself dressed, son. They need to talk with yer. Sooner we go, sooner you can get back."

Tom thought he heard a slight low growl from the boxer's throat, and felt Dean stiffen beside him, ready and willing.

"I got company."

"I'm sure you're worth waiting for, Mr Raye. When you're ready." Tom folded his arms across his chest. "As Mr Murphy said, sooner we get going, the better."

Joe Murphy stood at the doorway, reluctant to go farther, as Franklin turned and disappeared behind a door just open at the end of the hall. Tom had no such compunction and strolled in. There was a framed black and white picture of Muhammad Ali on the hallway wall, taken at the height of his powers. A quick

254   *Boxing Clever*

nudge of the first wooden door revealed a chrome and blue kitchen, ultra modern and, even to Tom's inexpert eye, expensive. Maybe they could confiscate the equipment – he was after one of those new pasta makers. The room opposite the kitchen was the lounge, all white, black and chrome. The effect was skewed by the collection of photographs and flowers in bright colours arranged on the top of a glass unit. Like a shrine.

He was just about to take a closer look when the door was pulled closed in front of him by a massive black arm. Tom turned to be hit by a glare of absolute fury and a man struggling to retain control.

"That's private," he hissed. "You don' have no business in there."

Tom didn't apologise, just held the man's stare and raised his hand in the direction of the front door. He was aware of his own breathing and a threatening scent, and willed himself not to swallow. A tiny sound at the rear of the flat shattered the invisible battleground – Franklin's eyes darted in the direction of the noise. A tall brown girl slunk across the hallway, presumably to the bathroom. Her head was tilted so the shoulder length hair draped over her face but not quite well enough to completely mask the swollen, darkened jaw.

Joe Murphy repeatedly tried to reach his son as they drove to the police HQ, followed by the requested patrol car, just in case. Tom was wedged uncomfortably in the back seat with Franklin – there was no way both he and Dean would have fitted in. Joe eventually spoke. He gave a sketchy outline of where he was and where he was going and the implicit instruction for his solicitor to follow him. He shut his phone with a snap.

The interview room was beginning to smell like a squash court by the time the solicitor arrived. Franklin Raye was clearly not very happy and Tom was pleased to see the sweat building on his face.

"Let's get started, shall we?" he said, and made the required announcement to the tape recorder.

'No comment.' 'No comment.' 'My client has no comment.' 'You have no evidence to charge him.' 'You must find some evidence or let him go.'

It was like a bloody mantra. Tom sat back in his chair and twirled his pen between his fingers. He started the questions again.

"We know that your client knows Otis King. We know Otis King knew Mr Mawhinney. We know that Mr Mawhinney wrote home about a friend, a boxer, called Frank. What I don't know is why Mr Raye is so unwilling to confirm that he did in fact know the dead man? Why the silent act?!"

Best boy. Don' you say nothin'. Gramps will make it all okay. Count, son. Count and breathe. Count and breathe. They can't take it all away, not now. In, out. In out. The clicking and fluttering in his head found a rhythm, and he concentrated, really, really hard.

Christ, he's fucking mental, thought Tom watching as the big frame began to rock slightly backwards and forwards. This could get dodgy. He looked at Joe for some enlightenment. Joe didn't seem to be concerned; maybe this was normal behaviour. He looked at his watch. Eleven-thirty. Time for one more try.

"Franklin." He lowered his voice so that it was like a caress. Bingo, eye contact. Of sorts. Tom leant forwards towards him.

"What was the nature of your relationship with Col Mawhinney?"

The fist was so fast and so accurate that Tom knew instantly that his nose was broken. Blood spurted down onto the table

256   *Boxing Clever*

and across the floor as he shot to his feet, trying to keep his hand to his face. Got you, you lunatic.

"Don' fuckin' call me a backender!" Franklin roared, trying to break free from Dean and Joe's grip.

Within a minute the room was full of uniformed officers trying to pin him down. Tom accepted the offer of a packet of tissues from the horrified solicitor and nodded as she said she would accept her client being held on an assault charge. Joe Murphy looked destroyed, constantly chattering, trying to find the words to reach his protégé, who was shaking, his nostrils flaring with each massive breath. Then suddenly, he was calm. When he spoke it was as a child, a bizarre expression on his face.

"I din' mean it, boss. I din' mean it. I'll work harder, I promise."

Fending off helpful offers of lifts and painkillers, Tom waited until Franklin had been escorted to a cell for the night before accepting Dean's insistence that he was taking him to A&E. Dean had been vocal about the boxer's behaviour – "a fucking headcase", a view no doubt in common with anyone else who had witnessed the aftermath of the punch. All Tom could think was... two cases as good as sorted. That'll keep The Rodent happy.

It was after one o'clock in the morning when his nose was back into some sort of shape. The adhesive tape was going to irritate him but now his most pressing worry was the sneaking closure of his eyes. His face was swelling in reaction to the trauma and it hurt. Thanking God for forethought – he had asked the doctor to alert Alice's ward sister that he was on his way up – he whispered his thanks to the nurse and went to sit by Alice's bed.

It was a form of confessional. He whispered the day's events, leaning against his palm, elbow resting on the green and white covered bed. It didn't matter that there was no response. The quiet twilight of her surroundings was just what he needed. He reached a decision. He would keep her out of it all from now on and support Frank all the way in getting Ellen's case noticed. He had to follow the proper channels. He had to believe in them.

Fortunately there was no wait for a taxi and he was home within ten minutes. Jack was waiting to greet him, the little body pressed hard against his legs as he wearily closed the front door. God, he could sleep for a week.

Three hours was all he managed. Whether it was the ache in his face or his stomach or his mind that woke him, it didn't matter; he couldn't contemplate going back to sleep. Jack chirruped in query from the foot of the bed as Tom sat groggily at the edge of it, wondering if his face looked as bad as it felt. He staggered into the bathroom and almost blinded himself with the light. Christ. He was almost unrecognisable.

He took a gentle shower, patting himself dry as if his whole body was battered. Two painkillers and a swig of cold tap water from the sink and then down into the kitchen.

The rhythmic kissing sound of the dough moving beneath his fists eased his mind and soon the smell of warm cinnamon began to fill the house as the puffy little rolls baked to a golden brown. Waiting for them to cool, he took his coffee into the lounge and switched on the TV. Twenty-four-hour international news. Forest fires in California took the top slot. The forthcoming Summit was mentioned only in passing even though there were only four days to go... Jumping up from the sofa so quickly that he dislodged Jack into mid-air, he ran upstairs to get dressed. To do *something*.

He saw Jack slither out through the cat flap as he buttered and packed up four of the still-warm rolls. He felt a bit guilty that he had no treats for him – he'd not be getting any at Alice's for awhile.

258   *Boxing Clever*

There was a sleepy attractiveness about the city early on a summer morning, he thought. The soft, bright light fed Tom's spirit as he drove along the quiet roads. He took out a roll and began to chew. Where to go first? Back to the hospital? Drive around Ardwick? To work? He went over the abortive interview with Franklin and recalled the manic look in the man's eyes before he delivered the punch. Definitely barking. He was looking forward to trying to get a confession out of him for Col and Andy Harris but, given the state of the guy before he was put away for the night, it promised to be hard going. He'd have to get both the Murphy's and the trainer in. Otis King, too.

The look on the face of the young WPC as he walked along the corridor confirmed that he looked a bloody fright.

"Shit! Who did you piss off?" Ryan was already at her desk.

Tom told her. Nasally. Ryan gave an appreciative whistle. "Press are going to love that. What else can we pin on him?"

"Pretty sure the Andy Harris death is down to him. Fuck, it hurts even to speak."

"Erm..." Ryan was unnaturally reticent. "Any news?"

He knew what she was asking and shook his head.

"What's the locker room talk?" he asked.

A shrug. "Well, you know...what I'd do if it was my girl, sister, whatever... stuff about The Rodent so far up the Region's arse he can't see straight. No one is bad-mouthing you, Tom."

It was so rare for Ryan to use his name that he took from her comments a mixed message of sympathy and blame.

He hit his keyboard and stared at the screen for inspiration. The small clock on the bottom right corner of the monitor told him it was too early to ring the housing department. But not George. He was going to pick off each of the men on the kidnap team to lobby for press coverage. Time was running out.

After an hour he had spoken to each of the men with no clear idea of level of impact or success. They should all be bloody politicians.

Dean sauntered in, chatting with Elliott and clearly in the middle of some tawdry joke when he caught sight of Tom's face.

"Christ! You didn't walk into a lamppost as well, did ya? You look ten times worse than last night."

"Thanks for the sympathy and for your information, it'll get worse before it gets better. Go and pull in Otis King. Let's get some more info on what's been going on with our Mr Raye and Col Mawhinney."

Dean said he had been surprisingly easy to find; the gods were giving them a break.

Tom looked at the young, handsome face, traces of the bruising still evident. Otis King was the first person he'd seen today who hadn't found some remark to offer about his face. Clearly Otis knew when to keep his mouth shut. Tom registered the downcast eyes and got ready for the 'no comment' routine.

"Col Mawhinney," he stated. "Friend of yours." A statement, not a question. "Why do you think someone decided to kill him and bury him – not very well, mind you – in a peat bog?"

The head flicked up. Tom knew terror when he saw it. He used it.

"Could be you next, Otis. Now'd be a good time to talk."

It was like a dam busting, a classic example of verbal diarrhoea. Tom didn't enlighten Otis that the object of his anxiety was in a cell about fifty yards away and probably sleeping like a baby. He talked about Franklin, the drug sales, the money. Martin Murphy had been paying him to keep an eye on the boxer but he hadn't told him about the drugs. Otis wanted the money. He was sweating freely now and gabbling like an excited teenager.

260   *Boxing Clever*

"I was thinkin' about getting moved to someone else, he was acting weird. I want protection!" he suddenly shouted as if understanding that he was in a very small space between a rock and a hard place. "Me mam will kill me if anything happens to our Leroy."

"Leroy?"

"Brother. Younger. Way of getting to me. Been done before."

"I don't think you need to worry about that," Tom started but Otis was shaking with insistence.

"He's not at our gaff – he's been staying at a mate's while his mam's on holiday." He gave an address and was so agitated that Tom wrote it down as if he was going to do something about it.

"Who was Franklin working for? How did he get in on the action here so quickly?"

A rap came on the door.

"Sir?" Tom looked round at the interruption. "The Super wants to see you. Immediately."

"We've had a call," The Rodent said without preamble. "Came through to me. Caller had been sent round the houses a bit and they weren't happy. They want to know why we haven't been on the TV. They want us to get on the news tonight and say," he looked down at his notes, "that the police are struggling with a major crime, that it's the work of a very clever gang and that we are waiting to hear from them."

"Bastards! Did they talk about Ellen?" Tom demanded.

"That was it. It may be professional and political suicide but I'm prepared to do it. Let's confer." He buzzed through to Margery and requested a teleconference. Immediately.

They had almost reached agreement when Tom's phone began to ring. He grabbed at it, the telephone console and Frank suddenly quiet.

"Yes?"

"Is that Inspector Tom Ashton?" A woman's voice.

He took a deep breath and shook his head at Frank. Into the phone, he said, "It is. And you are?"

She was a nurse, and she wanted to tell him that Mrs Roberts was completely awake and very anxious to talk to him. Very anxious.

He reminded himself of his decision to keep Alice out of this but he could not bury the hope that she just might... The telephone discussions were still circling on.

"For God's sake!" He stood to leave and stared down at the phone. "We've been thinking about using the media anyway. What's the problem? Because they asked first? I have to go out."

"Tom!" He heard the query and the command in his name as he reached the door but he opened it and walked through, closing it firmly behind him.

Alice plucked at the linen covering her chest. She had been helped into a slouching sitting position but her feet were still pinned by the bedding. Even though it hurt her ankle, she tried to wriggle her legs to loosen the sheets. It felt like an age since she had asked them to reach Tom and she was terrified of falling back to sleep. Her old bones ached with weariness. It was the fire of certain knowledge that kept her eyes fixed on the door, willing him to hurry.

She saw him just as the cheery plump nurse came across to plop a bowl of indefinable liquid and a bread roll on the wheeled tray table next to her bed.

"Tom!" The relief was marvellous. "Please, I know where she is! And," seeing the expression on his face, "don't start asking how I am or telling me to eat that up first." She pointed in disgust at the peculiar grey concoction.

He grabbed a chair and sat. "Well?"

262   *Boxing Clever*

She wanted to tell him the whole story but that could wait. "I saw the shadow of a face at the house I was mugged at. I don't know the address but I can describe to you exactly where it is. She's in there. I'm sure of it."

She gave him every detail she knew and watched as he wrote it down. That the taxi had turned left at the junction she and Tom had stopped at that time when she could see no further. She described the houses and a pub that she had passed, and then the house itself.

When she had told him all she could, it was like coming round from a dreadful fever. Weak and drained. But with that blissful awareness that it was going to be all right.

He wanted to go it alone but he needed someone at his back. Someone who wouldn't ask too many questions.

Dean was waiting at the back gates when Tom pulled up.

"I said we had a lead from Otis King. That we might need support. A patrol car will pick us up at the entrance to the estate but keep a distance." He looked at Tom. "Going to tell me what the fuck's going on?"

"A hunch, mate. If I'm wrong...Ellen's no worse off."

Dean sucked at his teeth. "Shit."

Tom negotiated the route with Alice's descriptions clear in his mind. He indicated to turn into the street with the pub on the corner, knowing that the house should be about one hundred yards on the right hand side. He gave a cursory glance up to the road sign on wall of the pub as he passed it and slammed the brakes on so suddenly that Dean rammed his hand onto the dashboard in alarm.

"What the −"

Tom stared. He had been given this road name before. Today. By Otis King.

CHAPTER 26

"I was given this road name this morning by Otis King." Tom spoke quietly as he re-engaged the gearbox and took the car forwards, slowly.

"I thought this was to do with Ellen – not the drugs stuff?" Dean wasn't the only one who was confused. But Tom still had the prickle of anticipation on the back of his neck; Alice was on to something.

Tom could see the police patrol car just turning into the road behind them as he pulled into the kerb just past the house perfectly described by Alice. He pulled off his seat belt and was out of the car as it rocked to its final rest.

"Keep behind me. And get ready to yell for back-up."

He was up the short path and knocking at the front door in seconds. While he was getting ready to break the door down, it opened to reveal a thin gap. Tom could see a youthful questioning face and got a whiff of powerful aftershave, and before the door could be closed, Tom threw himself against it. He pushed past a teenager who was in brand new oversized jeans and a hooded top.

"Who the fuck are you?! Get out!" The youngster had clearly been expecting somebody else. The family resemblance was there all right.

"You'll be Leroy King, then?" Tom shoved him against the wall of the hallway and ran to the stairs. "Your brother has been in to talk to me today. Worried about you, he was. I wonder

264   *Boxing Clever*

why?" Tom was halfway up the stairs before he heard the yell and felt a hand trying to grab his legs.

"Ellen!" he bellowed. "Ellen! It's Tom!" His words were almost drowned out by the shouts of fury from Leroy who suddenly let go.

"You're a fuckin' liar!"

Tom didn't care if he tried to do a runner because he'd heard a cry. It was her.

Dean began to shout up the stairs as Tom tried to open the locked door. He threw his shoulder against the panelled barrier and the thin wood gave a satisfying creak.

"Keep back from the door!" He grunted as the next impact shot back along his ribs. He stepped back, ready for the next charge.

"Let me, mate." Dean was at his shoulder.

"No! This is mine." *Crack!*

She was curled on the corner of the bed with her arms over her head as he broke through into the room. It was gloomy. There was some sort of white paint on the inside of the windows and it smelt stale.

"Ellen! Are you all right? It's okay, it's okay. Let's get out of here, come on."

He helped her to her feet, thankful that she seemed to be unharmed. She stared at his face in horror and he said quietly, "I'm fine. Come on."

She threw her arms round his neck and began to sob. As he held her, he stroked her greasy head and tried to ignore the sourness that reached his nostrils.

She insisted on going home to have a long bath and change into some fresh clothes before she would speak about it. Tom gently reminded her they would need evidence first if they had sexually assaulted her. She cried silently, but shook her head. He almost wept with relief for both of them.

She sat in the back of the car as close to him as she could, leaning against him with her hand clinging onto the fabric of his trousers, moving only to use his phone to briefly ring her parents. They had to do a detour to his house to pick up her keys and she didn't want to stay in the car with Dean even for those few minutes. Tom took her into the house with him and she cried all over again when Jack ran up to her, yowling in recognition.

She looked around her home as if waking from a coma in a strange country. She ran her fingers along the window ledge in the hall, and then took the few steps to stand staring at the sofa and bookcase.

"I didn't think I'd see this again." Her voice was low and wobbly. "Or you."

She turned to face him, her chin puckered and her eyes brimming all over again. She put up her hand to stop him as he moved towards her, arms outstretched.

"I need to feel clean. I need lots of hugs but not like this. I need to feel like me."

He promised to keep the doors locked while she was upstairs and it wasn't long before the scent of bath foam or whatever floated down the stairs. He sat in the kitchen with a mug of black coffee while he worked out what to say. Then he rang George.

Frank arrived with George at the house in time to see Ellen come down the stairs. Tom was amused to see The Rodent hang back awkwardly as if she was so fragile she might do something hysterical.

Instead she said, "I'm starving! I need to get something to eat and then we can talk."

266   *Boxing Clever*

She bustled round the kitchen, reclaiming her territory. It was like a bizarre tea ceremony with Tom perched alongside Frank and George at the pine table, watching as she offered and made green tea and prepared herself a toasted sandwich from bread in the freezer. As she pottered, she described how she had been fooled into approaching a car outside her house to give directions and was then bundled down by the back seat. She had only ever seen two of them.

Tom thought he could see her old spirit returning as she looked at George and asked, "What did they want from us?"

Her face displayed her confusion and then distress as she heard what had happened.

"Twenty thousand? Is that all?"

Frank moved in and began to explain that there had been reason to believe that the abduction had been politically motivated because of the timing but in the light of the arrests... He trailed off.

Tom said it. "It doesn't seem this is anything really to do with Vanpharma, or the Summit," he began, aware of her eyes boring into him, her mouth tight shut. "Even without speaking to the lads involved – it looks like this whole thing was a way of getting at us. The police."

She stared at him. "Because of you?" She was incredulous and a red blush began to rise up her pale neck. "I was kidnapped and had to endure a week in that smelly, poxy house with a dirty bathroom, because of you?"

She was on her feet and shouting now. Tears of disbelief rolled down her cheeks and she gave a hard laugh.

"There I was, trying to remember all the things we'd been told at work. Don't alienate aggressors, go along with demands, the company will look after you. Christ! I could have made a run from the car, or smashed the window! I thought others might get hurt! It was only because I had my period that they didn't try and rape me too!" She was openly sobbing now. "They wouldn't buy me anything. I had to use a roll of kitchen paper..."

The pointless little bastards. He jumped to his feet and tried to comfort her, but she pushed him away. George and Frank looked horrified and embarrassed.

"You need someone to come and stay with you. Maybe Fiona? There'll be a patrol car outside. I'm going to get those scrawny tossers to tell me just what this was all about. We can talk about all this in a little while?"

Not a good speech.

"Yeah, fine. You go and do your precious police work. Don't mind me."

He was perplexed. "Of course I'll stay if that's what you want!" He could see Frank nodding furiously. "Someone else can question them. I only thought..."

"Well you thought wrong." She stormed out of the kitchen and when he followed her, he could hear her on the phone again to her parents. She shouted past him to the others. "Would you drive me to Dorset, George?"

"I'll take you!" Tom said quickly. "If that's what you want." He walked through to where she was standing, and he could see the phone shaking in her hand. "But we have to have your statement first."

She stared at him, her mouth tight and white. "No." She was quite definite. "You do what you need to. I'd rather go with George."

He was all over the place. It was as if she suddenly hated him and while he could understand some of her anger, he felt penalised for wanting to punish those who had taken her.

He arranged for Ryan to come and take the full statement. Ellen didn't want him to be there. He stood helplessly as she

268   *Boxing Clever*

began to pack for her trip to Dorset while waiting for Ryan to arrive. Eventually, she turned to look at him.

"Thank you for finding me, Tom." There was no smile, no hug. "You know where I am if you need to talk to me."

He thought later, many times, that he could have stopped her going but he didn't. She was right. He needed to understand.

The debrief in Frank's office was a subdued affair. While there was relief at Ellen's safe return and the disappearance of a massive potential political threat, it was somehow unsatisfactory. For Tom, it was because of how Ellen had looked at him as she left and for Frank, it was professional.

"We have to find some way of gaining respect with these youngsters. I'm going to have to explain all this to the powers that be." The light bulb in his head must have flickered because he stared at Tom. "What were you doing at that house anyway?"

"Tip-off from Otis King. Thought it might be a drug den." It was thin, but it seemed to satisfy.

The cheers as he walked into the CID room helped. He still couldn't smile without pain but he did anyway.

"Thanks, guys. What have we got so far?"

Dean took the floor as various colleagues sat or stood around the room to listen. Tom heard that the DNA had come back with a positive match for Andy Harris and that the family were on their way up although they'd been advised to think carefully about wanting to see him. Frank had agreed for them to push for two charges of murder on Franklin Raye: Col Mawhinney and Andy Harris.

"We're doing that this afternoon, Tom. Want to be there?"

He did. "Who else is coming in? Need to talk Joe and Martin Murphy."

Maureen Devlin   269

"Joe's agreed to be here this afternoon but Martin is away in London apparently."

Tom could see the best bit was yet to come. Dean was practically salivating like a rabid dog. He stole the punchline from a baby-faced comic.

"There's more." He grinned. "When we got young Leroy in here, he was still shouting the odds that his big brother wouldn't ever talk to us filth. He was so sodding belligerent we decided to bring Otis through to see what his baby brother had been up to. Christ, you should have been there – we're talking fireworks!"

Ellen was going to be horrified when she learned that her imprisonment was purely due to Leroy wanting to get at the police so that he could impress his older brother. He saw Otis as the big Mr I Am, with money and clothes and jewellery, who hung around with Franklin Raye – who everyone knew was going to be as big as Mike Tyson. Leroy wanted credibility. He had wanted to be part of the big league.

"He was behind the stuff going on on Saturday as well. Figured it would do no harm to let some of his other mates know that we were going to be a bit thin on the ground. Should be able to pull in most of those guys as well now," Elliott added.

"For fuck's sake." Tom was depressed beyond measure. He welcomed back his old friend – stomach acid – as he digested the information. "It's a shame they don't use their intelligence in other ways. They've played us like a puppeteer." He thought for a minute then asked, "Did you find out if they had anything planned for the 25th if we'd not found her?"

"Reckon they would have just let her go, Tom," Dean said. "The 25th was when Leroy's mate's mum was due back from Tenerife."

270   *Boxing Clever*

Tom had to admit that Franklin was a superb actor when he wasn't totally deranged. The boxer was adamant that he hadn't killed anybody. He admitted that he had met Andy Harris, that he had dated his sister when he was in London.

"Heard there was an accusation of rape against you, Franklin?" Dean was taking the lead. "That was Andy Harris' sister, wasn't it?"

The solicitor stepped in. The woman from the first interview had obviously persuaded her male colleague to come in her place and he, fully briefed, was on form.

"There was no case to answer. You know better than that."

"Did you see Andy Harris after you came to Manchester?" Dean pressed on. "Tell me about the last time you saw Col Mawhinney."

The questioning was long and fruitless. Tom learned precious little about how Franklin had met Col except that Otis had introduced them. No, he hadn't killed him. He liked him. He didn't do it. All Franklin would say was that he didn't do it.

Tom tried. "How did you get Andy into the canal basin?"

"What basin? I didn't!" It was a rising wail and Tom stiffened. Maybe it was he who brought out the worst in this guy. The solicitor was trying to edge away from his client as the tension in the room rose noticeably.

"I wanna see Mr Murphy. And I want to go home. Now. Besides." He got to his feet. "I've got training to do."

Well, he's certainly lucid now, thought Tom. Even so, he could see they would have a hard time convincing a court that he was sane enough to enter a plea under the Mental Heath Act, never mind get a jury conviction.

"Sorry, Franklin. Not today," Dean said. "We need to talk about the assault next."

In the interview room opposite, Joe Murphy was clutching a plastic cup of what smelled like coffee, the female solicitor at his side. She had opted for the safer option then, Tom noted.

"Joe," he opened. "Franklin is in a whole heap of trouble. Tell me about Andy Harris."

The solicitor was getting up his swollen nose. She blocked any line of questions about Franklin, stating circumstantial evidence-gathering and her client not being answerable.

"Are you intending to charge my client, Inspector? He has answered all of your questions and it seems that you have no proven reason to keep him here any longer."

"I need to speak to Martin, Joe," Tom knew he was going to have to let the older man go. "Have you managed to reach him?"

The slight colouring was a give-away. "He's on business and tied up in meetings a lot. I've told him you want to talk to him. He knows."

"Tell him I want to talk to him tomorrow, Joe." Tom's nose was hurting, his backache was building and he wanted to go home. "If not, I'll have him on obstruction."

He left it until Tuesday afternoon before he rang Ellen. At least she had taken his call. He wanted to go down and see her but she was horribly resistant to the idea. He couldn't even get her to think about it.

"Can I call you again? Tomorrow?"

"Whatever."

"Dear God!" Alice stared at him in horror. "Did they do that when you found Ellen?" He smiled at the certainty in her question. He hadn't told her he had yet.

272   *Boxing Clever*

He shook his head and pulled over a chair to sit beside her bed. Her eyes, as bright and alert as they used to be, twinkled as she heard the reason why he was black and blue.

"Was Ellen okay?" she asked. "Can you tell me what it was all about?"

He did. He thought she deserved that at least.

"I don't know whether she wants me to keep ringing her or not." He chewed distractedly at one of the grapes he had brought in for Alice.

"Oh, yes." Alice was firm. "She's angry and you need to feel it. Don't forget, it's because of her relationship with you that she was taken in the first place."

He paused for awhile. "I've been in touch with her company. They're sorting out counselling for her. They're closing ranks and I feel that they're pushing me out." He gave a wry laugh. "Their guy, George, even suggested they were not only going to try and recover their money, but that they might sue the police because taking Ellen was not about them. That somehow we should have prevented it."

"Ridiculous!" Alice's irritation was comforting.

He didn't explain that he could have done exactly that; if he'd told Ellen about the thefts from cars, she would have put her laptop and organiser in the boot. "So." He concentrated on selecting another grape, keen to change the subject. "When are you coming out?"

She happily reported to him that they were going to let her go home the next day. Her scans were fine and her ankle was more aching than painful. She'd hobbled to the bathroom on her own this morning and that had been the clincher.

"They need the bed anyway. They've told my GP so that a nurse will come for a day or so to make sure I can get about. And I told them I had good neighbours."

He snorted. "One neighbour who got you in here in the first place. I'll come and pick you up. Jack'll be pleased to see you."

"What's going to happen to the man who did that to you?" she asked.

He was glad to stay a little longer, to keep talking. He gave a brief outline of Franklin's position.

"And he knew the man who sold the drugs to Mel?" she asked. "What a coincidence."

"More than that, Alice," he explained. "The guy who thumped me must be close to the head of a drug network to be able to get involved so quickly when he came up from London. There was no way he was existing on handouts from the gym owner. His flat reeked of too much money and no taste." He remembered the odd thing out. "He had a collection of photos and flowers in a sort of shrine."

Alice nodded, sagely. "Woman? Probably his mother or grandmother. Fixation. Think you'll find that they've died and when they did, he went off the rails."

A bell sounded to announce the end of evening visiting hours. Alice thanked him for coming and accepted his offer of a lift home the next day.

This was the first time that Tom had actually been in the ward with other visitors and it was strange to feel just like everyone else as he shuffled behind chattering relatives and friends through the fire doors. He turned and raised his hand in goodbye.

He knew his eyes were registering the colours of the day, but it was as if he was looking from inside someone else's head. He stood for a moment outside the hospital and lurched with a dreadful sense of loss. He didn't know what to do next. The Rodent had made it clear he needed to take a couple of days off; Ellen didn't want to see him; Dean had assured him they would

274   *Boxing Clever*

be following up all the other cases and told him to chill out. How exactly? His nose was settling down but it was still too sore, and his eyes too slitty to try and do anything really physical like squash. He rocked on his heels and stretched, registering the protest in his lower back and shoulders. God, he was wrecked.

He stood, hands clasped behind his back. The granite headstone glinted in the sunlight and he felt the hot prickle of emotion flood his eyes. It was almost thirteen years since Greg had died and Tom's world had been turned upside down. He bowed his head in respect. Then, not caring if anyone was watching, he pulled back his shoulders and executed a perfect salute. Sometimes I wished it'd been me, he thought. But now I'm so very glad I'm alive. Just wish that you were here too. And I'm sorry I haven't been here more often. He sat on the grass and, plucking away errant stalks, began to talk to his friend.

Much later and feeling easier than he had for months, he checked his watch. He had called the hospital and they had assured him that Alice would be discharged today, but asked him not to arrive before three pm. He thought about calling Ellen, to suggest they come up here sometime, but he couldn't bear to hear the rejection. Not today.

Alice was ready to go. She had been dressed since nine o'clock even though the nurse told her she wouldn't be able to go until the doctor had given the final say-so after lunch. Her beige raincoat, in need of a clean, lay across the bed. She tried to concentrate on the dire magazine that the lady in the bed next to her had passed across. She had no interest in knitting patterns and hated what she called 'old woman's fiction'. She hadn't told Tom yet, but she loved to read a good thriller. The higher the body count, the better.

Maureen Devlin   275

She had a cup of tea and completed the crossword puzzle in the magazine. Her neighbour had made a start but her spelling was so poor it was not surprising she had given up. She had just finished it when Tom arrived to take her home.

When he pulled up outside her house, he was chastened to see the tears rolling down her cheeks.

"I wondered if I'd ever come home again," she said.

He sat in her tidy lounge, Jack purring rapturously on the arm of Alice's chair.

"I was wrong to involve you Alice," he began. "I was desperate for anything to help and I got you hurt." He dropped his eyed in shame. "Ellen said the same thing to me. That she thought she'd never see her home again. I should have been protecting you both. Ellen was right. My ex-wife was right. My work rules the way I think."

"Oh, for pity's sake, Tom! Stop feeling sorry for yourself. I'm here and I'm fine. Ellen will be too. Don't forget it was me who sought you out in the first place. I can't control what I see, but I'm glad I could come to you. You did what you had to. No more now." Two little red spots had appeared on her cheeks as she spoke. "Now, go and call Ellen."

He defied anyone not to be lifted by the mood of the crowd. It was Thursday 25th July. An open-air concert to coincide with the start of the Summit was about to begin.

Dean and Fiona had insisted that he joined them in the city centre and they were standing, along with hundreds of others, in front of a massive screen near the site of the IRA bomb blast some years earlier. The city planners and architects had done a great job in rebuilding the shattered streets and new bars, restaurants, shops and a cinema had grown up around the old

Boxing Clever

cathedral. They each had a bottle of beer and Tom was grateful for the company of his friends and that of the happy and proud strangers standing alongside. The Manchester evening was warm and dry. There was a generous police presence, but Tom could see they were relaxed and enjoying the atmosphere.

The screen was relaying live coverage from the new stadium situated to the east of the city and Tom caught Dean's eye as various dignitaries made their entrance to the applause of the crowd. He couldn't comprehend what might have happened, because of two teenage boys...

Catcalls greeted the arrival of the Prime Minister and the cameras unkindly homed in on the grim expressions of the Premier and his wife. Tom laughed and took a generous swig of beer.

"My round next," he said.

"Good night, last night, wasn't it?" Dean asked as he arrived at work the next morning. "The morning nationals have really sung the city's praises. Feel dead proud." He held up a copy of the *Daily Mail.*

Tom knew exactly what he meant. He had decided he was going to try and persuade Ellen to come back home. The city was buzzing. It was what they had been trying to protect as well as to secure her release.

He was examining the case white board and was about to ask a question when his mobile phone rang and vibrated in his trouser pocket.

"Tom Ashton."

A grunt. "Mum told me I had to ring and say thanks." Jordan clearly found it an onerous task.

"Oh! Right. Glad they can do something for you." Tom made a mental note to congratulate his friend in the housing department. Pretty impressive work.

"Erm..." There was clearly more. "Something to tell you. Forgot the other day."

"Okay. Can you tell me now or shall I come round later?"

"Can you come round now? She's out."

He went alone. The rest of the team were all busy and he was glad of something to do that had a relatively low stress rating.

He stopped on the way to buy a couple of Danish pastries and fresh coffee as a gesture of appreciation for the boy's help.

Jordan was still in some pain, judging by the slow shuffle as he led the way to the back room, but he was looking better. When they had sat down, Tom opened the two brown bags and pushed one of them across to him. He sniffed at the coffee suspiciously and then took a cautious sip. He grimaced and poured two sachets of sugar in to the scalding liquid.

He waited as Jordan devoured his pastry and then eyed the one sitting on a paper napkin next to Tom's cup.

"All yours." He pushed it across and waited until the last crumbs had been licked off the sticky fingers.

"You wanted to tell me something. About Otis King?"

Jordan shook his head and took a deep breath.

"This is only 'cos of the house." Tom sat and said nothing.

"Mr Murphy gave me a bit of money to keep an eye on Franklin Raye. One of his spies he called me. Wanted to check what he was doing when he wasn't training and stuff. Saw him talking with that bloke who got killed and I followed him. The bloke. Not Franklin. He went to Canal Street, where all the poofs go. Mr Murphy was fuckin' livid. Franklin drinking with a ponce." He paused to take a drink. "I saw him on the day I got done. He was arguing with Mr Murphy and then some guys began to beat him up. They shoved him in a car. Think one of them saw me. Got grabbed from behind when I boarded away round the corner."

278   *Boxing Clever*

Tom was on the edge of his seat. "Are you saying it was one of Joe Murphy's goons who stabbed you?"

"Not Old Man Murphy," Jordan corrected him. "Mr Murphy."

Tom stood to help himself to think. "Let's get this straight. You were getting money from Martin Murphy to watch Franklin Raye. You saw Franklin drinking with Col Mawhinney before he then went off to the Gay Village. Col Mawhinney gets into an argument with Martin Murphy, you get stabbed and Col Mawhinney ends up in a bog."

Well, well. Maybe Franklin Raye is telling the truth.

"Will you provide a statement? We can do it here, no need to go to the station." A nod. "You've been a great help, Jordan. I'm going to call a colleague to pick up your mum first. I need to have a chat with your Mr Murphy."

Maybe it was the need to get rid of the whole burden or the sugar overload that prompted him to drop the final nugget.

"Franklin Raye's got a lock-up. A van came and he took two big bags out of it. I can show you if you like."

The Rodent actually rubbed his hands.

"Well, Tom, this is really very good work. There is enough to charge Franklin Raye with major drugs offences as well as the two murders. A good lead for Jordan Bell's stabbing too."

"Andy Harris' family are pressing to have charges of rape added to Franklin's troubles," Tom advised. "Seems the sister has had a change of heart with the news of her brother's death. She was paid a few hundred pounds to keep quiet and that has long gone. Martin Murphy paid it." He twirled his pen.

Frank looked at him closely. "What are you thinking?"

"We still can't get hold of Martin Murphy. Joe's been fudging that his son is away on business but I'm pretty damn sure he's done a runner. If he paid the sister to keep Franklin out of trouble, what else might he do if the brother shows up just as the boy was in line for his first major fight? They had invested a stack on his success. And if he'd kill once, who's to say he wouldn't top Mawhinney, thinking he might be gay and how that would look for Franklin in the press? We have Jordan to say they were arguing on the day he was stabbed. No evidence to say he knew about the drugs but if he was paying Jordan and Otis, he could well have been paying others."

Tom thought that the gym felt rather like an airport when a plane had just departed. The walls still echoed with the resonance of people, but there was little to do. A few men were going through their paces and Sam Jones was trying to show a youngish boy how to hit a small, round punchbag that was welded to the floor.

"Joe." Tom tried to be patient. "We need to talk to Martin. We have reason to believe now that he might be implicated in Col Mawhinney's death. This is not helping Franklin."

The rheumy eyes looked out of a grey and shrunken face. Joe Murphy was a broken man. He shook his head. "I don't know where he is."

The notice went out to all police forces and to the international agencies to track down and arrest Martin Murphy. The team was upbeat as they gathered at the end of the day to exchange the findings from their part of the investigation.

Elliott had been charged with getting to the bottom of the Murphy accounts. It appeared that Joe Murphy had handed the running of the gym and their various businesses, including a stake in the Salford Quays security firm, to his son a few years ago.

"It's like trying to unravel fishing line," Elliott reported. "But we can see from the accounts, such as they are, they were

280   *Boxing Clever*

in big trouble. Everything was mortgaged or in hock. It looks like Martin had been pinning all their hopes on Franklin hitting the big time from what the trainer told us."

"Enough that even the slightest threat to his plan had to be eradicated?" Tom asked.

Elliott thought so, and a number of colleagues muttered yes or nodded in agreement.

"That's all very well," Tom continued, as he closed the report and reviewed the facts. "It seems to ring true for Andy Harris, but for Mawhinney? Worried that Franklin had a gay friend or might be gay? Bit tenuous, never mind primitive. Any other ideas?"

Dean shifted his weight on the desk he was sitting on, to the sound of a resounding creak.

"Drugs?" he offered.

"Any evidence Murphy was supplying?"

"No." Dean was begrudging. "But that's not to say he wasn't."

The discussion carried on for awhile as ideas and hunches were debated and discounted.

Tom reached over and picked up the notes from Otis King's interview and began to read.

"You two-timer," he muttered under his breath. "In the pay of Franklin Raye to keep an eye on Col Mawhinney and in the pay of Martin Murphy to keep an eye on Franklin Raye. Don't believe that you didn't tell him about the drugs.

"Guys," he halted the noise and waved the paper. "We've missed something. Otis King was being paid by both Martin and Franklin. What if he did tell Martin not only about the drugs but also about Col being behind the death of the Mel Chadwick. Don't forget we were sniffing around as well by then. That would really bring the type of press attention he really didn't want."

Maureen Devlin 281

"I'd be delighted to ask him for some clarification," volunteered Dean. "Let's bring the whole thing down!"

Awhile later, Tom left the briefing room, confident that the cases would be solved and closed. Now he needed to sort his own mess out.

He rang Ellen to ask when she was coming back. She hadn't decided yet, she said. He said, again, that he was sorry and that he wanted the chance to make it up to her. That she was important to him.

She needed to think, she said. But if he fancied a drive down to Dorset...

THE END

About the Author

Maureen Devlin was born in Liverpool in 1957.

In 1979, she qualified as a pharmacist from the University of Leicester and, in her first professional role, turned an underperforming business into a highly successful concern. After gaining a PhD in pharmaceutical microbiology, Maureen joined GlaxoSmithKline (GSK), originally working in research and development, before moving on to customer relations. On leaving GSK, Maureen excelled in several roles, including working for the National Prescribing Centre and as an NHS consultant.

A lifelong lover of the arts, Maureen was a talented actress and a much-respected member of the Altrincham Garrick Theatre. She also enjoyed writing and was a regular contributor to the South Manchester Writers' Workshop.

Boxing Clever is the first of a trilogy of crime novels featuring Detective Inspector Tom Ashton. Tragically, Maureen's untimely death in 2009 meant that she did not live to see its publication.

Lightning Source UK Ltd.
Milton Keynes UK
177003UK00001B/2/P